Five years ago, when I began as an associate writer on *Love of My Life,* I asked the man who was then the head writer, "What does the producer do?"

"Clean up the shit," he had said.

Now it was my turn to wield the mop.

"Who?" I asked Cybelle. "Who are you afraid of?"

Cybelle leaned forward and whispered, "It's—he's my *sort of* husband."

Inside the office it was warm, but Cybelle—one of the sweetest and least demanding actresses I've ever worked with—was shivering and there was a look of absolute panic in her eyes. Alarm bells went off in my head. Cybelle was in a hot, front-burner story line that was keeping our ratings high. I didn't want to see her upset, but I also had an obligation to protect the show.

I came around to her side of the desk and pulled up the second visitor's chair. "Tell me about this 'sort of' husband. Why are you so frightened? If you don't want to stay married to him, we'll help you get a divorce."

"He'll never let me go, Morgan." Her body slumped in despair. "He really will kill me if he finds out where I am. Running away from him—that's the reason I dye my hair black, and why I wear green contacts on camera."

Starring on TV is a strange way to hide, I thought.

"Linda Palmer paints a vivid backstage portrait of the world of daytime drama . . . with spot on observations about the ins and outs of the broadcasting business."
—Barbara Rush, formerly of
All My Children and *Flamingo Road*

"Dotted with fascinating insider details about the soap world and its stars." —*Romantic Times*

Daytime Mysteries by Linda Palmer

LOVE IS MURDER
LOVE HER TO DEATH

love her to death

linda palmer

BERKLEY PRIME CRIME, NEW YORK

THE BERKLEY PUBLISHING GROUP
Published by the Penguin Group
Penguin Group (USA) Inc.
375 Hudson Street, New York, New York 10014, USA
Penguin Group (Canada), 10 Alcorn Avenue, Toronto, Ontario M4V 3B2, Canada
(a division of Pearson Penguin Canada Inc.)
Penguin Books Ltd., 80 Strand, London WC2R 0RL, England
Penguin Group Ireland, 25 St. Stephen's Green, Dublin 2, Ireland (a division of Penguin Books Ltd.)
Penguin Group (Australia), 250 Camberwell Road, Camberwell, Victoria 3124, Australia
(a division of Pearson Australia Group Pty. Ltd.)
Penguin Books India Pvt. Ltd., 11 Community Centre, Panchsheel Park, New Delhi—110 017, India
Penguin Group (NZ), Cnr. Airborne and Rosedale Roads, Albany, Auckland 1310, New Zealand
(a division of Pearson New Zealand Ltd.)
Penguin Books (South Africa) (Pty.) Ltd., 24 Sturdee Avenue, Rosebank, Johannesburg 2196,
South Africa

Penguin Books Ltd., Registered Offices: 80 Strand, London WC2R 0RL, England

This is a work of fiction. Names, characters, places, and incidents either are the product of the author's imagination or are used fictitiously, and any resemblance to actual persons, living or dead, business establishments, events, or locales is entirely coincidental.

LOVE HER TO DEATH

A Berkley Prime Crime Book / published by arrangement with the author

PRINTING HISTORY
Berkley Prime Crime edition / May 2005

Copyright © 2005 by Linda Palmer.
Cover design by Joni Friedman.
Cover art by Haydn Corner.

ISBN: 0-425-20295-X

BERKLEY® PRIME CRIME
Berkley Prime Crime Books are published by The Berkley Publishing Group,
a division of Penguin Group (USA) Inc.,
375 Hudson Street, New York, New York 10014.
BERKLEY PRIME CRIME is a registered trademark of Penguin Group (USA) Inc.
The Berkley Prime Crime design is a trademark belonging to Penguin Group (USA) Inc.

PRINTED IN THE UNITED STATES OF AMERICA

10 9 8 7 6 5 4 3 2 1

To D. Constantine Conte

I AM GRATEFUL ...

To Claire Carmichael (aka mystery novelist Claire McNab). Thank you for your hard work in teaching me the art and craft of writing mystery novels.

To Norman Knight: You are a genuine, heroic "knight."

To Morton Janklow: brilliant agent, great raconteur and loyal friend.

To Allison McCabe, extraordinary editor: You have creative x-ray vision.

To Warren Cowan, Monique Moss, and Richard Hoffman: Thank you for performing miracles on my behalf.

To Dr. Linda Venis, Director, Dept. of the Arts, Program Director, Writers' Program, UCLA Extension: Thank you for adjusting my schedule for book business.

To gifted photographer Gail Temple Colyer, who educated me about paddle wheel boats: One day we'll finally take that trip!

To the super-smart and diversely talented "test readers" who saw the manuscript first, and whose comments improved the book: Arthur Abelson, Carole Christie Moore Adams, Hilda Ashley, Henny Backus, Dr. Rachel Oriel Berg

Jane Wylie Boyd, Rosanne Kalil Bush, Ira Fistell, Richard Fredricks, Judy Tathwell Hahn, Nancy Koppang, Susan Magnuson, Mari Marks, Dr. Jeffrey Marks, Nellie Manda Monsrud, Jaclyn Carmichael Palmer, Dean Parker, Kathy J. Segal, Nancy and Terry Smith, Corrine Tatoul, and Kim LaDelpha Tocco. Thank you all for your help.

To Kay Partney Lautman and Virginia Voss Pohls: for giving "Aunt Penny" table decorating advice.

To Wayne Thompson of Colonial Heights, VA: the amazing man who inspired the character of "Chet."

To my "To Be Loved" teammate: Christie Burton.

As always, I'm grateful to Berry Gordy.

Chapter 1

"SNIPER PROOF," SAID my co-executive producer with a wide grin. "Twenty-six floors up is too high for anybody to shoot at you." Tommy Zenos indicated the beautiful nineteenth-century English partners' desk—his "Welcome to my foxhole" present to me. It had just been delivered in honor of my arrival. "Pick whichever half you want."

"I'll take the side next to the window," I said. After almost being murdered in my little home office a month ago, I no longer like the feeling of being enclosed.

The desk was gorgeous: green-tooled leather top, carved edges, and cabriole legs. English antiques are Tommy's passion. In addition, he brought two antique leather armchairs from his apartment for us, and a pair of Queen Anne chairs for visitors. I'd just been promoted from head writer of the daytime drama *Love of My Life* to head writer *and* co-executive producer. Because so much space is needed for taping facilities, Tommy and I were now sharing what had been *his* office in the Global Broadcasting building on Central Park West, in New York City.

"I need you here, Morgan," he said. "I can handle the practical stuff, but you're creative." He lowered his eyes and picked anxiously at his cuticles. "Besides, you're a good-looking woman who's not an actress. You're not after me for anything, so I can *talk* to you."

The intercom next to Tommy buzzed and I heard the voice of our assistant, Betty Kraft. "Your father's on line one."

Tommy blanched, his features twisting into an almost ludicrous expression. He lurched to his feet, shook his head, pointed to me and pantomimed picking up the phone.

I pressed the intercom buzzer on my side of the desk and said, "Betty, would you tell Mr. Zenos that Tommy's unavailable at the moment?"

"Will do," she replied, and disconnected.

Tommy flashed a grateful smile, then rushed out of the office.

Watching his fleeing back, it occurred to me he was not going to be the world's easiest office mate. Engaged four times but never married, he looks a decade older than his thirty-five years. I like Tommy, but he lives his life on an emotional roller coaster, and now we would share a small office, and one desk.

An hour later I was still alone at that aircraft carrier of a desk, editing scripts. Betty Kraft came into the office and closed the door. Tall and angular, with an explosion of gray corkscrew curls framing a rectangular face, she has piercing brown eyes and lips that curve into an expression of skepticism. Her attitude is: "I've seen it all and I don't let it get to me." According to Tommy, who adores her, she was a psychiatric nurse before landing her job at Global. "When you think about it," Tommy has said, "it's the perfect background for working in daytime drama."

Clutching an interoffice envelope, Betty looked grim. "From Lori Cole," she said. She balanced it on the palm of her hand. "I had Security check for explosives."

I laughed. "Lori Cole was only appointed VP Daytime last Friday. There can't be a problem already?"

"Don't be too sure. New executives are like dogs marking their territory. Sometimes they squirt the wrong target—like your leg."

I stood up, leaned across the desk, and took the envelope, but before I could open it, Betty pronounced five words that made my insides tighten.

"Cybelle wants to see you."

"Do you know why?"

"Actors never come to the producer's office just to say hello." Betty cocked one heavy eyebrow at me. " 'I'm not getting enough air time,' or 'I don't like my story line,' " she mimicked. "Or my personal favorite: 'I hate kissing my acting partner.' "

Five years ago, when I began as an associate writer on *Love of My Life*, I asked the man who was then head writer, "What does the producer do?"

"Clean up the shit," he had said.

Now it was my turn to wield the mop.

"Send her in," I said. "And hold my calls for a few minutes."

Betty nodded, and moments later ushered the actress into the office, closing the door behind her.

Delicate, stunning Cybelle Carter, with her jet-black hair and big round eyes, was one of the most popular young stars on our show. She greeted me with a soft "Hi, Morgan," and a nervous smile. As she perched on the edge of one of Tommy's Queen Anne chairs, I glanced at the Global Broadcasting Network envelope addressed to me. I was curious, but I didn't want to be rude to Cybelle. I put the envelope down unopened.

I looked up at her, but Cybelle was gazing at the show's genealogy chart, which was tacked on the wall behind Tommy's side of the desk. In the form of a graph, it stretches four feet wide and two feet high, diagramming all of the continuing characters on *Love of My Life* and listing who is connected—biologically or emotionally—to whom. This is an essential tool for keeping the relationships straight in a show that has been on the air five days a week, fifty-two weeks a year, for thirty years. *Love* was born the same year I was.

Cybelle grinned with delight. "There I am," she said, pointing to her place on the graph. Each character is represented by a small oval-shaped photo of the actor playing the part, the pictures hung like Christmas tree ornaments from their branches of the complex, multicharacter story.

She turned her attention from the chart to me. "I'm so glad they made you a producer," she said. "Tommy's nice, but it's great to be able to talk to a fellow woman about this problem I have."

"What is it?"

She hesitated for a moment, as though gathering her courage. "I'm really a natural blonde—like you, Morgan." She stroked a lock of the dark hair that made her resemble Disney's Snow White.

"That's unusual," I said. "When women color they usually go from dark hair to light, not the other way."

"Oh, but I *am* a real blonde." The urgency in her voice

startled me. "You can ask anybody who's seen me naked. Or . . ." she glanced around the office as if to make sure we were still alone. "It's just us girls—I could give you a peek."

"No, that's okay," I said quickly. "I'll take your word for it, Cybelle."

I'm a writer, not a gynecologist.

I decided to hurry Cybelle along by guessing why she had come to see me. "Do you want permission to go blonde on the show?"

Cybelle drew back as though she'd been struck.

"Oh, no!" Now there was desperation in her voice. "If I was a blonde again he could recognize me, and find me. Morgan, if he finds me, he's going to kill me!"

Chapter 2

I STOPPED FIDDLING with the Global envelope.

"Who?" I asked Cybelle. "Who are you afraid of?"

Cybelle leaned forward and whispered, "It's—he's my *sort of* husband."

It was a cold New York day in late November. Inside the office it was warm, but Cybelle—one of the sweetest and least demanding actresses I've ever worked with—was shivering and there was a look of absolute panic in her eyes. Alarm bells went off in my head. Cybelle was in a hot, front-burner story line that was keeping our ratings high. I didn't want to see her so upset, but I also had an obligation to protect the show.

I came around to her side of the desk and pulled up the second visitor's chair. "Tell me about this 'sort of' husband. Why are you so frightened? If you don't want to stay married to him, we'll help you get a divorce."

"He'll never let me go, Morgan." Her body slumped in despair. "He really will kill me if he finds out where I am."

Cybelle's eyes filled with tears. At any moment they would spill over the lower lids, cascade down her cheeks and ruin her TV makeup. I pulled several tissues out of the box on Tommy's side of the desk and gave them to her.

She took the tissues in trembling fingers and used them to block the flow.

With obvious effort, Cybelle regained control of her emotions. "Running away from him—that's the reason I dyed my hair black, and why I wear green contacts on camera."

Starring on TV is a strange way to hide, I thought. "You've been prominent on the show for a year now and he hasn't found you," I said.

"He wouldn't watch daytime TV, but in a few weeks my picture's going to be on the cover of *Time*!"

"Yes," I said, remembering the upcoming article. " 'The Junior Divas of Daytime.' "

Cybelle was one of four actresses chosen—the magazine had picked one each from four different shows—for a group cover shot. She was a natural choice for media attention; the audience loved her. According to the letters and e-mails that poured in to the office, and the fan chat room conversations we monitored, millions of viewers were hooked on the relationship between innocent Kira, the role played by Cybelle, and Cody, our dark knight, played by actor Link Ramsey. Kira and Cody were silk and chain mail—by any rational standard absolutely wrong for each other, and that made them the perfect combination for a daytime drama Super Couple.

"That magazine goes all over the world!" Cybelle was beginning to shake again.

"What's his name?" I asked.

The fear in her eyes was so powerful it was painful to see.

What in the world had happened to put her in this state?

"It's Philippe Abacasas."

The name meant nothing to me, but the moment Cybelle pronounced it, she shuddered and swung her head around, as though the very act of saying his name aloud would cause him to materialize, complete with razor fangs and death-ray eyes.

"It's okay." I patted her hand. "You're safe here at the studio."

I'm only a few years older than Cybelle, but the tone of my voice had the desired comforting effect. Cybelle took a long, deep breath and some of the tension left her body.

"Did you meet this Philippe here in New York?"

She shook her head. Strands of gleaming black hair brushed against her high cheekbones and the corner of her Kewpie Doll lips.

"In Houston," she said. "Four years ago, when I was eighteen. Houston's not my hometown, but it's where I was working as a waitress." Her words were spilling out in a rush now, as though she was relieved to share her problem. "This older man came in. He was wearing the most gorgeous suit, and was so *handsome*. He noticed me right away and asked to sit at my station. While he was deciding what to order, we talked about things. He said I was too special to stay in Houston. He invited me to go to San Francisco with him. He swore he wouldn't *do* anything— he just wanted to help me learn how to have a better life. The trip would be kind of a scholarship, he told me."

Oh, God. She fell for that.

"So I went," Cybelle said, "and just like he promised, he was a perfect gentleman. He took me to museums, and to fancy restaurants. He bought me beautiful clothes that he picked out. Then he took me to Paris, and to some more museums—I saw the real Mona Lisa. He had one of the famous designers make a dressmaker's form of my measurements. He said it was so he could order things for me while we traveled."

Her eyes were tearing up again, so I gave her more tissues and poured a glass of water from Tommy's carafe. I handed it to her and urged her to drink. She took a few sips.

"If you went to Paris, you had to have a passport. Did he get it for you?"

"No, I got one when I went to Houston," she said. "I wanted to see the world someday."

"It has your place of birth on it. If he saw that—"

"Those people don't know where I am," she said. I heard an unmistakable note of bitterness in her voice. "When I left Philippe I changed my name to Cybelle Carter." She looked at me, worried. "Do you think I'm a terrible person?"

"Of course not," I said reassuringly. "Go on with your story."

"He begged me to marry him. He said I was his last chance for happiness. Even though he was rich and I was broke, I felt sorry for him. Then the night we got married, he took something out from under the bed. One of the leather things that jockeys use—"

"A riding crop?"

Cybelle nodded. "Yes. Then he—"

A brisk knock on the door interrupted her. Jerry, the floor manager, opened it, coiled the top half of his body around the frame and said, "They need you on the set, Cybelle."

"Thanks, Jerry. She'll be there in a minute."

Jerry gave us a thumbs-up and withdrew.

Cybelle reached out and grasped one of my hands in both of hers. Her fingers were cold. "Please make up a past for me. The publicity people are after me for a full bio, the reporter from *Time* wants to interview me, and I don't know what to say. I can't tell them the truth." She took a breath and plunged on. "Morgan, you don't have any family—couldn't you maybe say I'm your little sister?"

I didn't see that coming. My voice was sharp when I asked her, "How do you know I don't have a family?"

"Gee, was it a secret? If it's a secret I'll never say anything—"

"No, it's not a secret," I said.

I just don't like being talked about.

Cybelle's eyes brightened. "Maybe we could say I'm from Europe someplace, and that my whole family died in an earthquake or in a war—and so that's why there aren't any records about me."

"You've been watching too much TV, Cybelle."

"Wars happen," she insisted. "Records get lost. I see stuff like that in the papers all the time." An obstacle occurred to her and she frowned. "But it has to be someplace where they speak English," she said, "because I don't speak any other language."

Under different circumstances, I might have laughed, but I had seen the real fear in Cybelle's eyes.

So I said, "Let me think about it."

Taking that as a yes, Cybelle squealed with gratitude and hugged me.

"I've got to go put in my contacts," she said, "but can we have dinner tonight and talk about it? With Johnny, too. You know Johnny Isaac, my agent? He doesn't know about

Philippe but I guess he has to now, so maybe you could tell him?" Her voice was begging me.

I would rather have a colon exam than tell Johnny Isaac his favorite client was married, and to someone who might be a dangerous nut, but I was co-executive producer now. "Handle it" was written in invisible ink at the bottom of my paycheck.

"Okay," I said. "You tell Johnny about dinner, but let's make it early. I have some rewriting to do tonight."

Cybelle was smiling as she hurried out of the office. It was as though once she dumped her problem in *my* lap she didn't have anything to worry about.

Now I did.

Chapter 3

AS SOON AS Cybelle left, Betty opened the door and stuck her head in. "Somebody wants to see you. A six-foot blonde with seven-foot legs. You better let her in so people will stop gawking and get back to work."

I knew Betty could be describing only one person. "Send her in!"

Into my new office, carrying a wrapped and beribboned bouquet of mixed flowers, swept a woman more stunning than the beauties that populate the network's shows. Silky blonde hair the color of Cristal champagne, and perfect legs that seem to go all the way up to her armpits. She was wearing a black and red dressed-to-devastate Versace suit with a deep V neckline. On her feet were a pair of Manolo Blanik foot fetishist's fantasies with the three-inch heels that increased her height to, as she likes to say, "five feet twelve." Because I am used to Nancy, I tend to forget the jaw-dropping effect she has on strangers.

"Betty, this is Nancy Cummings," I said, giving Nancy's hand a welcoming squeeze. "She's my lawyer."

Betty's eyes popped open. "Lawyer? Every time I think there's nothing left to surprise me . . ."

"This is Betty Kraft," I told Nancy, "the indispensable woman."

Nancy and Betty exchanged warm hellos.

"Morgan and I started as freshmen at Columbia together, a dozen years ago," Nancy said. "She's my best friend, so look out for her."

Betty took the flowers from Nancy. "I'll put these in water. Have a nice reunion, girls."

"I can't stay," Nancy said. "I'm taking a deposition in twenty minutes."

"Wearing *that?*"

Nancy smiled mischievously. "It rattles the opposition." One of my favorite things about Nancy is that she takes her work seriously, but never herself. "I just wanted to come by and wish you good luck in your new job," she said.

We were interrupted by the appearance of a good-looking young man in his early twenties in my doorway. With his light blond hair, star sapphire eyes, and easy smile, he might have been an actor, but I recognized him as Bud, Johnny Isaac's driver. He was carrying a double row of books that covered him from his waist to the handkerchief pocket of his dark jacket. A nine-by-eleven manila envelope was tucked under one arm.

"Hey, Miz Tyler." Aiming his dimpled chin at the books in his arms, he asked, "Where can I put these?"

Nancy glanced at the stack, arched one perfectly shaped eyebrow at me in amusement and said, "You're busy, sweetie. Talk to you later."

I said goodbye to Nancy and turned to Bud. "What's this?"

"From Mr. Isaac. There's a card in my pocket, but I can't reach it." His voice had a slight, pleasant drawl; he wasn't from New York.

"Here," I said, indicating one of the Queen Anne visitor's chairs.

Bud deposited the books on the sage green velvet seat cushion and fished around inside several pockets before he came up with a fold-over gift card from Barnes & Noble. He handed it to me and I read, "I heard you like caper novels. Thanks for being so good to Cybelle." It was signed "Johnny."

"That was very nice of Mr. Isaac," I said. In the pile I saw the names of some of my favorite mystery authors: Janet Evanovich, Nancy Pickard, Carolyn Hart, Jerrilyn Farmer, Sue Grafton, Robert Crais. A trove of treasures. "This is a great present. Thanks for bringing them, Bud."

"My pleasure, ma'am." He hesitated, looking down at his shoes, shifting his weight from one foot to the other. "I got some more errands to do for the boss, but . . ."

"What is it?"

He looked up at me and yanked the manila envelope from beneath his arm. "Would you look at this, ma'am?" Before I could respond, he'd opened the envelope and extracted an eight-by-ten glossy photograph. Of himself.

"Oh . . ." I said. *Oh, no* is what I was thinking.

"I drive and do stuff for Mr. Isaac, but I'm really an actor. Or, anyway, I want to be." There was a plea in his eyes. "Is this picture okay? For an actor, I mean?"

"It's very good." That was the truth. It was a headshot, taken at just the right angle to show Bud's even features, but without the retouching that tended to erase character and personality from a face. Skillful lighting emphasized his full head of blond hair. He was as attractive as any male model I'd ever seen, but unfortunately there wasn't anything in his face to distinguish him from thousands of other young men with bland good looks. I turned the picture over to glance at the traditional information page on the back of it. There wasn't much. It gave his name—Bud Collins—and vital statistics: five feet ten; one hundred and sixty-five pounds; blue eyes; blond hair; twenty-five years old. I was surprised to see he was represented by his present employer, Johnny Isaac, one of the most important agents in the business.

"Have you had any acting experience?" I asked.

"I'm taking lessons on my nights off, at the HB Studio, down on Bank Street. Do you know it?"

I nodded. "Some fine actors have come out of that school."

"Maybe you'll keep me in mind, if a part comes up?"

I didn't want to give him false encouragement, but the fact that he was studying at a respected acting school was a mark in his favor. "I'll give your picture to our casting director," I said. "If she wants you to come in for an audition, she'll call you."

Smiling happily, Bud gave me a thumbs-up and left. As he passed Betty in the doorway, he winked at her.

"That Bud's such a cutie," she said. "Like a Golden Retriever puppy. He makes me smile every time he comes over from the Isaac office to pick up scripts for Cybelle."

I showed her his eight-by-ten glossy. "Bud wants to be an actor."

The maternal light in her eyes went out. "Poor guy," Betty said sadly. She'd returned with Nancy's flowers, having arranged them in a cut glass pitcher I recognized as coming from the craft services catering table. When she put them on the desk she spotted the pile of novels.

"Are these what the puppy brought you?"

"A present from Johnny—mystery novels. Very thoughtful, but I don't know when I'll have time to read them." I saw her examining the titles with interest. "Borrow any of them you like."

"Thanks, I will." She moved back a step and looked pointedly at Nancy's flowers. She turned to me and shook her head in wonderment. "I'll say this for you, Morgan: you got guts, having a best friend who's that gorgeous."

I laughed. "Is that a compliment, or an insult?"

She just smiled at me.

I remembered the eight-by-ten glossy in my hand. "Betty, give this to Casting. Tell them I'd like Bud to get an audition when a part in his age range comes up."

"Will do." Betty studied the picture speculatively. "I wonder if he can act."

"If he can, I'd like to give him a chance."

"You're a softie."

"More like soft-*headed*," I said as Betty went back to her desk.

At last, I had a moment to read the note from Global's newest vice president, but before I could do more than open the flap on the envelope, Betty buzzed me. "There's a long distance call for you on line two," she said. "It's from The Hague, wherever that is."

"The Netherlands." I pressed the button for line two, but I didn't wait to hear the voice on the other end of the line. A warm smile was on my face and in my voice as I said,

"Hello, Chet." Kevin Chet Thompson, criminal psychologist and author of several best–selling books on crime, was the only person I knew at the World Court.

"Hi, gorgeous," he said. "Miss me?"

"You haven't been gone long enough."

"Four weeks—seems like a year to me."

"It can't be that bad," I said. "You only knew me for three weeks before you left." Chet and I met in early October, shortly after the murder of someone I worked with.

"It's been six and a half weeks since I kissed you," he said.

That reminder sent an involuntary little tingle through me, but I wasn't going to admit it. "I don't remember that," I lied.

I heard him chuckle. "Yes, you do."

Yes, I do. It was a terrific kiss.

I wanted to get off the subject of kissing. I was attracted to Chet, but I hadn't decided yet what to do about that.

"How are things at the war crimes trial?" I asked.

"Grim. Worse than grim. That's why I spend my free time thinking about how you felt in my arms."

"Hey, I'm at work—and if you're using your cell phone this must be costing you a fortune."

"I can afford it," he said.

"Do you know when you're coming back?"

"The day after Thanksgiving."

That would be this Friday, three days away. I kept my voice light. "Do they celebrate Thanksgiving at the World Court?"

"Sure—they hang a turkey," he joked. "Actually, friends of mine from the *New York Times* and the *International Herald Tribune* are putting something together. But I'd rather be with you." There was a pause. I thought we'd been disconnected, but then he spoke again. Now I heard a slight edge in his voice as he asked, "Are you spending Thanksgiving with *him*?"

"I'm going to have dinner at Penny's," I said. My voice acquired a matching edge, "with Nancy and the man who almost had to defend me for murder, and a few other peo-ple. And, yes, Detective Phoenix will be there. You *know* he lives there, so why are you asking?"

"I'd hoped the NYPD would have sent him away to charm school."

"Chet, I told you before you left that I'm not going to discuss who I see, or when or where."

"Are we having our first fight?"

"This is at least our third."

"Will you save Saturday night for me?"

I agreed. Our little storm was over, and we said good-bye. Affectionately.

Again, I picked up the envelope from Lori Cole, the new VP Daytime. This time I extracted the note without in-terruption. At the top was a notation that a copy had been sent to Tommy Zenos.

When I read Ms. Cole's communication—her dictate—it produced a rush of anger that made my face hot. This woman who had been hired away from another network with great fanfare, who had been a Global exec for less than a week, was ordering Tommy and me to fire one of our most talented actresses, Francie James.

I stormed out of the office.

Betty was at her desk right outside the door.

"Where's Tommy?" I asked.

"He called his father back, and now they're having yet another reconciliation lunch. This one's at the Four Sea-sons. Want me to page him?"

"No, don't disturb them. Just find me if he comes back before I do."

"The very minute. Where will you be?"

I answered her question with a question of my own. "Where's Francie James right now?"

Betty ran a finger down her copy of that day's master schedule, which listed what every actor in the cast of *Love of My Life* was doing, and where he or she was doing it, throughout the day.

"Francie . . . Francie . . . should be in Wardrobe."

"Then that's where I'm going," I said as I started across the floor.

An hour-long episode of *Love of My Life* is taped each Monday through Friday on the twenty-sixth floor of the Global Broadcasting Network building, in our two permanent facilities, Studios 35 and 37.

Trauma Center, the other Global daytime drama produced in New York, is taped directly below us; floors twenty-one through twenty-four house studios used for the news–magazine show *America in the Morning*; a game show; a late night comedy–variety hour and an afternoon talk show hosted by former child movie star, Kitty Leigh. Kitty recently started doing double duty by playing the role of a nightclub singer in our show. The rest of the network's schedule, which includes a third daytime drama, and the prime time comedies and dramas, are produced in Los Angeles.

Love's wardrobe department is on the far side of the floor from the production office, with the studios in between. I moved quietly toward Studio 35, where Cybelle and her romantic acting partner, Link Ramsey were taping a scene, a picnic lunch in the park. The "park" consisted of two portable trees, a plastic rock, and some Astroturf, but the scene would be shot mostly in close ups because faces full of longing, not shots of landscaping, are what keep the audience coming back for more.

Cybelle and Link were putting their hearts, or at least their talents, into one of my favorite scenes. It showed their characters getting to know each other better and, as they became brave enough to reveal secret things about themselves, falling more and more deeply in love. Although I would never admit it to anyone on the show, this was a scene I'd written from life—from my former life. I married Ian Tyler, a thirty-eight-year-old wildlife photographer, when I was nineteen years old, after knowing him for only one week. He was the real-life model for the man on that blanket, and I was the girl. We had fallen more in love every day of the almost six years we were together. I can't imagine ever loving like that again, so I relive those days through the characters played by Cybelle and Link.

I snapped myself out of the past and back into co-executive producer mode. Glancing at my watch, I saw the scene was running on schedule. That was especially important today because of the complicated action scene that had to be shot on location later. It had taken Tommy a while to work out the travel arrangements, and to rent the special location we needed, but this was one of our all-important Friday episodes. The excitement of the scene would be worth the trouble and expense.

I had devised a cliff–hanger tag for the show that sent Link and Cybelle diving into a lake to escape a mysterious gunman who was after Cody, the character played by Link. The "lake" would be a water tank located at an old movie studio in Queens. Link, tall and lean, insisted he'd do his own diving and swimming. Cybelle, though, was terrified of any body of water bigger than a bathtub, so her stunt double, Jeannie Ford, would go into the tank for her.

As soon as the love scene I was watching was completed, Link and Cybelle (accompanied by a different director, Cybelle's double, and a mobile crew) would head for Queens. There the makeup artist would wet Cybelle's hair and spray her face with baby oil, which photographs like beads of water. The director would shoot special close-ups of Cybelle that would be edited into the scene later, while Jeannie Ford would be photographed from the back, doing the swimming.

A prickling of the hairs on the base of my skull alerted me to the fact that I was not alone in the shadows. I turned my head to see Cybelle's devoted agent, Johnny Isaac, behind me. Further back, also watching the scene, was Bud Collins, Johnny's driver and newly revealed aspiring actor.

I moved to stand next to Johnny, and pantomimed opening a book while I mouthed the words "Thank you." He nodded acknowledgement, but returned his attention to Cybelle. And to Link, who was sucking Cybelle's fingers. I hadn't written that action in the script, but I wished I had. With his devilish smile, uninhibited sexuality, and idiosyncratic way of speaking his lines, Link was an actor who made a writer look good. And, I saw out of the corner of my eye, an actor who was making Johnny Isaac steam.

Johnny, about forty, has well-proportioned features, and the solid shoulders and arms of the boxer he had been when he was twenty. A successful talent agent, long divorced, he is rumored to have a massive crush on Cybelle. Tommy Zenos, who makes it his business to know everything about everybody, insists that Johnny has yet to tell Cybelle that he is "ga-ga in love with her," as Tommy puts it. He also claims that Cybelle is pretending not to know. So, Johnny's heart full of love is the metaphorical elephant in the living room no one ever mentions. I was not looking forward to telling him that Cybelle was married, and to a probable psycho who made her fear for her life. But I wouldn't think about that now.

I mouthed a silent goodbye to Johnny, smiled at Bud and worked my way through the nest of cables that criss-crossed the floor. Between Johnny's and Bud's presence on the set, and the heightened security following a murder in our building last month, I didn't have to worry about Cybelle's physical safety for the moment.

I had another urgent problem to solve.

Chapter 4

PASSING STUDIO 37, I saw lights being set, props being checked and several of the other contract actors on the show rehearsing their movements for upcoming scenes. Just as I reached the door to the wardrobe department, I heard the shrill voice of Costume Supervisor Dani Ryan, saying: "Francie, you've gotten fatter than a pig!"

I opened the door.

"Dani?" I didn't let my voice betray my annoyance. "May I see you outside?" I smiled at Francie James, the actress who was standing on the four-inch high circular platform used for costume fittings. Her face was flushed with embarrassment; she clutched a blouse against her chest as though the material would protect her from further verbal assault.

Dani Ryan, in her late thirties, is so thin she could be a

poster girl for anorexia. She put down her pins and tape measure and followed me out into the hallway where, for the moment, we had a tiny island of privacy.

"What do you need, Morgan?"

I kept my voice low because I didn't want to embarrass Dani by having her staff overhear what I was about to say. "Dani, I don't want you—ever again—to speak to anyone on this show the way you just spoke to Francie."

Dani instantly went on the defensive. "Francie's getting as wide as she is tall—I can't squeeze her into any of her costumes!"

"You're a great artist," I told her. That wasn't entirely an exaggeration; Dani *is* one of the most creative and resourceful costume supervisors in television. "I know Francie's become a challenge," I went on, "but I also know you can handle it." My admiring tone was Diplomacy On Parade. "Just between us, Dani, I'm changing Francie's story line, and she'll be in different costumes soon."

Very few people on staff are privy to information about future story lines, and even then only on a need-to-know basis. Dani was thrilled to be in the know. Before she could ask any questions, I said, "Take your staff and go have lunch downstairs in Global's dining room. My treat—so sign my name to the check. I'll talk to Francie."

"Okay."

"*I'll* talk to Francie," I repeated, with emphasis. "Just me."

Dani made a zipping motion across her lips. She opened the door to the wardrobe department, called to the two older women who were busy repairing and refreshing costumes, and summoned them out of the room.

As Dani and her crew disappeared down the hall toward

the elevator, I went into Wardrobe. Covering three thousand square feet, the wardrobe department houses thirty rows of clothing on rolling racks which are divided by signs indicating which *Love of My Life* character wears which outfits. In the corner immediately to my left, out of range of Dani Ryan's unforgiving three-sided mirror, Francie James had curled herself into a ball on a shabby old sofa. Although she wasn't making a sound, and her luxurious brown hair obscured her face, I knew by the shaking of her shoulders that she was sobbing.

I was struck by the beauty of Francie's thick and shining hair.

Francie, I realized, had the best hair of anyone on the show. I hadn't noticed before; she plays a legal secretary, and her hair is always coiled into a tight bun. I made a mental note to talk to the show's hairdresser about making an asset out of Francie's great mane.

"Francie. Hi."

She clenched her hands on the sofa pillow and sat up. Her face was so pale she looked sick as she said, "You're going to recast, aren't you."

It was a statement, not a question. She thought I was about to fire her for her weight gain and "recast" by hiring a slender actress to play her part.

"You are not going to be replaced, Francie." I glanced around until I spotted a box of tissues, pulled some out and handed them to her. She took them and wiped her eyes. I gave her a few more and she blew her nose.

I'd like to have the Kleenex concession on this show.

"I know I'm a mess—I've been trying to diet . . ."

"Let's not talk about weight or dieting for a minute," I said.

"That's easy for you to say, Morgan. You've got a great body, and it doesn't even matter because you're never on camera." Her tears started flowing again.

"Francie, come on, stop crying. I think you're going to like what I came to tell you. It's about what I'm planning for your character, Dinah."

"Planning?" She looked up at me with hope in her hazel eyes. She patted her stomach. "Are you going to get me pregnant on the show?"

"I have a better idea." I sat down on the sofa next to her. "Dinah has too much potential to waste her as Craig's secretary. I hate those awful, boxy suits you have to wear, and I don't like the way they do your hair. You have great hair, Francie, but we're not letting the audience see it. So, I'm going to have Craig try to force himself on Dinah, and when he does, I'm going to have Dinah surprise him by telling him to go 'F' himself—but in words we can say on the air."

That made her smile.

"You are beautiful, Francie," I said. "The camera loves your bone structure."

"Not any more. Billy Mills told me he was going to start shooting me with a wide-angle lens."

"That was cruel," I said, making a mental note to talk to Billy, one of our revolving wheel of four directors.

"Do you have any idea why you've gained so much weight?" I asked.

She nodded. "I've been taking diet pills for fifteen years. Then last year I finally let myself read about the side effects and I got scared, so I stopped taking them, but now I'm hungry all the time. I just eat, eat, eat."

"Look, Francie, don't worry about staying on the show. You're too good an actress; we're not going to lose you."

As I talked, I was getting an idea. I'd already planned, in my long-term document for *Love*, that Francie was going to leave the law office and break away from both her smothering mother character and from her lecherous boss on the show, sleazy lawyer Craig.

"We're going to put you in a much more entertaining setting," I said. "Behind the bar at the nightclub that Sean O'Neil's character, Nicky, just bought."

She sat up straighter.

"We'll have your fabulous hair falling loose around your face. And for your new work clothes, how would you like to wear some low cut peasant blouses?" I was sure she realized, without my having to say it, that those blouses would turn her large breasts from a costuming challenge into an asset. "At Nicky's, you'll listen to everybody's troubles and flash that wonderful smile of yours." Now came the sensitive part of my plan.

"Francie," I said, "would you like it if I wrote a weight loss story for Dinah?"

"I'd try to get thin on the show?"

"I'd like to incorporate your diet pill experience into the story. From what I've read, taking them for a long time can mess up a person's metabolism. I'll do some research to find out the facts, so we can deal with the danger of the pills as part of the story. And we'll work out a plan for you—*not* a diet. Over the course of a year you could slowly get to whatever *realistic* number you want, and inspire the audience at the same time."

She frowned. "What if I fail?" she asked.

"If you don't lose, that will be part of the story, too. You aren't what you *weigh*. You've made Dinah such an appealing character, you have millions of fans."

"You're really going to work out a weight loss plan for

me? You'll figure out how I can lose *and* stay off the
pills?"

"Yes," I said, with more confidence than I felt.

"When are we going to start? I'm supposed to spend
Thanksgiving with my parents in New Jersey. . . ."

"Go," I said. "Enjoy the day."

"But my mom's a fabulous cook." I heard a note of
panic in her voice. "Nothing she makes would be on anybody's diet."

"Don't say diet, Francie. Don't even *think* diet."

"Then tell me what I can eat at Mom's Thanksgiving
dinner."

"Whatever you want." I smiled. "Relax and have a
good time. We'll start your new . . ." I searched for just
the right word ". . . *fitness* program the day after Thanksgiving. I'll meet you at your place Friday morning. We'll
go for a walk and I'll lay out the plan. How's ten
o'clock?"

She nodded. "Great. Should I have breakfast first?"

"Of course," I said. "Stop worrying, Francie. It's a long
holiday weekend. No work. Have some fun."

Outside the wardrobe department a few minutes later I
leaned against the wall and took a deep breath. Francie
James had her spirit back. Now all I had to do was keep my
promise and come up with a weight loss plan for her that
wouldn't feel like a diet. No, scratch that. It wasn't *all*. I
also had to meet Lori Cole and convince her that firing
Francie was a bad idea. And there was another thing. *If Cybelle Carter's fear was real,* I had to find a way to keep her
mysterious husband from killing her.

The possibility of murder made me think of the other
man in my life—I mean other than author and criminal

psychologist Kevin Chet Thompson, who was currently at The Hague.

That other man was my favorite homicide detective, Matt Phoenix.

Chapter 5

AS I CAME into view, Betty Kraft gestured with her thumb toward the closed office door. "Tommy just got back," she said. She raised her eyebrows, flashing some signal, but I couldn't decode the message.

"What's the matter?" I asked.

Before she could answer, the office door flew open. "There you are!" Tommy was making wild scooping motions with both hands. "Come in, in, in."

Tommy's fits of extreme nervousness are usually triggered by encounters with his father. Alexander Zenos created three hugely successful daytime dramas. He is renowned for having done more than anyone except Agnes Nixon to combine social relevance with hot-blooded romance. And he is still doing it, two hundred and sixty episodes a year per show, year after year. He is unquestionably a titan in our business, but my guess is that Papa Zenos was an emotionally brutal father.

Tommy's red silk necktie was stained and askew, the top button of his pale blue shirt was missing, and he was nervously blotting his hands on a fistful of white paper napkins. When he turned to close the office door behind me, I saw a large bag from the Carnegie Delicatessen on the desk.

"You want corned beef with red cabbage slaw on regular rye, pastrami with Russian dressing on dark rye, or egg salad on an onion roll?" he asked, removing those items from the bag. He pushed aside piles of scripts to make room. "Also, I've got potato salad, Greek olives, and pickled tomatoes. And Diet Snapple."

Lean pastrami is one of my two hundred favorite foods. Inhaling the aroma, I reached for a couple of napkins and half of one of the thick sandwiches. Tommy pulled my chair around to the end the desk where he'd laid out the meal, and put a bottle of Snapple in front of each of us.

"I thought you had lunch with your father," I said. "Did he cancel?"

"No, we had lunch, but I can't *taste* anything when I eat with him. He has a hundred ways to tell me he thinks I'm a fat slob of a loser, without actually using those words."

"He should be proud of you," I said. I reminded him that our show was number three in the overall ratings, and number two with the precious eighteen to forty-nine-year-old demographic. "We're beating his *World Enough And Time*."

I've always liked the title of that particular Alexander Zenos creation, taken from a seventeenth century Andrew Marvel poem about a man pleading with his reluctant lady love: "Had we but world enough, and time, this coyness, lady, were no crime."

"Dad claims the ratings are rigged because our chairman of the board paid somebody off. Then he bragged that he's got better stunts planned for the February sweeps than we have."

I paused mid-bite. "He doesn't know what we're going to do! I haven't even told *you* yet! Assuming we get budget approval, I've worked out a story line that'll take us on a location shoot down the Mississippi River on a steamboat. Unless you're allergic to paddle wheels and catfish, you're going to love it."

Tommy didn't respond. I wasn't sure he was listening. When he looked at me, I saw defeat in his eyes. I took a bite out of my pastrami and waited for him to come out of his trance. Two mouthfuls later, Tommy's eyes unglazed. He focused them on the shelf behind me. "Hand me the Academy Players' Directory."

I turned and was about to take down the telephone-book sized catalogue of actors, when a thought struck me. "Why do you want it?"

"We have to replace Francie," Tommy answered through a mouthful of potato salad. He picked up the memo from Lori Cole and waved it with one hand. "Didn't you read this?"

"I read it," I said, "but I don't agree with it."

An expression of horror swept across Tommy's face; it was his automatic reaction to the thought of going up against an authority figure.

"But, Morgan, she *told* us to fire Francie. We have to do it because . . ." He scanned the note and read aloud: "Ms. James's weight is detrimental to the image of the Global Broadcasting Network." He looked up from the memo and put the executive-babble into his own words: "She's too fat for *Love*."

This from a man whose doctor told him recently that he's clinically obese.

I didn't say it. Stating the obvious to Tommy would not save Francie's job, nor save a good new story line.

"Tommy, we have plenty of romance and mystery on the show, but we've never done a diet story. Sex and diets sell. I'd like to use Francie's character for an on-air weight loss arc."

Tommy was intrigued; he stopped chewing. "You want to use Francie's weight gain to hook the audience into watching her *lose* weight?" He was smiling with delight at the possibility of striking a new vein of ratings gold. Suddenly the smile vanished. "But what if she doesn't lose weight?"

"I think she will, but if she doesn't, that will be part of the story, too. Anyway, if my weight loss plan doesn't produce the result she wants, by that time we'll have had months to dramatize how hard it is to lose weight, and how cruel people can be to those who don't look like the so-called 'ideal.'"

Tommy glanced down at his almost-finished corned beef, then back at me. "You've got a plan for Francie to lose weight?"

"Yes," I said.

Okay, technically that was a lie, but I thought of it as an *anticipation* of the truth.

"This plan—is it how you stay in shape even though you eat stuff that tastes good?" Tommy asked. Like Francie's had been, his voice was full of hope.

"I'm going to put the plan in the script. You can read it in a few days."

Just as soon as I figure it out.

Tommy picked up the egg salad sandwich. "So," he said, "you'll tell Lori Cole that we're keeping Francie?"

"You're the senior executive producer," I said. "Why don't you tell her?"

"Because you're the one with all the power."

That statement astonished me. "What power?" I asked. "VP Daytime outranks both of us."

Tommy smiled his *"I know a secret"* smile, a particular upturning of his lips coupled with a crinkling of his eyes that always precedes his telling me the latest hot news from the Global Broadcasting jungle drums.

"What?" I asked.

"She'll be afraid to cross you because"—he lowered his voice—"because everybody *knows* you're sleeping with our chairman of the board."

"That's ridiculous!" I said, sitting up straight. "I am *not* sleeping with Winston Yarborough." That was the absolute truth.

"I didn't expect you to admit it," he said. "Don't worry—I'm not going to say anything."

"It isn't true, Tommy. Where did you get such a crazy idea?"

My voice had risen with anger, but Tommy was still keeping his tone low and confidential as he used his fingers to check off several points to the theory.

"One, you're great-looking. Two, you're a widow so you're available. Three, you've been seen riding in the back of his limo," he said. "More than once." He shrugged. "It's obvious."

What Tommy, and whoever had seen me in Winston Yarborough's car, did not know—and what I could never tell anyone—was that, far from being romantically involved, I had been helping Yarborough do damage control. Global Broadcasting had faced a public relations nightmare because two people connected to the network had been murdered. We solved the problem and averted the damage. I have not seen or spoken to our chairman since.

"You, or somebody, took one and one and got eleven," I said. "The conclusion is *wrong*, Tommy."

Tommy was no longer sure of his bogus facts, but he didn't want to believe me. His voice was plaintive as he said, "You mean you and old Yarborough aren't . . . ?" He waggled his eyebrows as a euphemism for what he had thought.

"No, we are not." I stared at Tommy in amazement as his expression changed to doleful. "Are you *disappointed*?"

"Well, yes, I am, because if you're not sleeping with him, then you don't have any power and we're screwed."

I thought for a minute. Then I picked up the phone and buzzed Betty at her desk outside. "Betty, would you call Lori Cole's office and make an appointment for me to see her before she goes back to Los Angeles?"

There was time for one more bite of pastrami before Betty buzzed me back.

"The new queen's assistant—an officious twit named *Lawrence*—said, 'Ms. Cole doesn't have time to meet with Ms. Tyler.' " Betty's voice was colder than an ice pack.

"Tell *Lawrence* that this is urgent."

"I did. He wasn't impressed."

I pushed the rest of my sandwich away. Holding the phone against my forehead, I seethed. My face must have read "trouble," because when I glanced up at Tommy, his forehead was beading with sweat. His eyes darted to the remains of my lunch.

"Are you going to finish that?" he asked.

"No."

As he grabbed what was left of the pastrami special, I made a decision.

"Betty, please get Lori Cole's office for me."

On her end of the line, Betty gave a wicked little chuckle. "It'll be my pleasure."

In seconds a voice that sounded like a member of the British royal family announced, "Ms. Cole's office. Lawrence here."

"This is Morgan Tyler. I'd like to speak to Lori." For the purpose of intimidation, I deliberately used her first name, and did not acknowledge his.

"She is in a meeting," he said.

"Then I'll come over and catch her when it's over."

That shook him up. "Oh, no—don't do that!" I heard him rattling papers on his desk. "We have one *tiny* window of opportunity in her schedule. She could squeeze you in for a few minutes at eight o'clock tomorrow morning."

"Eight o'clock will be fine," I said in a voice sweet enough to rot a tooth. I hung up before *Lawrence* could.

Chapter 6

I DIDN'T HAVE either the privacy or the opportunity to telephone Homicide Detective Matt Phoenix of the Twentieth Precinct until later in the afternoon.

When he picked up I said, "Hi, it's Morgan. Did I catch you in the middle of a murder investigation?"

"We just cleared a case," he said.

"What's the score?"

"The bad guys are still ahead, but the good guys are closing the gap." There was a note of pride in his warm baritone. "So, Marmalade . . . I hope you're not calling because you found another body."

My penchant for finding bodies was a joke now, but a few weeks ago it hadn't been funny.

"Actually," I said, "I'm calling because you might help

prevent a murder. If someone I know really is in danger, I mean."

He was silent.

"Matt?"

"I'm waiting to hear a sentence I can understand. What's this about?"

"I'll tell you, but first could you use your sources to check out a man named Philippe Abacasas?"

"Spell it."

I did. "He's rich and European," I said. "I don't know if he's an American citizen."

"Do you know where he lives? Or where he is now?"

"No," I said, "but you wouldn't enjoy the challenge if I made it too easy for you."

"Nothing about you is easy, Marmalade."

Shortly after we met, Matt had remarked that my hair was the color of marmalade. It became his nickname for me.

"Don't call me that," I said.

"I can't call you 'Morgan.' It would sound like I'm dating a guy."

"Are we dating?"

"I've taken you out to dinner twice in the last three weeks, paid the check both times and escorted you to your door. Sounds like dating to me."

I smiled and changed the subject. "Speaking of dinner, could you join me and two friends this evening? Cybelle Carter—she's an actress on the show—and her agent, Johnny Isaac. You met him the same night you met me."

"A night to remember," he said, a playful lilt in his voice.

"Cybelle is the one I'm concerned about," I said.

"What have we got? A stalker? She could get a restraining order."

"It's more complicated than that. We'll explain tonight—if you can join us."

"Yeah, I'm free. In the meantime, I'll see what I can find out about this Philippe Abacasas."

"Thank you, Matt. Can you keep the inquiry quiet?"

"It's not a case," he said. "I'll call in a personal favor."

"I appreciate that. Maybe you'll be able to tell Cybelle she has nothing to worry about."

I heard a weary sigh on the other end of the line. When he spoke, the bantering tone was gone. "In my experience, it's pretty rare for a woman to be afraid of a man without reason," he said. "You sure you want to get in the middle of this?"

"If something happened to Cybelle, and I didn't try to help her, I'd never forgive myself."

"Are you worried about her as a *friend*, or because you need her on your show?"

"That's a rotten question," I said.

"Yeah, but what's the answer?"

Truth time. "It's both," I said. But I wasn't very proud of that.

"I'll check this guy out. Do you know what he looks like?"

"From what Cybelle told me, I have the impression that he's in his forties, good-looking, dresses expensively, lives high, travels first class."

I was silent for a moment, considering what else I should tell him.

"I can hear you thinking," he said. "Spill it."

"Cybelle's mystery man might have . . . unusual sexual habits."

"Define 'unusual'?"

"I don't know exactly," I said. Truthfully. "That's just a guess."

A riding crop under the bed sounds unusual to me, but I admit I haven't explored "the wilder shores of love."

I could hear a smile in his voice as he said, "One day I'd like to find out what you consider unusual."

"Don't you have criminals to catch?"

Matt chuckled. "Let me know when and where we're having dinner tonight," he said.

IT WAS A little after five when I left the office. Out on the street, I turned north and, invigorated by the cold November air, began the nine-block walk home. I live in a third floor co-op at the Dakota, the nineteenth-century gothic building at One West Seventy-second Street. Much of the classic horror movie *Rosemary's Baby* was filmed there. It's also the building where John Lennon lived until he was gunned down by a deranged fan right in front of the entrance. His widow still lives in their apartment on the second floor, which stretches almost half a block along Central Park. My home is directly above part of that apartment, though it's only one-third the size.

I collected my mail from Sally Hicks, a Columbia University theater major (as I once was) and the building's receptionist two days a week. She loaded me up with magazines, Christmas catalogues, scripts from my two out-of-town scriptwriters, packages from the Home Shopping Network and QVC, and several bills.

I was across the courtyard heading toward the entrance to my section of the building, when Sally called my name and hurried after me. She waved a small, flat package wrapped in shiny white paper.

"I almost forgot to give you this," she said, putting it on top of my pile. "It didn't come in the mail—a messenger dropped it off."

I thanked her and continued on toward the interior entrance, where, as usual, I ignored the elevator and sprinted up the two flights of stairs to my front door. Taking stairs and walking all over the city makes it possible for me to eat pretty much whatever I want.

Once inside my apartment, I dropped the heap of packages and mail onto the foyer table. I intended to go straight to the bedroom and deal with the pile later, after I showered and changed clothes, but the small messengered package intrigued me. It was secured by a gleaming silver bow, like a wedding present. I would have thought it had been delivered to me by mistake, but I saw my name written beneath the bow in a calligrapher's script. I examined it closely. My name was the only marking on the paper.

Opening the package, I discovered it was a DVD of the classic Hitchcock thriller, *Vertigo*. I turned it over, looking for an attached card or a note, but there wasn't one.

In the three years since becoming head writer of *Love of My Life,* I've received dozens of unexpected gifts. Some of them are from sponsors, some are from actors who want me to hear ideas for enhancing their roles. They get thank you notes, but no input. Other packages are from people who hope that a clever present will persuade me to read their writing samples and hire them to write scripts. I return those, with a note telling the senders that I *will* read their writing samples if they'll send them to the production office at the Global building, marked to my attention.

This was the first package that had come without identification as to the sender. It made me uneasy. I had the creepy feeling that someone had sent me a message, and it wasn't "Happy Birthday." I put the DVD down on the table and went into the bathroom to take a shower before changing for dinner.

In the bathroom I did something I'd never done before: I locked the door.

Chapter 7

JOHNNY ISAAC TOLD me he'd made a seven P.M. reservation at Tuscano, on Mulberry Street between Hester and Grand in Little Italy. I left word for Matt.

Little Italy is one of my favorite neighborhoods, so I didn't mind the five-mile taxi ride downtown. I got there eight minutes early, but as my cab pulled up, I saw Johnny standing at the front door, watching the street. He spotted me in the cab and hurried over to pay the driver before I had a chance to open my handbag. He must have added a generous tip, because the driver gave him a ringing "Thanks, man."

As Johnny opened the cab's back door and offered his hand to help me out, I asked, "Where's Cybelle?"

"Freshening up."

"Thank you so much for that wonderful collection of mystery novels," I said. "I'll be enjoying them for months."

"I figured they'd last longer than a few dozen roses," Johnny said. He opened the restaurant's front door and stood aside so I could precede him.

Tuscano was small; there were only twelve tables, covered with red cloths over white cloths, placed far enough apart on the terra cotta floor tiles so that conversations could be relatively private. The kitchen was separated from the tables only by a waist-high brick partition, which was topped by a serving counter of polished oak.

Three young chefs, who resembled each other enough to be brothers, and probably were, worked the stoves, grilling vegetables and meats and fish, boiling pasta and stirring sauces in large pots. An older woman with crimson hair—a shade not found in nature—supervised them. When she saw Johnny at the entrance, her welcoming smile turned her face from aged to ageless.

Johnny guided me to a table set for four and helped me off with the black wool cape I wore over a red cashmere mock-neck sweater and black suede pants. He was pulling a chair out for me when Cybelle returned from the rest room. He seated her, and then sat down himself.

He asked what I'd like to drink.

"A glass of wine," I said. "Red. Whatever the house wine is."

"The food here is northern Italian, but the wine is Sicilian. I think you'll like it." He signaled one of the two waiters over, ordered the red Sicilian wine for me and for himself, and a glass of white for Cybelle. He didn't have to ask her what she wanted.

Cybelle was so nervous that her "Hi" to me was barely audible.

As soon as the waiter left to fill the wine order, Johnny inclined his head toward the empty seat at our table. "Who's our fourth?"

"Matt Phoenix," I said. "You met him—"

"I remember. Phoenix the cop." He glanced from Cybelle to me and asked, "What's going on?"

Cybelle hunched her shoulders and shivered. Johnny looked at her, concerned. "You okay, baby?" She nodded in reply, avoiding his eyes.

"Just how bad is—whatever this is?" he asked.

"Cybelle has been wanting to tell you something," I said, "but she's worried that you'll be angry." I looked at Cybelle for confirmation, but she was avoiding my eyes, too. "The problem—"

At that moment, Matt Phoenix arrived. Six feet tall, with muscular shoulders, dark hair, and eyes dark as fresh brewed coffee, he was dressed casually in gray slacks and a navy blue blazer over a dove gray crewneck sweater. Attractive though he was, my attention focused on the envelope he clutched in one large hand.

"Sorry I'm late," he said. Johnny half rose from his seat, reached across the table, and the two men shook hands.

Matt smiled at me, said a quick "Hi," and turned to Cybelle. "Hello, Ms. Carter."

Cybelle nodded at him and forced a smile. It wasn't a good performance, but she was trying to be social.

Matt sat down next to me, across from Johnny, and Cybelle. The waiter brought our glasses of wine, and Matt said he'd have a glass of the red, too.

The lady with the crimson hair greeted Johnny in Italian, and he responded in kind. The only words I understood were the first four: "*Buona sera, cara Lucia.*" He must have said something flattering to her after that because she fluttered her eyelashes flirtatiously and blew him a kiss.

Johnny turned to us and said, "There's a limited menu, but it's all good." He indicated a chalkboard on the far wall. "It's posted over there if you want to choose, but Cybelle and I just let Lucia bring us whatever she recommends."

"Works for me," Matt said. I nodded my agreement. The waiter returned with Matt's wine, and Lucia left to instruct the chefs about our meal.

When we were alone again, Johnny said to Matt, "Okay, let's hear it."

"I came in late," Matt said, and ceded the floor to me. I aimed what I hoped was a reassuring smile at Cybelle. She had tightened up so much she had managed to make her size-two frame seem even smaller.

"Cybelle needs our help," I said. "Four years ago, when she was eighteen and living in Houston, she met a man . . ."

I saw Johnny's jaw muscles tighten. Briefly, I told him and Matt about the mysterious man Cybelle had married for a short time before running away from him. I left out the part about the riding crop.

"What's the guy's name?" Johnny asked. His voice was a hiss.

"Philippe Abacasas," I said.

Matt raised one hand in the classic "stop" gesture. "That's not necessarily his name." He opened the envelope and removed several faxed pages. "According to Interpol, Philippe Abacasas has no police record. His Swiss passport says he was born forty-one years ago, in Zurich. Profession listed as 'businessman.' " Matt paused for dramatic effect. "There's just one problem. Philippe Abacasas died at the age of six months."

Cybelle came out of her trance. "I don't understand," she whispered.

"I'm guessing that he searched a graveyard until he found the name of a male child who had been born in a year that would match his own age, then, using that name, got a copy of the child's birth certificate and used that to get a passport."

"Which one?" Cybelle asked.

That got Matt's attention. "What do you mean?"

"One day he forgot to lock his briefcase. I was curious, so I lifted the lid. There were several books that *looked* liked passports, all in different colors. Before I could pick them up, I heard him coming back, so I closed the case and pretended to be reading the paper."

"If he had passports from different countries," I said, "it might have been for different identities."

Johnny's voice was soft, but his eyes were hard. "So we don't know who he really is."

Cybelle asked, "Does this mean the marriage wasn't legal?"

I wanted to know the answer to that. So did Johnny.

Matt frowned. "It's a tricky matter," he said. "People can use names other than their own if it's not to defraud. Somebody should talk to a lawyer about this situation."

"I will," Johnny said.

I'll bet you will.

Perhaps it was Matt's presence, but Cybelle seemed to be gaining courage. She sat up straight and her words weren't tentative anymore. "Even if I'm not really married to Philippe," she said, "there's still the *other* problem." She didn't elaborate, so I picked up the story.

"Cybelle thinks that if he finds her, he's going to kill her."

Johnny reached over and covered Cybelle's hands with one of his. His other hand was on the table, balled up into a powerful fist. Suddenly I wondered who I should be more concerned about—Cybelle's husband or Johnny Isaac.

Then Johnny surprised me.

Chapter 8

"IF WHAT'S-HIS-NAME COMES near you," Johnny said, "I'll be like a pit bull with a tooth ache." He let go of Cybelle's hands, unballed his fist and *smiled*. The expression was so unusual that before I could stop myself, I said, "You have such a nice smile, Johnny; I've never seen it before."

"I'm a much more fun guy than you probably think."

"That's true, he is," Cybelle said earnestly.

He grinned and squeezed her hand gently. "Thanks for the endorsement, baby. Now let's have a good time, like normal people."

As we ate, Johnny began to warm up more. In answer to Matt's casual, making-conversation question about the talent agency business, Johnny said, "I started out in a friend's living room, because I couldn't afford an office. I only had one client—a foul-mouthed, alcoholic comic who signed with me because he knew I had to keep him working, or I'd starve."

As though on cue, two waiters arrived with an array of main courses: vermicelli puttanesca, chicken cacciatore, and stuffed eggplant rolls.

When portions of each had been distributed on our plates, Matt asked Johnny, "So who was he, your first client?"

"Louie Monk."

My eyebrows lifted in surprise. "He was a big TV star when I was in junior high."

Johnny nodded, and his lips curled in a smile full of irony. "Even the sleaziest clubs in the country wouldn't book him anymore—so I put him on television."

"How'd you manage that?" Matt asked.

"The salesman's trifecta: a lie, a bit of blackmail, and a publicity stunt." He grinned at Matt, his expression part pride, part bad-little-boy. "That stunt could have got me arrested, if I'd been caught."

"Did you kill anybody?" Matt asked.

"No."

"Then I'm off duty. Whatever you say in an Italian restaurant can't be used against you in a court of law," he joked.

Cybelle was round-eyed with wonder. She gave Johnny a gentle poke on his forearm and said, "Come on, tell us."

"Okay, the short version: I needed a script for Louie, so I started hanging with film students in the Village. The minute I let it slip that I was an agent looking for a story that could be a TV series, they were all over me. I found it—"

"*Home Free*," I jumped in. "About the homeless man who inherits a boarding school for girls!"

Matt and Cybelle stared at me blankly.

"It was a funny show," I said.

"The script started out as a drama about an orphanage for Native American kids," Johnny said. "I made a few little changes."

"Didn't the writer object?" Matt asked.

"A twenty-five-year-old-guy still living with his parents? He would have agreed to anything to get his name on the screen. Anyway, I cleaned Louie up, took sanitized pictures, stuck 'em in the new script and went to GBN, which was my first choice among the networks. When I told them that David Lorenzo was going to produce it, they bought the show on the spot."

"Who's David Lorenzo?" Matt asked.

"Fifteen years ago, he was the most successful producer on TV. Had the golden touch. Networks scrambled for anything with his name on it. Making the network deal was easy. My real problem was that I'd never met Lorenzo when I sold him as part of the package. While I had some information that kept Louie in line and off the sauce, I didn't have any leverage with Lorenzo, so I appealed to his greed."

"Tell me the part that would have got you arrested," Matt said.

"Lorenzo came on board when I told him I already had a network deal, and offered him a free ride," Johnny told us. "We shot the pilot, and it looked pretty good. Louie was great—you'd never know what a sleaze he was in real life. But then it was like somebody dropped a safe on our heads. We found out the network had given us the *worst* time slot on TV: nine P.M. on Wednesdays. Turned out the president of the network had a personal beef with Lorenzo—involving a woman that Lorenzo had forgotten about—so he took the show *intending* to put us in the 'suicide slot,' against two monster hits on CBS and ABC. He felt he could do it because Louie Monk was a nobody. He wouldn't have dared to torpedo a major star."

I groaned in sympathy. "That's awful."

Matt looked around the table at each of us. "It's a rotten business. Why are you people in it? For the money?"

"For the love of the fans," Cybelle said softly.

"For the fun of telling stories that get audiences to come back day after day, year after year, because they want to find out what happens next."

"I'm in it for the kick of the battle," Johnny said. "I like it when the other side fights dirty."

"What happened to your show?" I asked.

"I figured our only chance to stay on the air was to make Louie a star *before* the show went on," Johnny said. He slid a wry glance at Matt. "That's when I got the gun."

Matt put down his fork. "How'd you get a gun? And where is it?"

"Relax, Detective. The guy who sold it to me has been dead for ten years, and when I didn't need it any more, I took it apart and dropped the pieces in separate parts of the Hudson River."

Johnny's story suddenly brought back a fragment of something I'd read a long time ago. "Didn't somebody try to kill Louie Monk?"

Johnny looked pleased. "Not kill, exactly," he said. "Somebody *shot* at him, twice, but Louie was never in real danger. It was a publicity stunt—and it worked. Louie's face, and the name of our upcoming show, led the news on all the channels, and his picture made the front page of every paper except the *New York Times* and the *Wall Street Journal*. When we went on the air two weeks later our ratings were huge. GBN gave us a better time slot, and we ran for seven and a half years, until Louie got so impossibly demanding, no amount of money was worth dealing with him anymore."

Matt regarded Johnny with narrowed eyes. " 'Somebody' shot at him?"

Johnny flashed an impish grin. "You nailed me, Detective. I confess. I couldn't trust anybody else with the man's life. And I sure as hell couldn't trust anybody else to keep quiet about it."

"You're so amazing, Johnny." Cybelle's face was radiant.

Johnny looked as though he'd just been awarded the Nobel Prize for Agenting.

When dinner was over, Johnny insisted on paying the check. While he was doing that, Matt wrapped my cape around my shoulders, and helped Cybelle into her long, faux mink. Eyeing Cybelle's coat as he added a tip to the bill, Johnny said, "She could have real mink if she wanted."

Cybelle shook her head. "Not if it means little things have to die."

"I agree," I said. "My favorite fur is wild acrylic."

"We're lucky guys," Johnny joked. Matt's reply was a noncommittal grunt.

Johnny and Matt exchanged cards, and agreed to keep in touch in case either learned anything more about Philippe Abacasas.

As we headed toward the exit, Johnny brought up the rear. "You know why I enjoy taking this one out to restaurants?" he asked, nodding toward Cybelle. "I like to walk behind her, and watch people turn around to look because she's so beautiful."

Cybelle lowered her eyes modestly and made a *shushing* gesture at Johnny, but I could see she enjoyed his com-

pliments. Now that I had gotten to know Johnny Isaac a little, I liked him, and I hoped Cybelle wasn't going to break
his heart.

I remembered a passage from *The Great Gatsby;* it was
Nick's observation about Tom and Daisy Buchanan. "They
were careless people," Nick had said, "they smashed up
things and creatures . . . and let other people clean up the
mess. . . ."

That line made me wonder if Cybelle would turn out to
be a *real* Daisy Buchanan: a woman who could sail through
life leaving men broken and bleeding in her wake.

Chapter 9

THE FOUR OF us exited Tuscano into the chilly November night. With his right arm protectively around Cybelle, Johnny raised his left and waved. Twenty yards down the block, the headlights of a black Lincoln Park Avenue flashed on in response to his signal, and the vehicle's engine ignited.

The Lincoln glided to a stop in front of us and I saw Bud was at the wheel. I gave him a little wave. He tipped his cap at me.

Johnny asked, "Can we drop you off?"

"My car's across the street," Matt said, folding my hand in his. "I'll take Morgan home."

Even though our fingers were separated by two sets of gloves, having my hand in Matt's made my heart beat faster. I missed the incomparable closeness of two bodies pressed together, with no barriers between—what I lost when Ian died.

MATT AND I didn't say a word to each other on the ride up-town, but there was an electrical charge between us so strong that my face felt hot. My stomach was fluttering with nervous anticipation. I wanted to know what it felt like to be in Matt's arms, but I was frightened, too. It had been five years since Ian was killed, since I had touched a man's bare skin.

The car came to a stop. I looked up, surprised to see we were across the street from the Dakota.

We got here too fast.

"Would you . . . ?" My voice sounded hollow to my ears. I cleared my throat and tried again. "Cof—coffee? Would you like . . . ?"

In the spill from the street lamp I saw him smiling at me. "Yes," he said softly. "I would like . . . coffee."

I turned away, fumbling for the door handle, embarrassed that I couldn't find it. Matt leaned over, his arm brushing lightly across my breasts, and released the lock on the door.

He held my hand as we darted across the street to the building's entrance. I waved briefly at Frank, the Dakota's night security man, as we hurried into the empty courtyard and through it, heading for the interior staircase on the right that leads to my apartment.

At the foot of the stairs, Matt pulled me into his arms and kissed me. Kissed me breathless. We held each other tightly, our lips parted, our tongues beginning to explore—

"Hey, Miz Tyler!"

Frank's gravel voice shattered the moment. I jumped,

and discovered he was behind us, wheezing from his run across the courtyard. He realized what he had interrupted and said, "Oops! Sorry."

I mustered a shred of composure. "Yes, Frank?"

He motioned with a cardboard box in his hands. "Uh-hhh, this is for you." He handed it to me. It was about the size and shape of a shoebox. It bore the return address label of one of the television shopping networks.

I looked at it curiously. "When did this come?"

"A messenger brought it a couple hours ago."

"Thank you, Frank," I said.

"No problemo." He added, "Have a nice night," and hurried back across the courtyard.

I looked at the box, puzzled.

"What's the matter?" Matt asked.

"This is strange . . . I don't have time to shop, so I buy most of my clothes from the shopping channels . . . but I can't think of anything I've ordered that would come in a package this size." I shrugged and started up the stairs. I made it to the third step when Matt called, "Wait."

He bounded up the steps. "Let me see that." He took the box from me and started back to the courtyard.

A knot was beginning to form in the pit of my stomach as I followed him down—why would mail order come by *messenger*?

Matt held the box at the far edges. Very gently, he swooshed it from side to side. We heard a faint noise, like shards of china brushing against each other.

"Sounds like something's broken," I said. "And I *never* buy anything fragile by mail."

Matt set the box down on the cement floor of the courtyard, squatted next to it and took a Swiss Army knife from his pocket. I leaned over to see what he was doing when he slit open the tape that secured the top of the box.

"Get away!" he yelled, standing up and shoving me back.

One of the cardboard flaps was moving. I saw the dark, glistening form of a reptile rise from the interior. The arrowhead shape of the skull was an unmistakable identifier of a poisonous snake. From its posture, I knew that the unseen portion of its body was coiled to strike.

"Jeez . . ." Matt whispered, staring, mesmerized.

With horror, I realized Matt didn't know the snake was about to strike. Acting instinctively, I grabbed the thing from behind by its neck, just below the fangs. Squeezing hard, so the fangs couldn't touch me, I flung my arm up as high as it would go, and snapped the snake downward in a whip-cracking motion that broke its neck. The snap was so violent I was afraid I'd dislocated my shoulder.

"Good God, Morgan—are you crazy?"

"It's a mature rattler, about four feet long." I dropped the dead body back into the box. "I learned about snakes in Africa," I said. And then I started to shake. We were safe, but tears started streaming down my face.

Matt wrapped his arms around me, holding me tight against him, murmuring in a husky rasp: "Marmalade . . . Damn it, Marmalade . . ." His chin pressed down on the top of my head.

My breathing began to slow. Regaining control of myself, I lifted my face to look up at him. "Guess this means we're not going to have coffee after all," I joked.

"Not tonight, honey. After I see you upstairs and check out the apartment, I'm taking this package to the station house."

I nodded. There was nothing to say.

While my sexual experience has been limited to just one man, I know enough about the male gender to understand that when a woman saves a man's life it tends to dampen his lust.

Chapter 10

HAVING SOMEONE SEND me a live rattlesnake made for a bad night's sleep, but it put me in the perfect frame of mind to deal with Lori Cole, the network's newest "suit." To use a cliché that I try to avoid in my writing, I was spoiling for a fight.

I'd been awake since four, roused by a thought that must have been banging at the door of my subconscious for some time. Maybe for years. I didn't want to be a "good girl" anymore. In the kitchen I brewed a particularly strong pot of coffee and examined—for the first time, honestly—just how I had been living that label: "good girl."

As a child, being "good" was a survival tool for life in pretty dreadful foster homes and, later, in a Catholic boarding school. When I married wildlife photographer Ian

Tyler, I was a "good" wife because I abandoned my own plans and lived *his* life. I didn't blame Ian; I had given myself to him, no strings attached. Then, with no warning, Ian's life was over, and I had to decide what to do with the rest of mine. I found the answer back in New York City. I submitted a play I had written in college to the Global Broadcasting Network's "Be A Daytime Drama Head Writer" competition—and won. Daytime drama is an endless novel, and I have always loved big, fat novels. For me, writing in this form is a perfect fit. I love creating the multilayered romances and mysteries that are the hallmark of our show.

At last, I am living my own life, and it's good.

And now some new executive hire is trying to muck things up, and I'm supposed to let her?

Not while there's life in my body, sister.

WITH LORI COLE'S memo clenched in one hand, I didn't so much walk as *storm* the nine blocks along Central Park West from the Dakota to the Global building. By the time I reached the lobby, at ten minutes before eight, I was so revved up for the confrontation that I slammed the button for forty-three with the side of my fist.

The corridors of the forty-third floor are lined with poster-size photographs from Global's TV series, old and new, but I gave them barely a glance. Executive offices were spaced along the width of the building, with desks for assistants outside the executives' doors. At five minutes to eight, only one such desk was occupied. It didn't take Sherlock Holmes, or even Miss Marple, to deduce that the skinny young man with hair of a color I call "actress blonde" was Lori Cole's *Lawrence*.

He looked up, startled, at the emphatic sound of my high-heeled boots stamping down the corridor toward him.

"Is Lori in there?" I nodded toward the closed door behind him.

He straightened his posture, lifted one carefully shaped eyebrow, and asked, "And you are . . . ?"

"*Not* in a good mood." Striding past him, I opened the door.

"Wait! You can't—"

I was inside the new Daytime VP's office before Lawrence could finish the sentence.

The woman sitting at the desk was thirty-four, according to the bio that accompanied the announcement of her joining GBN. Everything about her was narrow: face, nose, torso, arms, and hands. Her brown hair, cut to fall just below her tiny ears, was thin. She was dressed expensively in a dark green wool suit and a beige silk blouse. Beside one small hand with skin so pale it was nearly transparent, was a mug of what I guessed (judging by the packages lying next to it) to be herbal tea. One of my personal mottos is: never trust people who avoid caffeine.

When I barged in, Lori Cole was reading a *Trauma Center* script, and making notes in its margins. I slammed her memo down on the top of the desk and watched with satisfaction as she flinched.

Her cool returned quickly. "You must be Morgan Tyler. I've heard about you." Her voice was pleasant, but her glance darted toward Lawrence, who was standing in the doorway awaiting instructions.

"Apparently you haven't heard enough." Pounding on the memo for emphasis, I said, "You want us to fire one of the most popular actresses on *Love*. Have you ever *watched* our show?"

Lori Cole signaled Lawrence to leave us alone. After he'd closed the door, she said defensively, "I've seen some tapes."

"Francie James has been on the show for *six years*. Our audience has been through her miscarriage, her abandonment by her husband, losing her home, and her mental breakdown. She's a three-time Emmy nominee. And you want to fire her based on having looked at a few tapes!"

Lori Cole wasn't going belly up just yet. She stood, braced her hands on the top of the desk and said flatly, "Francie James is ugly." She added, as if it were the final word on the subject, "*Fat* and ugly."

I switched my tone from angry to imperious. "You sound like the foreman of a jury that's just convicted her of murder."

Red spots appeared on Lori Cole's pale cheeks. "Good analogy. She's murdered her career with her stomach."

"No, Lori—she's given us a golden opportunity to draw an even bigger audience because people will want to see her lose weight on the air. I've planned a weight loss story that's going to get us the kind of media coverage we couldn't buy."

Did I just snarl at a network vice president? Yep, and I enjoyed it.

Lori Cole frowned. I sensed wheels turning in her mind and I wondered whether she was going to back down—or call Security and have me thrown out of the building.

She stretched one blue-veined hand toward the telephone, where I noticed that a light was flashing. I'll never know what she was going to do, because before she touched the instrument, Lawrence opened the door.

"Mr. Yarborough is on the line—for Ms. Tyler," he whispered.

"Tell him I'll call him back," I said.

Lori Cole gasped. So did Lawrence, and his hand flew up to his mouth. Both of them stared at me, round-eyed with shock at my audacity in putting off *the founder of the network*. The new vice president recovered first.

"Lawrence," Lori Cole said sharply, "don't keep the chairman of the board waiting on the line. Give him the message."

Moving like a robot, Lawrence backed out of the room.

Lori Cole turned to me, and her face morphed into one of the widest smiles I'd ever seen. "Morgan, sit down, please." She lowered herself into her own chair and gestured to the one nearest me.

I sat.

She indicated the sofa and coffee table seating arrangement to one side of the room. "Would you be more comfortable over there?"

She was sucking up to me big time.

"No, I'm fine right here," I said.

"Your diet story sounds *fabulous*," Lori Cole purred. "I can't wait to hear all about it. Oh—would you like a cup of my lemon grass tea?"

I'd rather have a cavity drilled.

"I'll take some coffee, if it doesn't come from a vending machine," I said.

She pressed the intercom button and instructed Lawrence to fetch coffee for me from the Starbucks in the lobby of the building next door. "And bring back all the stuff that goes with it," she added.

Apparently, nothing was too good for the woman who dared to tell Global's chairman that she would call him back.

* * *

AFTER WINNING THE battle to keep Francie James on the show, I found a deserted office far enough away from Lawrence for privacy, and called Winston Yarborough back from my cell phone. I got his assistant.

"I'm afraid Mr. Y's in a meeting now, Mrs. Tyler, but he wanted to know if you would be available to come to a small dinner party he and Mrs. Yarborough are giving this coming Friday night. It's the night after Thanksgiving. He knows that it's short notice, and he hopes you're not going away for the weekend."

"No, I'm not," I said. "And I'm free on Friday. Can you fax me the directions to their house in Greenwich?"

"They'll be here in town, so the party will be in their suite at the Carlyle."

"What time?" I asked.

"Drinks at seven, dinner at eight," he said. "Oh, just one more thing. It's sit down, for ten, so Mr. Yarborough asked that you come alone."

"I was planning to," I said. "I'll see them Friday night. I look forward to meeting *Mrs.* Yarborough."

I fervently hoped that she hadn't heard any rumors about her husband and me.

If she has, I might need a food taster.

A few minutes later, while I was at the newsstand in the lobby picking up all the magazines that contained diet articles, my cell phone rang. It was Matt and he sounded glum.

"What's the matter? Didn't you find any fingerprints on the box with the snake?"

"Only yours and mine, and Frank's." I remembered that they had my fingerprints in their database from when I was a murder suspect.

"You have Frank's prints?"

"Last night I asked him for a sample so I could eliminate them. He agreed right away. Nice guy. Incidentally, about the messenger who delivered the box—Frank didn't get a good look because he was on the phone writing down some instructions from one of your neighbors."

"Do you know where the rattler came from?" I asked. "You can't just order one from QVC."

"I'm investigating." His voice sounded strained.

"Matt? I can tell there's something else. What's wrong?"

I heard him take a deep breath.

"Before I got in this morning, G. G. went out on a homicide call . . . I just heard from him—and I'm on my way over there now. Honey, I'm afraid I've got some bad news."

My Starbucks coffee turned to acid, lurched against the walls of my stomach and started to rise into my throat.

"Oh, God," I whispered. "Who . . . ?"

"Cybelle Carter. The medical examiner says it looks like she was poisoned."

I dropped the pile of magazines onto the lobby's terrazzo floor and ran toward the revolving brass doors to the street.

Chapter 11

I SPRINTED ACROSS Central Park West in the middle of the block, frantically searching for a taxi going uptown. A bus driver blasted his horn at me, and yelled something obscene, but I ignored him. Cybelle was dead, and I hadn't done anything to protect her.

The driver of a taxi that looked about ready for the compacter spotted my madly waving arm and began to slow down. Before I reached the cab, a large, red-faced man wearing a plaid scarf around his neck darted out from between two parked cars and grabbed for the passenger door's handle. Too furious to stop and think, I seized him by the back of his coat and pulled hard.

"Get away from this taxi!" My wild yell astonished us both.

Plaid Scarf gaped at me, put his hands up, palms out in a defensive posture, and backed away.

"Okay, lady—take it easy."

"This is *my* cab," I said, yanking the rear door open. I climbed in and told the driver, "One Hundred West Seventy-ninth Street."

The driver was staring at me in his rearview mirror while the idling vehicle, desperately in need of a tune-up, rattled and shook.

"Go—now!"

"Yes, ma'am," he said. He pulled out into traffic and floored the accelerator, clearly anxious to get to my destination so he could be rid of the crazy woman in his back seat.

Cybelle lived at the Commodore, an apartment house built in the early nineteen hundreds. I had never been to her place, but I knew the address because we had talked about living just a few blocks from each other. From half a block away on West Seventy-ninth, I saw a pair of uniformed police officers standing beneath the canopied entrance to One Hundred, blocking the door. Two other officers were setting up sawhorse barriers to keep the unauthorized away. Pedestrians were stopping to ask questions, but the officers just shook their heads.

Vehicle traffic was slowing, clogging the street, as people in the cars craned their necks in an attempt to see what was happening.

"Let me out here," I said. Snatching some bills from my wallet, I tossed them to the driver through the narrow opening in the security pane that separated us, and jumped out of the car. I covered the distance to the Commodore and got there just as a dark sedan, red police bubble on top flashing and siren shrieking, bulled through the looky-loo vehicles and screeched to a stop. Matt Phoenix leaped out, and was fast enough to stop me at the sawhorse.

"I told you to go home," he snapped.

"I didn't hear you, but I wouldn't have done it if I *had* heard you."

"Big surprise," he said. But his voice was softer now. He cupped my elbow in one large hand and steered me through the gathering crowd, past the police guards who saw the gold shield pinned to his lapel and moved aside for us to enter. He stopped just inside the door and turned me around to face him.

"You don't want to go up there," he said.

"I've got to! Cybelle came to me for help, and I didn't do anything for her." A new thought struck me with the force of a blow. "Oh, God—*Johnny*. Does he know? Is he up there?"

"G. G. said there was no one there except the bod—except Cybelle—and the maid who found her and called the police."

I shook myself free of his hands and started toward the elevator, where another uniformed officer stood guard. Then I stopped. "What apartment?"

"I'll take you up." He nodded to the officer, who pressed the button for the third floor.

On three, doors were open up and down the hall, with tenants leaning out to see what was going on. When we stepped out of the elevator, curious eyes focused on us.

"Go back into your homes," Matt said. "Please. We'll come to talk to you soon." His tone was polite but it rang with authority, and had the desired effect. Cybelle's curious neighbors retreated.

The door to 3C was open. Another uniformed officer stood guard.

Cybelle's living room was neat and lovely. Feminine, like Cybelle herself. The one thing in the room that stood out as clearly not belonging was the burly figure of Detective First Grade G. G. Flynn, Matt's partner at the Twentieth Precinct. At fifty, G. G. is older than Matt by a dozen years, and shorter by four or five inches. He is also a good thirty pounds heavier than Matt, and while Matt's dark hair is abundant, G. G.'s has thinned to a fringe. My friend Penny, who is also Matt's aunt, told me once that George Gordon Flynn was "nicer than he seems to be the first ten or twelve times you meet him." It had taken a while, but I have come to realize that she was right.

G. G., who was at Cybelle's antique writing desk, wore thin rubber gloves as he studied her appointment book. He looked up when we came in, slipped the book into a plastic evidence bag and came over.

"Sorry about your friend," he said to me. I nodded, or thought I did. He turned to Matt. "Most of the pages in her date book have been ripped out. It's going to the lab." He stripped off the rubber gloves and jammed them into a jacket pocket. "I'm gonna start the canvas," he said as he headed for the front door.

"I'll join you in a few minutes."

G. G. lumbered past us, out into the third floor corridor.

Beyond Cybelle's living room, I glimpsed a dining room. Down a short hallway was the closed door to what I guessed was Cybelle's bedroom, but the action—a team of crime scene investigators—was taking place in the kitchen.

I stopped in the doorway and forced myself to look at the object of interest to those technicians. Matt continued into the kitchen, speaking softly to a man from the Medical Examiner's office. I had seen him before, at another crime scene, two months ago. He was standing next to the slender form that lay face down beside the small kitchen table. Her luxurious black hair fanned out over the black and white diamond-patterned floor tiles. She was wearing the expensive pale blue silk pajamas I recognized as one of Tommy's gifts to the female members of our cast last Christmas. Her feet were bare . . .

Her feet.

"Something's wrong," I said. Matt glanced up from his conference with the man from the M.E.'s office.

"Cybelle wears a size six shoe," I said. "She must wear an *eight*."

Matt gestured to the nearest crime scene tech. "Let's turn her over," he said.

I held my breath as the two men very gently lifted her by her shoulders and reversed her position. The long black hair fell away from her face. I gasped. Her features were twisted into a horrifying expression, but even so I knew that—

"This isn't Cybelle Carter," Matt said. He stood up and looked at me questioningly. "Do you know this woman?"

"Her name is Jeannie . . . something," I said. I shook my head, embarrassed and angry at myself because I couldn't remember her last name. The poor girl deserved at least that minimal dignity. Then it came to me. "Jeannie *Ford*. She's worked on the show a few times, as Cybelle's body double. In fact, she did the water stunts for us just yesterday."

Suddenly, from behind us, came a piercing scream.

I whirled to see Cybelle, her eyes bulging with horror as she stared at the body on the floor. Johnny Isaac was beside her, his mouth open in shock. Just behind them, Johnny's driver stood frozen and bug-eyed. He dropped the suitcase he was carrying. Cybelle's scream became a high decibel, primordial wail. Johnny pulled her tight against him, but she didn't stop wailing until she fainted in his arms. Johnny yelled, "Bud—brandy!" and Bud took off in the direction of the living room.

Chapter 12

SPRINGING TO JOHNNY'S side just as Cybelle collapsed, Matt lifted her unconscious form in his arms. With Johnny hurrying ahead to open the door, Matt carried Cybelle down the hall and into her bedroom. The man from the Medical Examiner's office and I followed like tails on a kite.

"Gently, gently," Johnny said, as Matt lowered Cybelle onto her canopied bed. I saw that the rose velvet duvet cover and the pink damask top sheet had been turned down at the corner. The bed had been made ready, but it had not been slept in.

Bud came rushing in with an open bottle of Courvoisier in one hand and a crystal tumbler, half full of amber liquid, in the other. Johnny reached for the glass, but the man from the Medical Examiner's office shouldered him out of the way. Johnny moved aside and Bud, clutching the bottle against his chest, backed up to stand against the wall. The M.E.'s man took a capsule from his jacket pocket, snapped it open and waved it beneath Cybelle's nostrils.

Responding immediately, she moaned and scrunched up her nose. Her eyes blinked open. I saw that she was trying to focus on the circle of men hovering above her.

Johnny's face was whiter than Cybelle's. "Is she all right?" It sounded more like a demand than a question.

"She will be, in a couple of minutes." The M.E.'s man pressed two fingers lightly against the pulse in her right wrist and nodded to himself. "How do you feel, Miss?"

"What . . . ? What happened?"

As I stepped into Cybelle's bathroom and soaked a washcloth in cold water, I heard Johnny say, "You fainted, baby."

Returning to her bedside, I leaned in and put the cold cloth across Cybelle's forehead. She looked up at me gratefully and murmured her thanks.

Johnny challenged the M.E.'s man. "Aren't you supposed to ask her what her name is or something?"

He shrugged. "I don't usually get to work on live people."

"That's a damned insensitive remark," Johnny snapped.

"So sue me—but I'm Civil Service," he said as he left the room.

Cybelle held the cold cloth against her brow with one hand and with the other she squeezed the fingers on Johnny's right hand. "That was Jeannie?"

"Yes," I said gently.

"What was she doing here?" Matt's voice wasn't quite as gentle, but I was glad he wasn't being "bad cop" with her.

Cybelle tried to sit up. Johnny helped her. I saw a little color beginning to return to her cheeks. "Yesterday she had a fight with her boyfriend. She was afraid he was going to beat her up, so I gave her my key and told her she could stay here." She glanced at her devoted agent. "After what we talked about at dinner last night, Johnny thought I should stay at his place."

"I've got a nice guest room," he said hastily.

A girl lay dead in the kitchen, but Johnny was thinking about protecting Cybelle's reputation.

Johnny gestured in the general direction of Bud. "We came back here this morning so Cybelle could pack," he said. "We're flying to Hawaii at noon for the Thanksgiving break."

"Cancel the tickets," Matt said. "Nobody connected with Jeannie Ford leaves town until I say so." Good Cop Matt had turned into official, officious Detective Phoenix.

Johnny scribbled his home address and phone number on the back of his business card and handed it to me. "If you want to reach us, we'll be at my place," he said. He looked at Cybelle. "That okay with you, baby?" She nodded.

Indicating the card in my hand, Detective Phoenix told Johnny: "I need that information, too." Then he turned to me and said, "Go home."

Never again, I vowed, will I let another person treat me like a child. Because we were not alone, I restrained myself from responding with a tart comment. Instead, I shot him an angry glare. It hit its mark. He clenched his teeth and glared back at me. I could feel him steaming, and took an unfamiliar—and perverse—pleasure in the fact that I could make him mad. I had never made Ian mad. When I had time, I'd have to think about that.

On my way out, I stopped at the kitchen door. A photographer was taking pictures of poor Jeannie while crime scene techs were bagging Cybelle's garbage and packing up the only items in her refrigerator: chocolate pudding and Diet Snapple. The M.E.'s man, who was closest to the doorway, was making notes.

"What kind of poison do you think it was?" I asked.

"From the look of the body, I'm guessing strychnine," he answered while he was writing. "But it'll take an autop—" He stopped and looked at me. "Who are you?"

From behind me, Matt said, "She's a civilian, and she's not supposed to be here, Mel. She's leaving *right now*."

Matt took my arm, but I shook him off and stalked toward the open doorway to the hall. He caught up with me and said, "I'll call you later."

I left the apartment without replying.

WEDNESDAY BEFORE THANKSGIVING was a half-day. There was no sense in going to the office. As soon as I got home, I telephoned Tommy Zenos and told him what had happened to Jeannie Ford.

"That's terrible!" I could hear the genuine sorrow in his voice.

"I'm afraid there's more," I said. "But you'll have to keep to yourself what I'm about to tell you, at least until the police are ready to let the information out."

"Oh, I won't say a word. I promise."

I wasn't sure Tommy, addicted to gossip, could keep that promise. I told him the bare minimum: that Jeannie had been at Cybelle's apartment, and that Cybelle had stayed the night with a friend.

"Was Cybelle with Link Ramsey?" Tommy asked.

"No."

"Then she must have been with the lovelorn agent."

"That's not really any of our business, Tommy." To divert him from asking any more questions, I told him I had some *good* news. "We don't have to fire Francie. Lori Cole endorsed our weight-loss story."

"How in the *world* did you manage that?"

I was glad he couldn't see the expression on my face: lip curled, eyebrow lifted—*ham on wry*.

"I used my charm," I said. Assuring him I would keep him posted throughout our long holiday weekend, I wished him a happy Thanksgiving and said goodbye.

My next call was to Winston Yarborough. When I told his assistant that the call was urgent, he put me right through.

"I'm sorry to disturb you, Win." Weeks ago, when we were working together, Global's founder and chairman had insisted that I call him Win. I honored his request, but it still felt awkward on my tongue. Briefly, I told him about Jeannie Ford's death, that it looked as though she had been poisoned, that she had been staying in Cybelle's apartment, and that if the poisoning turned out to be deliberate and not an accident of some kind, the probable target was Cybelle Carter.

He listened, then said, "I'll call you right back. Are you in the office?"

"At home. The number is—"

"I have the number," he said.

He called back in a minute and a half.

"I've told Nathan Hughes, and instructed him to call you for details in five minutes."

Nathan Hughes is the head of public relations for GBN. An artist whose medium is language, he can "spin" like a world champion ice skater.

"I'm afraid I'm unfamiliar with Miss Ford's name," Winston Yarborough said. "Did she work for us?"

"She's been Cybelle's body double on the show a few times, but she's not a regular employee."

"Nathan will get her work history and emphasize her employment with companies other than Global. It might have to be mentioned that she was a friend of Miss Carter's, to explain the place of her death, but Nathan will know how to downplay it."

He meant that Jeannie Ford was going to be "downplayed."

"If she was murdered, and it turns out that Cybelle was the intended victim," I snapped, "I don't think we'll be able to keep the lid on that."

The chairman's voice softened. "Morgan, please don't believe I'm thinking only about the image · of our company," he said. "I'm deeply concerned about Miss Carter's safety. I will be happy to pay for her accommodations wherever you think she will be safe, and for any amount of personal security for her. You decide what is best, and order it in my name. Cost must not be a consideration."

I thanked him for that, and we said warm goodbyes.

Intentionally, I hadn't told him about the rattler. First, I didn't know if it had anything to do with Cybelle's problem. Second, I didn't want Winston Yarborough hiring an army of personal security for *me*. The thought of losing my freedom of movement was worse to me than the arrival of a dozen deadly snakes.

Nathan Hughes telephoned exactly five minutes from the time he'd been told to call me. I pictured him standing next to the phone with a stopwatch in his hand.

When I was finished speaking, he said, "I'll take it from here. Thank you, Morgan."

My conversation with Nathan Hughes was the last of the reports I had to make to the company. Now it was time to look after myself. While the Dakota was among the safest buildings in New York, the Commodore was supposed to have been safe, too. No place is *impossible* to get into.

I opened the bottom drawer of my bedside table and took out the silver Glock 19 Ian had given me years ago in Africa. Because we spent time in some dangerous places, he taught me how to use it, and beamed with pride when I became proficient. "Proficient" had been his word. In truth, I was a better shot than he was. The Glock's overall length is seven and a quarter inches; four and a half of those inches are barrel. The stock grip is made of a single piece of injection-molded plastic. A light weapon, it weighs about a pound and a half with a full .40 caliber magazine.

It had been too long since I'd aimed at a target. Time to sharpen my skills. I found the telephone number of Targets, the shooting range where I used to practice. Located in Spring Valley, New York, Targets is about thirty miles north of Manhattan, off I-87. I called to make an appointment. Their available time was two o'clock Sunday afternoon. I booked it.

Chapter 13

IT WAS PAST one-thirty in the afternoon. I went into the kitchen and took out a can of tuna fish, a small red onion, a jar of Miracle Whip, and a container of my friend Penny's homemade sweet pickle relish. I pictured Penny across the park, in her own kitchen, preparing marvels for tomorrow's Thanksgiving dinner. Chopping an onion and mixing it together with the tuna, Miracle Whip, and a spoonful of relish, I wished that I'd learned to cook.

I was halfway through my lunch, chewing slowly as I reviewed what I had learned about Philippe Abacasas from Matt's source at Interpol, and what Cybelle had told me in the office. Something was picking at the edge of my consciousness, and then I realized what it was. I went to my bedroom and took the suede jacket I had worn earlier from its hanger and searched through the pockets until I found Johnny Isaac's card with his home telephone number.

Johnny picked up on the second ring. After greeting him, I asked to speak to Cybelle. She must have been close by, because she came on the line immediately.

"Hi, Morgan . . . Is everything all right?"

"There's nothing new. I wanted to ask you a question. You said Abacasas had a dress form made for you at a fashion house in Paris. What house was it?"

"Robert Glassel," she said, using the correct French pronunciation. "It's on Avenue Victor Hugo. Is that important?"

"Probably not. I just wanted to get a complete picture."

"Okay," she said.

Johnny came back on the line. "You doing anything tomorrow for Thanksgiving?" he asked. " 'Cause if not, you could come have dinner with the three of us."

"Three?"

"My driver, Bud, will be with us. I put him on bodyguard duty, until I can interview some pros."

"I do have Thanksgiving plans," I said, "but I appreciate the invitation."

"Any time," Johnny said.

I thought about the name Cybelle had given me: Robert Glassel. One of the top French couturiers. If Philippe Abacasas was a regular customer they might have an address for him, but from what I'd read, French couturiers were almost as secretive about client information as were Swiss banks. My advantage was that I knew another one of Glassel's customers: Nancy Cummings. I reached Nancy at her law office and asked if she could come over that evening.

"I need to pick your brain," I told her. "It's important."

"My brain is yours," she said immediately. "I'll be there

at seven, with salad. We have to save calories for tomorrow's dinner at Penny's."

After we hung up, I counted to five, picked up the receiver and listened for the "beep, beep, beep" of voice
mail, signaling that I had a message. No beeps, no message. It was two-thirty in the afternoon and Matt Phoenix
still had not called.

To hell with him.

I pulled an old fleece-lined jacket out of the closet,
grabbed my wallet and keys and left the apartment.

Once downstairs in the Dakota's open courtyard, I realized it had gotten considerably colder. The sharp air stung
my face, and I thought I could smell a hint of coming snow
in the air. I should have worn a coat instead of the jacket,
but I was too impatient to go back upstairs and change.

At the entrance to the Dakota, I turned right and walked
west until I crossed Columbus Avenue, which, as usual,
was choked with vehicles and pedestrians. Horns honked
and voices shouted, but those sounds are so usual in New
York City that I no longer pay attention to them. They were
background, "white noise," as I headed for my objective:
the well-stocked newsstand halfway further down Seventy-
second Street.

I greeted the nice old man from whom I've been buying
magazines for several years. "Hi, Bert."

Bert responded with his familiar cheerful grin, that exposed the gap between his two front teeth. "How 'bout the
new *Modern Bride* magazine? I sell 'em to pretty girls for
half price."

"The mood I'm in, just give me a copy of *Guns and
Ammo.*"

He frowned with concern. "You serious?"

"No," I said. "Actually, I'm looking for women's magazines today. Everything you've got that has a diet story in it."

He gave me a quick, appraising glance. "You don't need to go on a diet."

"Thanks for the compliment. I need the articles for work."

His hands partially covered by fingerless blue wool gloves, Bert rummaged through his current inventory, and then through the pile he'd put aside to return. It took only a few minutes for him to put together a stack of fifteen magazines that had a wide variety of diet stories featured prominently on their covers. Fifty-six dollars' worth. I gave him three twenties and told him to keep the change.

He chuckled and saluted me with newsprint-stained fingers. "More customers like you, I can go home early."

By the time I was within a few yards of the Dakota, the stack of magazines had grown so heavy that my arms were aching. Then I saw something up ahead that made me stop short.

Matt Phoenix was standing on the left side of the entrance, directly below the bas relief portrait of the bearded man, carved in profile. It looks like a mug shot of Santa Claus.

Matt saw me, hurried forward and took the magazines. "We need to talk," he said. "Upstairs."

Chapter 14

MATT FOLLOWED ME across the courtyard and into the interior stairway where he had kissed me the night before. All at once I remembered how good it had felt to be in his arms, and to hold him in mine. Then I got a grip on myself; it was not an appropriate time to be thinking about that.

Still, I wished I hadn't eaten those onions earlier.

We both stopped at the foot of the stairs. I glanced at Matt and saw that he was looking at me. It was obvious from the hint of gentleness in his eyes that he was remembering last night, too, and how close we had come. It was an awkward moment.

"The arrival of that snake certainly was ill-timed."

"Not funny," he said sharply. I think it came out more emphatically than he had meant it to, because he immediately softened his tone. "You could have been killed."

I started up the stairs. "There was one good thing about last night."

"Yeah," he said quietly. "I enjoyed that part, too."

"I meant the *interruption*." I put that delicately, I thought. "It made me so angry, I took it out on a network executive this morning."

We reached the third floor. I unlocked the door to my apartment, preceded Matt into the foyer and turned on a light to chase away the gloom of the late November afternoon.

"Where do you want these?" Matt asked, shifting the weight of the heavy pile of magazines from his right arm to his left.

"In the kitchen."

At the kitchen doorway, I gestured toward the round oak breakfast table in the middle of the room. "Put the magazines there. Would you like some coffee?"

"Yeah, that'd be great."

While I fit a filter into Mr. Coffee's basket, spooned in freshly ground Kenya beans and clicked the switch to "On," Matt fanned the magazines out, face up. "I didn't think you had this much time to read," he said.

"They're research for a story line I'm creating."

He scanned the covers and immediately said, "Something about dieting."

"You're a good detective."

"I wish all our cases were that easy," he said.

I shook my head. "I don't believe it. You'd be bored in no time."

He sat down in front of the single place mat. "You've got me pegged as an adrenaline junkie?"

"I think the reason you decided to be a homicide detective is more complicated than that." I took another place mat out of a drawer, and put napkins on the table.

"At least you're thinking about me," he said. "But don't make guesses about me and I won't guess about you. If we want to know something, we'll ask. Deal?"

"Deal," I said.

I took a small wooden tray from a cabinet below the coffee maker and put two tall ceramic mugs onto it.

"I like the sound and the smell of coffee brewing," Matt said.

"If you're hungry," I said, "there's some tuna salad in the refrigerator. I could make you a sandwich."

"No, thanks. I had hot dogs with G. G. a little while ago."

"Penny said that G. G. and his wife are coming to Thanksgiving dinner. I'm looking forward to meeting *Mrs.* Detective G. G. Flynn. I've been wondering what she's like."

"A good woman," Matt said. "She keeps him sane."

"That's got to be a full-time job." Matt smiled at me. He knew that I had come to appreciate his irascible partner.

The coffee ready, I filled our mugs, but before I could pick up the tray, Matt was beside me. His shoulder brushed against mine and I felt an immediate little tingle.

"I'll take that," he said, picking up the tray. He carried it to the table and waited for me to sit down before he did.

I placed a mug in front of each of us and asked, "What have you found out about Jeannie's death?"

"Her boyfriend, a lowlife named Hal Meeks, is in the clear. He was in jail on a drunk and disorderly bust from night before last. His mother bailed him out a couple of hours ago."

"Then he was behind bars even before Jeannie knew she'd be staying at Cybelle's." That was not good news. "Any word from the coroner about the cause of death?"

Matt's expression was grim. "Strychnine. It's a nasty

way to die." He did not add the gruesome details, but I remembered how Jeannie's features had been twisted in agony. I shuddered and put down my mug.

"Do they know how the poison got into her system? Or where it came from?"

"They found traces of strychnine in an empty container of Swiss Chocolate pudding in the trash," he said.

Chocolate pudding. I realized the terrible significance of where the poison had been placed. "It *was* Cybelle somebody tried to kill."

Matt instantly became all business. "Tell me what you're thinking."

"Everybody who works with her knows Cybelle has a thing for chocolate pudding," I said. "Tommy Zenos makes sure the catering people bring it on the days she tapes."

"That stuff's all fat and sugar," Matt shook his head. "How's she stay so thin?"

"She doesn't eat a lot of it," I said. "Some days that's *all* she'll eat. Link—the actor who plays opposite her—makes jokes about it. His nickname for her is Puddin' Pop."

"So you're saying a lot of people know she likes the stuff."

I nodded. "It was bad enough to imagine her weirdo husband found out where she is and tried to kill her. I don't want to think it could be someone I work with."

Matt nodded. "G. G. found Cybelle's household receipts in a kitchen drawer. Two days ago, she bought three containers of pudding from a gourmet shop. Jeannie Ford ate from one container. They found poison in all three."

I knew I was clutching at one last straw, but still I had to ask, "Could this be a product tampering case? A psycho with a grudge against the food company?"

"We're checking that out," he said, "but, frankly, it's not the likeliest explanation. You know what that means."

"Someone really *did* try to kill Cybelle."

There was a terrible irony in the fact that Jeannie Ford, who had been Cybelle's stunt double in life, had substituted for her in death.

"I'll need to get a list of all the people who work on your show," Matt said. "Addresses and phone numbers."

Matt must have known that my first instinct would be to resist, because he added: "I can get a subpoena for the information, but it'll be quicker if you just give it to me."

I knew he was right. I gave in. "I have a personnel list here. Wait a minute."

Returning to the kitchen a couple of minutes later, I handed him two single-spaced pages of names, addresses, and phone numbers.

"Thanks," he said.

"Just don't treat these people like criminals."

Whatever Matt might have replied was interrupted by the ring of my telephone. "Excuse me," I said, reaching for the receiver. "I'll make this quick."

"Take your time. I'll pour myself some more coffee."

In response to my hello, I heard Chet's voice. "Hi, gorgeous."

"Hi." I glanced at Matt. He was facing Mr. Coffee, with his back to me, but I guessed that he was listening. I turned halfway around, giving myself a miniscule amount of privacy. I asked Chet, "Where are you?"

"Still at The Hague. That's why I'm calling. I'm afraid I can't get back for our date Saturday night. I'm stuck here for another week or two."

"That's disappointing."

"For me, too."

"What's happened?"

"I'm finally getting an interview I've been chasing. Can't be more specific on the phone," he said, but I heard the excitement in his voice.

"I understand." Even though my back was to him, I sensed Matt was watching me. "Well, good luck with it."

"You sound strange," Chet said. "Something wrong?"

"In this business, there's always a problem." I tried to sound flippant, and was immediately ashamed of myself because that answer trivialized the death of a human being. I decided to stop being phony. "It's nothing I can talk about right now," I said.

"Ah. You're not alone, are you?"

"No."

"Is Inspector Tight-Lips there?"

That did it. "I said I'm not going to talk about it right now. If you make another crack like that, I might not talk to you at all!"

"Maybe I should call later, when you're in a better mood."

"*Fine*," I said. We exchanged cool goodbyes. I slammed the receiver in place and took a deep breath.

"Whew," Matt said. I turned around and saw he was smiling at me. "I thought *I* was the only person who could make you that mad. Should I be jealous?"

I wanted to wipe the smirk off his face. Instead, I took the mug out of his hand and said, "Go investigate something."

I heard him chuckling as he headed down the hall toward the front door.

Chapter 15

NANCY CUMMINGS ARRIVED at seven in a cloud of tantalizing floral scent. She'd changed from one of her dressed-to-destroy-the-opposition business suits into a black cashmere exercise outfit that had never absorbed a bead of sweat.

She handed me a take-out bag from the *uber* snobby restaurant located on the ground floor of the midtown building that also houses the powerful law firm in which she is an associate. The restaurant is rumored to prepare take-out only for current and former U.S. presidents, and, apparently, for Nancy Cummings.

"It's their special salad," she said. "Seven different kinds of lettuce."

"I can only think of two kinds."

"I can only think of four, but I'd never admit it to them."

Her expression changed to one of concern as she looked at me closely. "You don't look hungry," she said.

"I'm not."

I stashed the elegantly boxed salads in the refrigerator and we adjourned to the den where we slipped off our shoes and propped ourselves up at opposite ends of my big, forest green velvet couch. I watched Nancy as she adjusted the pillows for maximum comfort. She always chooses to sit at that end of the couch, her back to the table lamp. The backlight creates a halo effect that turns her pale blonde hair to gold.

I filled Nancy in on what had happened to Jeannie Ford, and about my concern for Cybelle. I told her what Cybelle had confided to me.

"His name, at least the name she knows him by, is Philippe Abacasas," I said. "He had a dress form made for her in Paris, at Robert Glassel. If you still shop there—"

Nancy nodded, understanding what I wanted before I could ask. "I'll find out what I can. My business should loosen Robert's tongue, but if it doesn't, I'll play the lawyer card."

"Thanks," I said.

She stared at me. "Okay, girlfriend, what else is going on?"

I told her I had almost gone to bed with Matt.

"Hallelujah." She clapped her hands. "I told you a long time ago that women don't throw themselves on their husband's funeral pyres anymore—at least not in New York." Peering at me as though she was studying some alien creature, she said, "What do you mean, *almost?* What stopped you?"

Then I told her about the episode with the rattlesnake.

"Jeez-us, Morgan!" She was horrified for me—and insisted on hearing everything. I told her what little I knew. It took a few minutes, but I finally convinced her that the rattlesnake was just a stunt, unlikely to be repeated. Finally, she calmed down, and then a wicked little smile curled her lips. "Killing a snake in front of a man—that's a real *downer*. Pun intended."

I laughed, and that felt good. "There's more," I said.

Nancy has been my best friend since we met at the start of our freshman year at Columbia. Near the end of our sophomore year, she was sitting next to me the first time I saw Ian Tyler, who'd come to Columbia to give a lecture on wildlife conservation. He and I never took our eyes off each other during that lecture. One week later, we were married. If anyone could understand what I was about to say, it would be Nancy.

"You know Ian was my first. The truth is, when we got married I was a nineteen-year-old girl who fell for a handsome, exciting, famous man twice my age. It was my good luck that infatuation evolved into love, but . . ."

"But what?" She was leaning forward, urging me on.

"But we were never equals. He was my husband, my mentor. . . . He told me once—we were in bed, we'd just made love, and it was wonderful, it always was. He said I was 'a woman made for a man.' I took that as a compliment, until late last night. Now I finally have to admit what it was that he had meant."

"What?"

"That I was a woman who always did what *he* wanted to do. We went where he wanted to go, lived the way he wanted to live. Don't misunderstand me, Nance, I'm not blaming Ian. We had a fantastic time together. It's just that I don't want to give my life over to somebody else again."

Nancy smiled. "I'm so proud—my little girl is all grown

up at last. This calls for a celebration. Break out the Oreos. We'll have one cookie each."

I returned from the kitchen carrying a tray with two Oreos on a napkin and two glasses of milk. Nancy had her fingers laced behind her head and she was leaning against the back of the sofa. While her eyes were aimed in the direction of the window, I knew that she wasn't gazing out at the lights of Central Park. Nancy was in her favorite thinking position.

She looked up when I came into the den.

"Tell me about anything unusual that happened before you received the snake."

I passed Nancy a glass of milk, put the Oreos on the napkin between us and began to scroll my mind back.

The Oreo was halfway to my mouth when I remembered. "Somebody sent me a DVD of *Vertigo*," I said.

"The Hitchcock movie?"

I nodded. "It was wrapped in white paper, silver ribbon, my name written in calligraphy. No card."

Nancy sat up straight, her own Oreo forgotten. "Let's see it."

The DVD was on the entry table, not twenty feet from where we were sitting in the den, unwrapped, but resting on the paper and ribbon. I handed the items to Nancy, who examined them carefully.

"Let's play it," Nancy said. "Maybe it'll give us a clue as to who sent it to you."

"And *why*." I put the DVD in the machine and pushed "Play."

It was a good movie, justifiably called a classic. It would have been easy to relax and enjoy it, but Nancy and I were too intent on finding answers to do that.

We watched the character played by Jimmy Stewart fall in love with an elegant mystery woman who died—a death for which he blamed himself. Wandering aimlessly, trying to recover from his loss, he was stunned to see another woman, one who resembled his dead love. Her hair was a different color, she wasn't elegant, but she looked enough like the woman he lost that he followed her and persuaded her to go out with him.

A few minutes later, Nancy and I leaned forward simultaneously as we stared intently at the screen. I pushed "Pause."

"Jimmy Stewart picked out her clothes," Nancy said. "He changed her hair—"

"He *transformed* her, Nancy. Just like Philippe Abacasas transformed Cybelle."

"We've made a connection," she said. Nancy high-fived me. Then she looked puzzled. "What do you think it means?"

"When I'm creating mystery plot lines for the show, the *what* is always a lot easier to figure out than the *why*."

Nancy sighed. "It's the same thing in my law practice. *Why* people do what they do—that's the bitch."

I pushed "Play" again. We watched the rest of the movie. When it was over, we were silent for a few moments.

Lines of concern creased Nancy's brow. "Jimmy Stewart killed that woman."

"No, he didn't," I said. "Her death was an accident."

"All right, I'll rephrase: it was his *obsession* with her that killed her. Whether it was murder or the law of unintended consequences, that poor dumb girl in the movie is just as dead. And your actress had a horrifying near miss."

"I've got to figure out who has a motive powerful enough to make him—or her—try to kill Cybelle."

"You better think fast, Morgan. Some unknown person or persons sent you two packages. They were messages of some kind—and one of them damn near killed you."

Chapter 16

I HAD TROUBLE getting to sleep that night. Not even turning the TV on to the Home Shopping Network and QVC could relax me. It was "Craft Day" on one network and "The Patio and Garden Festival" on the other. I have never been any good at crafts; I can't put contact paper in a drawer without creating strange little lumps. As for patio and garden products, the closest I come to having a garden is the eighteen-inch mini-balcony outside my living room window, where there is barely room for a potted geranium.

At some point, though, I did fall asleep, because I began to dream.

I was in the dream, but I was also watching myself in the dream.

The scene was all white. Large, powerful overhead lights shone down on me. I was lying on a hospital bed and people in white masks were bending over me but somehow I knew that I wasn't in a hospital. One of the masked figures was washing my hair—no, coloring my hair. Another was smoothing creamy makeup on my face. I tried to tell them that I didn't want my hair dyed, and that I never wore makeup—mascara usually, but never makeup. I tried to tell them, but they didn't hear me—or maybe they just wouldn't listen.

The scene changed and I was walking down a hallway, wearing a pair of Nancy's very high heels and one of her glamour suits. Gone were the nearly blinding overhead lights. Now there was only a single light shining on my newly platinum hair. I was me, but I wasn't me anymore. I was the girl in Vertigo, newly transformed. I wanted to scream, but I couldn't make a sound. I struggled to wake up, but the dream was too strong. I was compelled to keep walking toward the door at the end of the hall, toward something I knew I didn't want to see.

The door opened to reveal the silhouette of a man. Light was behind him so I couldn't see his face, but he was tall, like Jimmy Stewart, with Jimmy Stewart's rangy build. He saw me—the new me that wasn't me at all—and he smiled. I knew he was smiling because a light from somewhere glinted off his white teeth, even though the rest of his face was in darkness.

He whispered to me. It was Jimmy Stewart's recognizable drawling rasp. "Now you're perfect," he said.

I tried to tell him that he wasn't seeing me, but I couldn't speak. Then he reached out with elongated arms, like tentacles with hands at the ends of them. He fastened his fingers around my wrists and drew me toward him. Closer . . . closer . . . Now I was struggling to breathe. I wanted to run, but my feet were too heavy. I couldn't move. Slowly, he turned into the light and at last I saw his face. I screamed!

I screamed until I forced myself awake.

Sitting up in bed, damp with sweat and with my heart pounding, I realized I was in my apartment, surrounded by familiar objects. The inch-high red numbers on the face of the digital bedside clock told me it was ten minutes to five in the morning. For confirmation, I glanced over at the bedroom window, which faces east, and saw a thin sliver of pale gray dawn coming through where the heavy blue velvet drapes don't quite meet. I could breathe again. I was back in reality. My racing pulse began to slow to normal.

Safe. I made myself remember the final image in the dream, the sight that had frightened me so much it propelled me awake. The man in the doorway, the man with Jimmy Stewart's silhouette and voice was not the actor from *Vertigo*. The man was *Ian*.

I took the longest shower of my life, shampooed my hair, and then shampooed it again. Still, the image of Ian's face in the dream remained.

IT WAS NEARLY six-thirty when I carried a huge mug of coffee, the pile of diet-story magazines, and a white legal pad and pen into the den and settled myself comfortably on the padded window seat. Below me, an excited crowd was gathering along Central Park West to watch the annual Macy's Thanksgiving Day Parade. On both sides of the street, people of all ages maneuvered for the best viewing positions at the curb. Fathers hoisted small children onto their shoulders.

Thanksgiving Day. It was cold, and so clear I thought if

my windows faced west instead of east, and I squinted, I could see past New Jersey, all the way to . . . whatever's immediately west of New Jersey. My years out of the country have weakened my grasp of East Coast geography. I promised myself to check a map and refresh my memory. Right now I had work to do. If there was time before I had to be at Penny's at four o'clock, I would come up with a plan for Francie to lose weight slowly and steadily, without giving her the sense of deprivation that drives so many dieters to kick their programs and binge. But first I had to start outlining the new scenes that would get Francie out of her job at the law office and into the nightclub setting which would be the foundation for the new romantic story line I was planning for her.

Francie hadn't had a love scene since she gained weight. Part of that was because I had been resting her character, Dinah, since her last big dramatic story line a year ago, while I concentrated on bringing other characters forward on the canvas. To be perfectly honest, though, with the change in Francie's appearance, I hadn't been looking for potential romantic partners for her. I was ashamed of myself for having fallen into the general prejudice against creating love stories for larger women. Now I could do something about that by inventing a new male character who would be attracted to Francie *before* the weight loss became apparent. In fact, we could make the audience worry about whether or not this new man was sincere, or if he was going to give her another heartbreak. The story possibilities excited me, and I began to scribble notes on the pad. Soon, I had filled up several pages.

* * *

THE SOUNDS OF the crowd below grew louder as I heard the first strains of a band marching down Central Park West from the north, heralding the beginning of the parade.

I was jotting down diet tips and ideas. When I looked up, I saw the first huge balloon cartoon figures bobbing and floating past my third floor perch. The balloons were so close I was sure I could touch them if I opened the window and leaned out. I resisted the impulse, and instead settled back against the window seat alcove to enjoy the parade for a bit.

Now that hours had passed since the weird dream that had awakened me, I could think about it calmly. Dissect it, as I would a scene I was writing. The genesis, of course, had been watching *Vertigo* with Nancy before I went to bed.

Thinking of Nancy, I smiled at the one part of the dream that was amusing: the thought of me wearing one of Nancy's super glam, cover-of-*Vogue* outfits. Me, whose wardrobe consists mostly of sweaters and shirts and blazers and jeans. Nancy is three inches taller, and built like a fashion model. Her closet is safe from me.

Then I remembered something. Eleven years earlier, I *did* wear one of Nancy's designer numbers. It was a simple silk dress, the color of fresh cream. We let it out in the bust and raised the hem a couple of inches. It was the prettiest dress I'd ever seen.

Nancy gave it to me—to wear for my wedding to Ian.

Chapter 17

AT TEN MINUTES to three I put down my pad and pen and went to my bedroom to choose an outfit to wear for Thanksgiving dinner.

In deference to Penny's muted elegance, and Nancy's flamboyant chic, I decided against wearing slacks. Instead, I took a burnt orange suede boot skirt out of the closet, and paired that with a butterscotch cashmere sweater, to be topped off with my chocolate suede blazer. Orange, chocolate, butterscotch . . . I felt salivary glands go on the alert; I'd been reading too much about food and dieting.

As finishing touches, I cinched a wide brown leather belt around my waist and, because I was going to walk to Penny's, I put on a comfortable pair of brown ankle boots with two-inch heels—just the right height for the long skirt. A few strokes with a hairbrush, a few swipes with a lipstick, two quick dabs of my favorite perfume, and I was out the door.

THE BLEACHER SEATING was being dismantled, and the crowds that massed along Central Park West to see the parade were long gone. Their litter remained, but a sanitation crew was already busy cleaning the street, which was virtually empty of people. Nor did I see many moving cars. I guessed that most New Yorkers were either staying home today, or had already reached their destinations. It was so quiet along Central Park West, I could hear the click of my heels on the pavement. I liked the illusion of being almost alone in the city, which is why I have never joined the stampede to leave town on long holiday weekends.

Although the sun was still shining, the temperature had fallen to the mid-forties. I pulled the suede blazer tighter around me, folded my arms across my chest, and walked faster. At the quickened pace, the cold was stimulating instead of uncomfortable. It was a long hike to Penny's: down Central Park West to Fifty-ninth Street, then east along Central Park South to Madison Avenue, and up Madison to Sixty-eighth. Cutting directly across Central Park to the east side of Manhattan would have been quicker, but then I wouldn't get any exercise at all before the big meal.

Penny Cavanaugh and Matt Phoenix—aunt and nephew, even though Penny, at forty-one, is only three years older than Matt—live in Matt's narrow, four-story townhouse on East sixty-eighth Street, between Madison and Park. When he first told me his address, I was afraid that Matt, the first man to whom I had been attracted since Ian died, must be a dirty cop if he owned an East Side townhouse. It was a relief to find out that I was wrong. The house had been left to Matt by his grandfather.

It was a few minutes past four when I reached Sixty-eighth and walked the last half block to Matt's red brick house with the white trim. Terra cotta pots spilling over with red geraniums flanked the short path to the entrance, where a big orange pumpkin nestled against the corner of the black lacquered front door. An artfully arranged sheaf of wheat fanned out from beneath the polished brass doorknocker.

I rang the bell.

A woman I'd never seen before opened the door. Everything about her was theatrical: her pale oval face and huge brown eyes were surrounded by an explosion of curls in a shade I would call I-Love-Lucy red. Her emerald earrings were extra large, her green satin dress was extra tight, and the neckline plunged to a spot below her breasts. Her figure was as voluptuous as a woman's in a *Playboy* magazine cartoon. If I had to liken her to a movie star, it would be Jessica Rabbit.

She smiled at me. "Hi."

Her voice was low and breathy, and slightly husky. "You must be Morgan. I'm Brandi. Brandi with an *i*."

I slipped off my gloves and took her outstretched hand. It was softer than mine. I made a mental note to use hand cream more often. "Hello," I said. "Am I late?"

"No, honey, you're just the last one to get here. Come on in."

Brandi stepped back and closed the door behind me. "Can I take your jacket? It's nice n' warm inside. Matt made a fire."

Matt. Could this Brandi be here with Matt? He might have a girlfriend. He never said that he didn't. We weren't sleeping together—*almost* doesn't count. While I have lived like a nun for the past five years, I shouldn't believe that Matt has lived like a monk. Still, the thought of Matt having a girlfriend now hit me like a blow to my stomach.

I pasted a smile on my face, as I stuffed my gloves into a pocket and shrugged out of the blazer.

Brandi was watching me as she took my blazer and opened the hall closet.

"You haven't got a snowball's idea in hell who I am, do you, honey?" She saved me the awkwardness of admitting that I didn't by adding, "I'm Georgie's wife."

"Georgie?"

"Georgie," she repeated, as though repeating the name was the same as explaining. She saw that I didn't get it yet. "G. G. Flynn," she said. "Matt's partner at the cop shop."

"Oh," I said. My smile at her became sincere. "It's nice to meet you."

She winked, and cocked her head in such a knowing way I felt exposed.

"You got nothin' to worry about, honey. Matt's not my type," she said as she made room in the closet for my blazer. "My Georgie is the only man for me."

It was hard for me to imagine gruff G. G. Flynn as any woman's "only man for me," but some response was required, so I said, "He's . . . a very good detective." I was immediately ashamed of the lameness of that remark, but Brandi seemed pleased at the compliment, nodding in agreement.

Trying to find something else to say, I asked, "How did you two meet?"

"He busted me."

I didn't have time to absorb that, because she closed the closet door and headed toward the living room. I followed in her undulating wake.

Everyone was there except Penny. Nancy was sitting comfortably curled up on one of the deep brown velvet couches that flanked the fireplace. Nancy's personal "only man for me"—criminal defense attorney Arnold Rose—sat beside her. Arnold is several inches shorter than Nancy, with thinning dark hair, and a soft little belly, but Nancy has told me that in her opinion he is *the* most attractive man in New York. "You'll see that when you know him better," she's said. For this holiday dinner, Arnold was wearing a black sports jacket and a pale gray cashmere sweater, which was the casual version of his working-day black lawyer suits and pale gray shirts.

Opposite Arnold, on the facing couch, was G. G. He was gritting his teeth and glaring at Arnold over the top of one of Penny's flower arrangements.

Matt was at the bar in the corner, pouring drinks. He smiled when he saw me and came forward to give my hand a quick squeeze. "You look good enough to eat," he whispered. For others to hear, he said, "Happy Thanksgiving."

Arnold and G. G. stood when Brandi and I came into the room. Arnold hurried over to give my cheek a quick kiss, while G. G. greeted me with a wave.

"Thank God you got here when you did, Morgan," Nancy said. Her tone was wry, amused. "Arnold and G. G. were about to challenge each other to a duel."

"We disagree about the need for an adversarial justice system," Arnold said as he resumed his seat next to Nancy and took her hand. "Homicide detectives and criminal lawyers are natural enemies."

G. G. growled, "Probably shouldn't be invited to the same Thanksgiving dinners."

"Lawyers have a right to eat, too," Brandi said.

"Yeah? Show me where it says that in the Constitution."

"Now be a good boy, Georgie." Brandi sat down next to him and his expression changed from a heated glare at Arnold to a beam of pleasure at his wife. In the months that I've known him, I have never even seen Detective G. G. Flynn *smile,* let alone beam. Looking at the two of them together on the couch, I thought of the movie *Shrek.* Brandi and G. G. were the princess and the ogre, an unlikely couple who fell in love.

"Where's Penny?" I asked Matt.

"In the kitchen."

"I'll go see if she needs any help—"

"You won't do any such thing," Penny said as she came into the living room. She gave me a hug of welcome. "Everything's under control."

Penny is the kind of woman who starts out attractive and becomes lovelier as you get to know her. Her pretty, heart-shaped face is virtually unlined, and is nicely framed by shoulder length hair the color of rich, dark chocolate. Penny is interested in everything and everyone, which makes her good company. The sparkle in her eyes makes her look closer to thirty than to forty.

On many of the surfaces around the living room, Penny had placed carvings that depicted scenes of early American life. I was particularly impressed with a pair of painted statues next to the fireplace: a Pilgrim couple about three feet high. "Where did you get those?" I asked.

"I made them out of clay. Matt cut the wooden circles they're standing on."

"The house looks like a dream of Thanksgiving," I said.

Matt winked at Penny. "She has a whole closet dedicated just to holiday decorations. Wait'll you see what the place looks like on Groundhog Day."

As Matt poured glasses of wine, Penny sat down on the

couch next to Arnold, and gestured me into the adjacent wingback chair.

Frowning in sympathy, Penny said to me: "I head about that poor girl. How awful."

Matt shook his head at Penny. "G. G. and I are off duty," he said. "No talking about murder."

I raised an eyebrow at Matt. "What are you? The conversation police?"

Penny and Nancy laughed, and Matt had the good grace to smile.

"Do you have any suspects?" Penny asked Matt.

"Not yet."

G. G. sat up straight, rotated his shoulders to get the kinks out, and looked at Penny. "Enough of this small talk. When do we eat?"

PENNY'S SPECTACULAR TABLE decorations featured Pilgrim figurines arranged around harvest produce and fresh flowers flowing from a cornucopia. She had turned seven shiny red apples into place cards by painting our first names onto them.

"Edible paint," she assured us, as we found our places at the circular table and sat down. Penny had put me between Matt and Arnold, with Nancy on the other side of Arnold. She had put Brandi and G. G. on either side of herself, diplomatically seating G. G. and Arnold as far away from each other as was possible in a small dining room.

At Penny's request, the group of us held hands while she said grace. Thanks having been given, we then raised our heads to *ohhhh* and *ahhhh* at her holiday feast. Golden turkey, moist and so tender we could cut it with a fork, sausage and apple stuffing with walnuts and water chestnuts, fresh corn, green beans, baked yams with honey and raisins, a cranberry mold, home-made biscuits—and flower jelly.

"*Flower* jelly?" With narrow-eyed suspicion, G. G. examined the little individual crystal jars at each of our place settings. "Flowers are poisonous. We got one poison case already."

Chapter 18

"THESE FLOWERS ARE *not* poisonous!" Penny said with a touch of heat. "I used begonias and violets and citrus blossoms. They're perfectly safe. I know which flowers to avoid."

In spite of Penny's firm assurance, Nancy, Arnold, Brandi, G. G., and even Matt started at the little jars, hesitating.

Somebody had to support Penny. Quickly, I spread some jelly on a biscuit and took a bite—and a big leap of faith.

"This is delicious," I said. And it was. As the others tried it and praised Penny, I felt Matt take my hand under the table and give it a gentle squeeze.

"Which flowers are poisonous?" Nancy asked.

"I have the whole list in the kitchen, but some of them

are azaleas, daffodils, lily of the valley, poinsettias and mistletoe—both the mistletoe leaves and the berries."

"So mistletoe can kill you," G. G. said. "That figures."

Brandi gave him an affectionate poke in the side. "Oh, *poor* you." Brandi smiled teasingly and said to the rest of us, "Bullets couldn't bring this old buffalo down, but a kiss under the mistletoe did him in."

I stared in wonder at G. G. Flynn. Tough as leather, his heavy face was dominated by a nose that had been broken more than once and a star-shaped scar that indented his right cheek, but when he looked at his wife with unconcealed love, he seemed ten years younger, and almost unmarked by life.

CONVERSATION DURING DINNER ranged from what might happen next in the Middle East, to rising property taxes, to the Knicks' expensive new center. Things went well until dessert. Then, halfway through his second piece of Penny's raspberry and blueberry pie, G. G. glanced across the table at Arnold Rose and declared, "We got to get rid of that Miranda ruling."

Before Arnold could reply, Penny and Brandi jumped in to change the subject and avoid an argument. They both turned to me, but Brandi got in the first word. "My favorite character on your show is Cody," she said. "I can't decide if he's a good guy or a bad guy."

G. G. grunted, but Brandi gave him a playful tap and said, "Hush, now."

Penny picked up the conversational ball. "Last year, when Sylvia had that terrible accident and was in a coma for weeks with her face all bandaged up—when the bandages came off it was another actress. What happened?"

"The original Sylvia wanted to leave the show to get married and go with her husband to England," I said, "so we let her out of her contract."

"Somebody new playing the same part—doesn't the audience get confused?" Arnold asked.

"They adjust pretty quickly, if they like the new actor. But there are some characters that you just can't recast, because the particular actor has a quality that's unique. If we lose one of those rare performers we have to retire the role, sometimes for years."

"Or until the actor finds out he doesn't have a big career in movies or primetime and decides to go back to you," Nancy said.

The telephone rang and Matt got up to answer it in the next room.

When he returned, he wasn't smiling. "The report came back on the prints they got off the torn appointment book in Cybelle Carter's apartment."

G. G. was half out of his chair. "We got somebody to talk to?"

Matt glanced at me before replying, signaling I wasn't going to like his answer.

"They're Johnny Isaac's prints," he said.

G. G. was up all the way and heading for the door. "Let's pick him up for questioning."

I put my napkin down and stood up. "I'm going with you."

"No, you're not," Matt said. "This is police business, not show business."

I felt my face flush with anger, but the concerned expression on Penny's face stopped me from telling Matt what I thought about him. Instead, I took a calming breath and said, "I don't believe Johnny would try to kill Cybelle. He adores her."

"Life isn't as neat as you can make it in a script."

That remark made my blood boil. I turned to Arnold. "I think Johnny's going to need your help."

Arnold asked Nancy, "Do you mind?"

"Of course not."

He leaned over to give her a quick kiss on the cheek. She whispered something in his ear, then drew back and said to him, "Call me here later."

He smiled at her and nodded.

"I'll be here, too," I told Arnold as he hurried after the two detectives.

Brandi glanced around the table at Penny, Nancy, and me, smiled devilishly and said, "Now it's just us chickens. What'll we talk about?"

"Men," Nancy joked.

Penny smiled at that. "You girls talk, I'll listen." She stood up and began to clear the table. Nancy, Brandi, and I rose to help her.

"I like your Arnold," Penny told Nancy. "Is it serious between you two?"

"He's wonderful, Penny. I'm so happy. I want everybody to be as happy as I am. You're next."

Startled, Penny looked up from stacking dishes. "What do you mean?"

Behind Penny, I started shaking my head vigorously and making hand motions to stop Nancy. She saw me, but didn't get the message.

"I want you to meet this great guy in our firm," she said. "He's—"

Penny's face lost its color. She gripped the stack of

plates so tightly that her knuckles turned white. "I know you mean well, Nancy." There was a slight tremor in her voice. For a moment, I thought she was going to cry, but she held herself together. "I can't let you introduce me to some man because I'm already married."

"But I thought—"

"I'm not free, Nancy. But thank you for the kind thought." Clutching the stack of dishes, Penny turned and hurried into the kitchen.

Nancy looked at me. "You told me Penny was a widow."

"She is," Brandi said. She glanced toward the kitchen and lowered her voice. "But she thinks her husband—his name is Patrick—she thinks Patrick is coming back."

"Coming *back*? Back from where?"

"Why, from the dead."

"I should have told you about this," I said to Nancy.

"Yes, you should have. What's going on?"

Even though I heard water running in the kitchen, I lowered my voice even more. "Patrick's plane exploded over the ocean seven years ago. Because his body was never recovered, Penny believes he's still alive and that one day he'll walk through the front door with an explanation."

"Like maybe he was really in a secret government crime-fighting organization and had to go undercover," Brandi said. "Anyway, that was Frisco's excuse to Felicia on *General Hospital.*"

Brandi leaned in closer to Nancy and added the part that I left out. "Penny got the idea about Patrick from the stories because so many people come back from the dead, like Luke and Laura, and Erica Kane's father, and two or three of Erica's husbands, and Stefan DeMera, and Roger Thorpe, and just about all of those crazy Cassadines, and—"

"I get the picture," Nancy said. She turned to me. "The last thing I want to do is upset Penny, but this type of hope can't be good for her."

"She'll start living again, when she's ready," I said. "*I* did."

Nancy, Brandi, and I joined Penny in the kitchen. Our intention was to help her clean up, but when we looked around, we were amazed to see there was nothing to do. The sink and the counters were spotless.

"Where are all the dirty pots and pans?" I asked.

"I wash them as I go along. Then all I have to do is put the dishes in the washer." Penny was her warm and cheerful hostess-self again.

We got another surprise when we saw she was carving a juicy, golden and intact turkey.

"Is that a *second* turkey?"

"Yes." She expertly sliced the meat and scooped out enough stuffing to fill five Tupperware containers. "I made it so I could send you all home with leftovers. Don't you think the best part of Thanksgiving dinner is the leftovers?"

"The best part of Thanksgiving is being with friends," Nancy said.

Brandi nodded. "You sure said an eyeful, honey."

THE ELEVEN O'CLOCK news had just begun when Arnold Rose finally called. Penny handed the phone to Nancy and I picked up the kitchen extension.

"It took some fancy talking, but Isaac isn't under arrest," he told us.

"*Did* he tear the pages out of Cybelle's appointment book?" I asked.

"Yes, he admitted to that, when they told him his fingerprints were on it."

"Why would he do such a thing?"

"He claimed he was worried about Cybelle, about what
that husband of hers would do if he found her. Isaac's excuse is that he tore the pages out to frighten her just enough
so that she would come and stay with him, where he could
protect her."

"That's a stupid story," Nancy said.

"Yes, it is, but after spending several hours with him,
I'm inclined to agree with Morgan that he wouldn't physically hurt the woman."

"What do the police think?" I asked.

Arnold's reply gave me concern for Johnny. "At the moment," he said, "Isaac is their only suspect."

NANCY AND BRANDI waited at Penny's for their respective
men to take them home, but I said my goodbyes and hurried outside to find a taxi.

I saw the roof light of an empty cab at the corner of
Sixty-eighth and Madison, hailed it, and gave the driver
my address.

There was very little traffic on the streets. As the cab
sped through Central Park, I leaned back against the seat
and thought about love.

Love had cracked granite-hard G. G. Flynn open and
exposed his vulnerable core, and it had pushed a smart
man like Johnny Isaac into doing something stupid. Love
was making Nancy Cummings glow, and had turned steely
criminal lawyer Arnold Rose into Don Quixote, ready to
rush off to fight for anything that mattered to her.

Lost love was keeping Penny Cavanaugh a captive of

her past, and for years it had prevented me from living like a healthy adult woman. No longer. I was ready to dive again into the uncharted waters of romance. When the time was right, I decided to help Penny do the same thing.

Chapter 19

FRANCIE JAMES AND I had agreed to meet at her place in Greenwich Village on Friday morning at ten, to begin the weight-loss plan I had devised for her. I pulled on a heavy sweater, workout pants, and running shoes, and took a cab to her address on Waverly Place, an attractive tree-lined street of early twentieth–century townhouses that have been turned from private homes into upscale apartments.

It was five minutes to ten when the taxi pulled up in front of Francie's building and I got out. Like its neighbors, 135 Waverly is four stories high with a gray stone façade, tall, narrow front windows and a short flight of concrete steps leading to the entrance. Francie told me her apartment occupies the first floor, with a basement apartment below, and two other floor-throughs above her. The three above ground floors share the common front door;

the basement apartment has a separate entrance, which is a few steps below the sidewalk.

Although I haven't been to his place yet, I know that Chet Thompson rents an apartment on this street, where he stays when he comes into the city from his house in Connecticut. Chet's building is four doors down from Francie's, but I knew I wouldn't run into him because he was still at The Hague. I'd been short with him the last time he phoned, but the thought of him filled me with a delicious feeling of anticipation, even though I didn't know what our relationship was going to be. It's confusing, after six years with one man, and then five years with no man, to suddenly find myself attracted to *two* men. Eventually, I'll have to make a choice, but I need to know them better before I do. Of course, if I take too long, they might not be waiting.

I share one important thing with the characters I throw into jeopardy on *Love of My Life*: I don't know what is going to happen next in my life, either.

Francie answered the door on the first ring. She was dressed in new gray sweats and Nikes, and a red terry headband swept her thick, golden brown hair back from her face. Smiling, she stepped aside to invite me into her apartment.

The living room was decorated in a harmonious mixture of soft colors and fabrics. A few good antiques, or excellent reproductions, were scattered among the contemporary furniture. A large, comfortable-looking sofa was opposite the fireplace. A pair of club chairs faced the window, with their backs to the interior wall. They formed the end of an L-shaped seating area around a big wooden coffee table that had once been a door.

A long, narrow library table was behind the sofa, covered with magazines and newspapers. There were quite a few attractive features in the room, but by far the most appealing to me was the huge gray Persian cat that draped itself gracefully across the papers on the table. Two more cats—a small black one with white feet and a big gray tabby—peeked at me from atop the arms of the sofa. All three cats had thick coats shiny with good health.

"What gorgeous cats," I said. The Persian, perhaps accustomed to compliments, looked at me, yawned and closed its eyes.

"Thank you. They're my babies." She picked up the tabby, cradled it against her chest and brought the cat over to me. As I stroked its glossy fur, it began to purr.

I asked Francie, "Did you have a nice Thanksgiving?"

"It was great. My sister just found out that she's pregnant so all the attention was on her. Nobody ragged on me about my weight."

The tabby wiggled in Francie's arms. She put it down gently.

"Well, are you ready to start?" I asked.

"Do you want to look in my fridge? To see what I have in there, and tell me what to throw out?"

"No," I said. "You can eat whatever you want."

"Then how am I going to lose weight?" Her voice was a wail of despair.

"Trust me. You will lose weight, if you follow my plan. First: do you have a bathroom scale?"

"Sure."

"Step number one: get rid of it."

She looked puzzled.

"I don't want you to weigh yourself," I said.

"But how can I tell if I'm losing?" Her eyes registered sudden comprehension. "Oh, you mean by my clothes? When they start feeling loose?"

"That's it."

"But shouldn't I check my weight, just to be sure I'm on track?"

"Absolutely not." My voice was firm. "This is an essential part of the plan. If you start weighing yourself, it's not going to work. Before, when you tried to diet, you checked the scale, right?"

She nodded.

"And the longer you stayed on the diet, the more and more frequently you stepped on the scale?"

"Yes, but it got so discouraging—"

"That's exactly the point. Checking to see if you've lost a pound—that's a stresser. When we're stressed, we start eating. It's easy for a taste to turn into a binge. So, no weighing yourself. Let's go for a walk. As soon as we get rid of that scale, you'll hear the rest of the plan."

"I'll go get it," she said.

After we deposited Francie's scale in a nearby dumpster, we strolled through Greenwich Village. At Washington Square Park we paused to watch the skaters. When we began walking again I increased our pace a little bit at a time, while I explained the principles of the plan I'd devised.

"For step number two," I said, "name your favorite foods."

She closed her eyes and *hmmmmmed* with pleasure. "Ice cream, every flavor except mint. And Godiva chocolates, potatoes, bread and butter, every kind of pasta, beef stew, anything Chinese, fried chicken, chocolate cake."

Her list was making me hungry. "Now," I said, "of all the things you like best, which one would be easiest to give up?"

She thought for a moment. "I guess . . . bread."

"How would you feel about giving up bread? *Only*

bread. Eat all the rest of your favorite things, but just pretend that bread doesn't exist."

"I could do that. But if I can still have ice cream and chocolates and potatoes, how can I lose weight?"

"Just give up bread. See what happens."

"Sounds too easy."

"Trust me, Francie. Here's step number three: when you have a meal alone at home, *don't read while you eat.*"

Francie was so surprised she came to an abrupt stop. "But I study my lines while I eat. Or I catch up on magazines and newspapers—"

"Study your lines in the bathtub, or in bed, or lying on the sofa with your cats curled up around you. Just don't read while you're eating." I started walking again, urging her along with a little tug on the sleeve of her sweatshirt.

"Can I watch TV?" she asked.

"No. Listen to music. Look at what's on your plate."

She shrugged and gave in. "Okay, no reading, no TV. But just tell me why not?"

"When we read or watch TV, we don't really enjoy what we're eating. We barely taste it. Our brain processes what we're reading or watching, and the result is that we eat more than we realize, more than we really want. We go past the point when hunger is satisfied. The worst part is that when we're not aware of what we're eating, we miss the enjoyment."

"That makes sense."

We walked in silence for a few minutes. Glancing at Francie, I saw an expression of concentration on her face. Finally, she came to some internal conclusion.

"I'm going to do it—follow your plan exactly. No stepping on a scale, no bread, and no reading or TV during meals."

"There is just one more thing," I said.

She laughed. "You sound like Columbo, in those old TV reruns." She lowered her voice, cocked her head and produced an excellent imitation of actor Peter Falk as the rumpled detective: "Oh, sir, there's just one more thing . . ."

I grinned with admiration. "That's very good. Do you do anybody else?"

"Some singers, and Al Pacino." Giving me Al Pacino's Michael Corleone stare, she lowered her voice again and whispered, "Freddo, you broke my heart."

I clapped my hands. "That's terrific. I'll see if I can work that talent into some of Dinah's new scenes."

"Great," she said. Her eyes were shining. "Now, Lieutenant Columbo, what was that *one last thing?*"

"Step number four: walk every day. Walk whenever you can. Five minutes. Ten minutes. It would be great if you could eventually work up to forty-five minutes a day, but you don't have to do it all at once. Three fifteen-minute walks are just as good."

In her enthusiasm for the plan, Francie herself had picked up the pace of our amble, and had edged slightly ahead of me. "I'll get a treadmill," she said, "so I can keep walking when the weather's bad."

"If you follow the plan, you will lose weight." I made my tone casual, because I didn't want her to get so keyed up that she would rush the process and, as a result, burn out. "We're in no hurry, Francie. This new story line unfolds over the course of a year, so don't pressure yourself for quick results, because they won't last."

"I can do this," she said, nodding. She was talking as much to herself as to me. "I really can do this."

We walked for nearly an hour before we were back in front of Francie's building.

As I hailed a cab going uptown, I told her to call me if she needed any support or reassurance.

Leaning against the back seat of my taxi, I smiled. What Francie didn't know was that I was willing to bet she would cut *way* down on the other favorite foods she listed once she began to lose weight. I was also sure that by not reading or watching TV during meals, she'd naturally eat less because she'd be aware of what she was tasting. Last, by telling her she could eat anything she wanted—except the one item she herself had proposed to give up—I hoped that in time, as her looks improved and as exercising became part of her everyday life, she would *want* to alter her eating habits and so would choose a healthier menu.

That was the real secret of the plan.

Chapter 20

BACK HOME, THE first thing I did was check for messages. No message from Matt, but Johnny Isaac called to thank me for sending Arnold Rose to his rescue, and Brandi Flynn left a message saying how nice it was to meet me. I returned those calls, and then settled down to work on new story for the show.

By the time I had to shut down the computer to dress for Winston Yarborough's dinner party, I'd sketched out the mysterious new man (I was going to call him Ben) who was about to enter the life of Francie's character, Dinah:

    Ben and Dinah meet late one night, in
    the rain, when Dinah discovers him uncon-
    scious in the alley behind Nicky's night-
    club, apparently the victim of a mugging.

Nicky, who's closing up, hears Dinah's
cries for help, and rushes outside. Together they carry the unconscious Ben out
of the rain and into Nicky's club.

Ben's face is dirty, his hair is matted
with blood from a blow on the head, and
his clothes are soaked through. Even in
this condition, Dinah sees that Ben is a
very attractive man. Nicky notices that
he is well dressed. He's not the kind of
man anyone would expect to find lying face
down in an alley.

While Nicky goes upstairs to awaken
Doctor Glenn, who lives in an apartment
on the floor above the club, Dinah wraps
Ben in a warm, dry blanket, then gently
begins to clean his face and dab antiseptic from the club's first aid kit on his
wound. She speaks to him softly, urging
him to wake up.

Her voice seems to reach him because
Ben opens his eyes. He sees Dinah, leaning over him, tending to him. Obviously
confused, he gazes at the unfamiliar sur-
roundings and asks where he is.

Dinah tells him that they're in
Nicky's, a nightclub, that it's after
hours and that she found him lying in the
alley, unconscious. She asks what happened to him.

Ben replies that he's not sure. . . .
He searches through his pockets. Near
panic, he tells her that his wallet is

gone . . . if he had a wallet . . . He
doesn't remember, but he's sure he must
have had a wallet. Everyone has a
wallet . . . don't they?

Dinah asks his name. He admits that he
doesn't know who he is . . .

Dinah takes his hands—looks at his wrists,
sees a tan line and tells him that it looks
as though he usually wears a watch, but he's
not wearing a watch now.

He doesn't remember a watch. . . .
They must have taken it when they hit him
over the head and robbed him.

They? What does he remember about his
attackers?

Nothing. All he can recall is two figures coming out of the darkness . . .
Everything else—everything before that—
is a blank.

He struggles to sit up. Dinah helps him
to sit in a chair. He lifts his hands to
examine them—and stares as though he's
never seen them before. He's not wearing
a ring of any kind. His hands are strong,
and callused—but his nails are well kept,
recently manicured. It's the first of many
contradictions about this man who doesn't
know who he is, nor what happened to him.
He goes through his pockets again, but
doesn't find anything that would provide a
clue to his identity.

Doctor Glenn, hair rumpled, hastily
dressed, enters with Nicky. He examines

Ben and observes that he's had a nasty
blow on the head, and probably has a concussion. He tells Nicky to call the hospital for an ambulance. Ben stops Nicky
from making the call. He insists that
he's feeling okay, that he doesn't need
to go to the hospital.

Doctor Glenn disagrees, but Ben is
adamant—he refuses to go to the hospital.
Nor will he let them call the police. He
assures them that he will be all right.
To prove it, he tries to stand up, but
the effort is too much for him, and he
passes out. Nicky catches him just before
he crashes to the floor.

Dinah, very worried about the serious-
ness of his injuries, sides with Doctor
Glenn. She hands the telephone to Glenn,
who calls for an ambulance.

In the hospital, Ben will meet a few of
the other continuing characters in the
story, and this will begin the weaving of
Ben into *Love of My Life's* tapestry.

Dinah persuades Nicky to hire Ben to
work in the nightclub with them. It will
be a surprise when Cody brings Kira to
the club one night. Cody is stunned—and
not happy—to see Ben, because he recognizes Ben from somewhere in Cody's own
dark past. It will be clear from the expression on Cody's face that whatever he
thinks of Ben, it is not good. This is
intended to send a shiver of alarm though

the audience. I want them to worry about
what their beloved Dinah is getting herself into by befriending this attractive
and seemingly needy stranger, who might
turn out to be dangerous to her.

The expression on Ben's face when he
sees Cody will be enigmatic. We won't be
sure whether or not Ben recognizes Cody.
Later, when Ben is alone, he has a quick
memory flashback. He *did* recognize Cody—
but he doesn't know from where, or under
what circumstances. However, Ben realizes
that Cody's failure to mention that they
know each other is a bad sign. Ben worries
about what he might have done that he
can't remember. He's concerned that he's
going to bring trouble into the life of
the woman who has been so kind to him,
Dinah.

Ben's fears will force him to follow
Cody when Cody and Kira take off for
their high-octane adventure-chase-thrill
ride aboard a riverboat.

Dinah, her worry about Ben increasing,
will follow Ben. This will plunge both
couples into jeopardy, during which Ben
and Dinah begin to suspect that they are
developing serious feelings for each
other. This is a complication that scares
both of them because Ben doesn't know
what he's done that could bring harm to
Dinah, and Dinah is terrified of falling
in love because she's embarrassed about

her weight gain. She's sure that a man as good-looking as Ben couldn't possibly find her attractive. When he kisses her, and she pulls away, he will think that it's because Dinah is suspicious of him. Finally, she will confess her fear, and he will be astonished because he finds her lovely just as she is. But if she really doesn't like the way she looks, and she wants to change, he'll help her. Ben will give Dinah essentially the same plan I gave to Francie, and he will urge that whatever change she wants to make should be a *slow* change.

When we're back in the office on Monday, Tommy and I will start searching for a charismatic actor to play Ben, and as soon as we have some candidates we'll bring them in to audition with Francie, to see whose personality clicks with hers. Link Ramsey and Cybelle Carter as Cody and Kira make magic in their scenes together. Now we'll need a Ben to strike sparks with Dinah—I have a bumpy ride in store for those two. Combining an obstacle-filled romance with a weight-loss story should keep our ratings high during February sweeps.

Big numbers will give us some protection against further interference from Lori Cole. While I won the battle to keep Francie James on the show, the new head of daytime did not take defeat well. I saw the hostility in her eyes and knew that I had made a dangerous enemy.

Nancy called just as I was ready to leave for Winston Yarborough's party. Her voice was breathy with excitement.

"I found Philippe Abacasas for you!"

"Hey, Nancy Drew—that's fantastic. Details, please."

"Robert Glassel came through for me," she said. "Abacasas keeps a permanent suite at the Hotel Baur Au Lac in Zurich, but all of the bills for the clothes he ordered from Robert were sent to Abacasas care of his bank—Bank Leu, that's also in Zurich."

I tried to keep disappointment out of my voice. "It's valuable information," I said, "but Cybelle ran away from Abacasas three years ago. He could be anywhere."

"Robert saw him in Zurich, in a restaurant, *the day before yesterday*." Nancy's tone was triumphant.

"That's great work, Nancy!"

"Okay, what do we do next?"

"I'll call Matt and tell him what you found out."

"If he doesn't get off his tight NYPD duff, I can get a Swiss operative to keep an eye on Abacasas," Nancy said. "Or find out if he sent anyone to New York with strychnine in his carry-on."

I laughed. "You're really getting into this, aren't you?"

"Detecting is a hell of a lot more fun than corporate law," she said. "Of course, in corporate law people aren't inclined to send us rattlesnakes. Speaking of which, where does that investigation stand?"

"Matt hasn't been able to find the source of the snake. Frankly, since Jeannie Ford was murdered, it's not a high priority."

"Well, it's a high priority for *me*," Nancy said. "Since you came back from playing Sheena, Queen of the Jungle, you've brought a lot of fun into my life. I don't want to lose my best friend again."

I said goodbye to Nancy and I dialed Matt's number at the Twentieth Precinct.

When he picked up, I said, "Nancy's contact at the fash-

ion house in Paris told her that Philippe Abacasas is in Zurich, and that he lives at the Hotel Baur Au Lac."

"Who is this?" His tone was droll.

"Very funny. I think Nancy did a great job in finding
that out."

"Maybe. We'll see."

His apparent indifference made me want to shriek. I
must have made some noise of exasperation, because he
said, "I heard that. If you start screaming and hurt my ear,
that constitutes assault on a police officer and I'll have to
put the cuffs on you."

"In your dreams," I said. Softly.

Before he could reply, I hung up the phone.

Chapter 21

BECAUSE OUR FOUNDER and chairman is known for seldom doing anything for purely social reasons, I was certain Winston Yarborough's dinner party would be a business evening.

I chose, with particular care, a new dress from a French boutique on Madison. Black silk, long sleeves, waist cinched with a wide black belt, a jewel neckline, and a high white satin collar and matching white satin cuffs. It cost more than I like to spend, but I rationalized that when I removed the collar and cuffs, I would have the equivalent of two outfits.

It was ten minutes after seven when I got out of the cab at Madison and Seventy-sixth Street, in front of the elegant Hotel Carlyle. Winston Yarborough, who has a home in Greenwich, Connecticut, keeps an apartment in the hotel.

A doorman in uniform stood at the imposing white wood and canopied entry. A pair of long white canvas drapes trimmed in gold bracket the canopy, nicely framing the black and gold façade. For anyone who doesn't recognize this famous hotel at first glimpse, "The Carlyle" is spelled out in gold script on each side of the canopy and above the revolving door.

Although I have been to the Café Carlyle and to the Carlyle's Bemelman's Bar for various celebrations over the years, it wasn't until I met Winston Yarborough that I went upstairs, to one of the hotel's luxurious suites.

Crossing the opulent lobby, I headed directly for the elevators, and recognized Yarborough's chauffeur standing in front of the private car at the end of the row. He saluted me and I said hello to him. He opened the door to the Carlyle's gilded cage for me and pressed the button for the Yarboroughs' floor.

When the elevator stopped, the door slid open and I heard music: instrumental arrangements of Broadway show tunes. I recognized the songs because Ian had a large collection of original cast recordings—many nights we played his albums in the African bush on our little battery-powered machine. I stepped into the sumptuous foyer of the Yarboroughs' Tower Suite to the strains of "Wouldn't It Be Loverly." A butler was there to take my cape and guide me up the two steps to the living room, which was furnished with fine antiques and museum-quality art. The last time I was there, Yarborough had had three glorious Turner landscapes on the living room walls. Tonight the Turner over the fireplace was gone, replaced by a Cézanne still life.

Looking at that painting, I remembered something I'd learned in an art appreciation class at Columbia. Unlike most young artists, Cézanne didn't have to live the cliché of the painter starving in a garret,; his father was a wealthy banker who left him a fortune. Cézanne's boyhood friend was Emile Zola, who grew up to become a famous novelist. Cézanne, whose talent was unappreciated by the public for most of his life, was a bitter loner. When he thought that the much more successful Zola had made thinly disguised references to his failures in one of his novels, Cézanne was furious. He ended their friendship, even though Zola had been his longest and most loyal supporter. It occurred to me that I might be able to use their fractured relationship as the inspiration for a *Love of My Life* story line. I'd have to file the thought away; I was on duty as a guest.

Six people were already in the Yarbrough's cream and apricot living room. Patrician, sterling-haired Winston Yarborough stood talking to two men who appeared to be in their fifties. The face of the heavier one was vaguely familiar, but I couldn't place him. All three wore dark suits; together, the trio made me imagine a coven of bankers.

Three women had gathered on the other side of the room. Two were thin and stylish in little black dresses and big white diamonds. The third was an orange-haired Amazon. Wearing a Flamingo pink satin dinner suit, she stood out like a neon sign blinking in the darkness. I recognized her because her face was on the cover of the current *Newsweek;* she was Dolly Naughton, the thirty-eight-year-old recently elected Governor of Texas.

Seeing her made me realize why the beefy man with Yarborough looked familiar—he was Governor Naughton's husband, wealthy ex-pro quarterback Billy Naughton, TV pitchman for a top-selling beer. Without his camera makeup, Naughton had the red-veined nose of a serious drinker.

Winston Yarborough smiled with delight when he saw

me, left his conversation group and extended his arms in welcome.

"Morgan, my dear. I'm so pleased you're here." He grasped my shoulders, kissed me lightly on the cheek and stepped back to survey me. "How beautiful you look. That dress is very becoming."

"Thank you."

At that moment, the thinnest and most diamond-laden of the women noticed us together and frowned. Her hair was unnaturally black and the skin of her face was unnaturally tight. She was as stunning, and as artificial as an airbrushed photo in a fashion magazine. Her features were delicate and so well-proportioned, I guessed she must have been a spectacular beauty before she began to use the services of colorists and plastic surgeons. With a drink in one hand and a cigarette in the other, she disengaged from her group and glided toward us like a lioness stalking prey.

"You must be Morgan . . . *Taylor*," she said. Her voice vibrated with good breeding, or expensive schools. "I'm Cecile Yarborough. Win's wife." She waved the cigarette as though it were a scepter and slid a sideways glance at Yarborough. "You didn't tell me your little writer is so pretty."

Between giving me the wrong last name, and using the put-down *little writer*, I suspected she had heard the rumors about her husband and me, but I couldn't blurt out, "Mrs. Yarborough, we're not having an affair!" Suppose she *hadn't* heard the gossip, and was simply being unpleasant?

"Win, darling," she said. "The caterer's having a meltdown. Go talk to him, won't you?"

He nodded. "I won't be long," he said to me as he left us.

Cecile Yarborough assessed my black dress and white collar and cuffs.

"What an appropriate costume," she said. Her tone was glacial. "You look just like a pilgrim."

Fortunately, the elevator door opened behind me and another couple arrived, diverting her attention. The woman, in her forties and letting her brown hair go gray, was on the "super thin, little black dress and diamonds" team, but she looked a bit drab standing next to that swaggering Prince of Charisma, the network's number one anchorman and glamour boy Jeff Norman. Cecile Yarborough cried, "Darlings!" as she abandoned me and rushed to embrace them.

I wasn't alone for more than a few seconds. Winston Yarborough returned from his mission and took my arm.

"Come," he said, "I want you to meet the other guests."

I exchanged polite hellos—until we reached Wilma Barton, the much younger, golden blonde wife of Jerome Barton, the new Chairman of the Federal Communications Commission. When he told her what I did for the network, she grabbed my hand in a fierce grip. Shooing Yarborough away, she pulled me toward a private corner of the room.

"I just adore *Love of My Life*," she gushed. "I have so much sadness in my own life—my husband's teenage children just *hate* me! Oh, I don't know what I would do without your stories."

Her face was flushed and her voice quivered with excitement as she leaned close to me. "It's fate that we met tonight. Fate, that's absolutely what it is. I have so many ideas for you!"

"I'm sorry, Mrs. Barton, but I'm not allowed to accept—"

"Kira should get pregnant with Cody's baby," she rushed on. "And somebody— you can figure out *who*— forces her to have an abortion, but she doesn't want an abortion because she loves Cody, so she works it out with the doctor that he'll just take her little baby and plant it in another woman's womb. Maybe in Sylvia's. I cried all day after Doctor Glenn told Sylvia she'd never be able to have a baby. She'd be thrilled when she finds out that she's carrying one, wouldn't she?"

I gaped at Wilma Barton; she took my stupefied stare for fascination.

"Oh, I'm just *bursting* with wonderful ideas," she said. "I know I could write, if I only had the time!"

By eight-thirty dinner had yet to be announced. I did a quick head-count in the room and discovered that there were nine of us assembled. Yarborough's assistant had said there would be ten for dinner, so someone was missing. I assumed we were waiting for him, or her.

Smiling politely at the boisterous husband of the Governor of Texas as he complained about the many inconveniences of being married to a politician, I nodded with sympathy and murmured "Ummm." But actually, I was listening to the score of *Brigadoon*. Lovers Tommy and Fiona, doomed to be separated in time by a hundred years, were saying goodbye when I glimpsed the elevator door slide open. I turned my head enough to see a lone man step out into the foyer.

The new arrival was absolutely one of the most attractive men I have ever seen. A couple of inches under six feet tall, thick dark hair, a powerful torso and a face that was too rugged to be labeled handsome, he was something better than handsome; his features radiated masculinity. Winston Yarborough's tenth guest wore a black Brioni suit tailored to perfection, but unlike the other men in the room, in their uniform of shirts and ties, this man wore a white silk turtleneck sweater. He was polished, without being slick.

Yarborough saw the late arrival and hurried across the room to greet him warmly. Conversation had stopped and all eyes were on Yarborough and his guest. Guiding him into the middle of the living room, Global's chairman announced, "I would like you all to meet our guest of honor, one of Global Entertainment's most important stockholders: Philippe Abacasas."

Chapter 22

I WAS IN such a state of shock I didn't hear Yarborough introduce him to the others. Then it was my turn.

"Philippe, this is Morgan Tyler."

Philippe Abacasas stared at me with eyes the liquid gray of the Indian Ocean along the white sand shoreline of Mombasa.

"It is my pleasure to meet you," he said at last.

When he took my hand, the sensation of his skin against mine was thrilling. He was about to say something else when the Yarboroughs' butler opened the double doors to the dining room and announced dinner.

Abacasas lowered his voice. "May we have a private conversation later?"

Before I could reply, Winston Yarborough steered me away, saying genially, "You'll have to wait to get to know this lady, Philippe. I'm taking Morgan in to dinner." As the chairman's hand cupped my elbow, I saw Cecile Yarborough aim an icy glare at her husband's back.

THE DINING ROOM was a festival of gardenias, lilies, and tall white tapered candles. Thanks to my trips to auction houses with Tommy Zenos, I was able to appreciate the exquisite early Victorian mahogany dining table and the fine mahogany George IV dining chairs, the seats of which were upholstered in pale yellow damask that matched the fabric on the walls. The shade was the perfect backdrop for the many flickering candles, which suffused the room in a golden glow.

Cecile Yarborough presided at one end of the table, with her husband at the other. Jerome Barton, the new chairman of the F.C.C., was on her right and Abacasas on her left. Winston Yarborough's dinner partners were Wilma Barton and Governor Dolly Naughton. I was diagonally across from Abacasas, between the F.C.C.'s Barton and anchorman Jeff Norman. Directly across from me was Hazel Norman. About as animated as wallpaper, she was gazing off into space.

I yearned for this dinner party to be over so I could talk to Abacasas, but I consoled myself with the thought that in this distinguished company—the chairman of the Federal Communications Commission, media titan Winston Yarborough, Jeff Norman who'd just returned from a dangerous assignment in the Middle East, and the flamboyant (but reportedly brilliant) Governor Naughton—I'd hear some interesting conversation about the world beyond show business.

Just as we were served the first course—artichoke

hearts with caviar—Hazel Norman came out of her trance and looked around at the other female guests. She leaned forward across the table and, in a voice loud enough for everyone to hear, said to me, "I'm the only *first* wife in this room."

Cecile Yarborough, after throwing a stiletto-sharp glance in my direction, said to her other guests, "Everyone knows Win was married before. When people ask me which Mrs. Yarborough I am, I tell them I'm the *final* Mrs. Yarborough."

A moment of uneasy laughter. Then the tension was broken as various guests began to chat in pairs. Jerome Barton, seated on my left, leaned forward toward Jeff Norman, who was on my right. Speaking across me in a quiet, confidential tone, Barton said, "Jeff, now that you're back in the U.S., there's something I want to ask you."

At last, I thought, *I'll hear about the Middle East*.

"Did you get hair plugs?" asked the F.C.C. Chairman of the anchorman.

Governor Naughton turned away from Winston Yarborough to join their conversation. "I want Billy to get rid of his silly comb-over and get plugs," she said, "but he's afraid it's going to hurt."

Inside my closed mouth I gritted my teeth. For *this* I put on high heels?

Never had a dinner seemed to go on for so long.

I pasted on a smile and retreated into my own thoughts. Here I was, in the same room with the mysterious, and possibly dangerous, Philippe Abacasas—and he wanted to talk to me *privately*.

Did that mean he knew Cybelle's whereabouts? He must. But he hadn't contacted her directly, so what was he up to? So many questions were swirling in my head, I could barely taste the courses that arrived on a succession of plates. Finally, dessert was served. I glanced at Abacasas. He was looking at me. Our eyes met for an instant, then I broke the contact. Noticing that the other women at the table had hardly touched their dessert—chocolate mousse with fresh raspberries—I rather defiantly ate mine. I caught Abacasas looking at me again. He winked conspiratorially, and asked his hostess for a second helping of the mousse. The man was so attractive that I would have enjoyed our silent communications.

Except for the fact that he was *Philippe Abacasas*.

Coming face-to-face with Abacasas, when he was supposed to be in Zurich, and learning he was a major stockholder in the parent company of Global Broadcasting, had piled one incredible coincidence on top of another. I don't believe in incredible coincidences as a rule, but I *do* believe in seizing opportunities. Abacasas and I would have our private chat.

FINALLY, THE LAST drops of coffee (yuck, *decaf*), port, and brandy had been sipped and swallowed. The party was over. Abacasas did what I hoped he would do; he intercepted me on my way to say good night to our host and hostess.

"As we are the only two who are unaccompanied, will you allow me to see you home?"

I had the insane impulse to say yes. I slapped it down.

"No, thank you," I said.

With a smile he asked, "Then will you have a drink with me? In some well-lighted place, surrounded by people, where you will feel safe?"

There was humor in his eyes, but they bored so deeply

into mine that it was almost a caress. I felt my cheeks flush with embarrassment.

"You think I'm afraid of you?"

"I am the one who is afraid." His voice was warm, his tone conciliatory. "Human relationships are complicated. People say things—you may have formed an incorrect impression of me."

There it was.

"If you have formed a negative opinion," he said, "please grant me the opportunity to correct it."

"We can go somewhere and have *real* coffee."

"Excellent," he said.

Abacasas had a gleaming black limousine and a uniformed driver waiting outside the Carlyle. At the sight of his boss, the driver hurried to open the back door.

I shook my head. "There's a coffee bar just around the corner," I said.

"Follow us," Abacasas told the driver.

It was an odd sensation to walk the equivalent of half a block with a limo creeping behind us at five miles an hour.

When we reached the establishment I had in mind, Abacasas saw the name on the window and nodded in recognition. "Rick's," he said. "Like in *Casablanca*."

He strode to the car and told the driver to park and come inside to have coffee and something to eat. Then Abacasas opened the door to Rick's and stepped back for me to precede him. It was a quiet night; there were only two other couples and a man by himself. He was hunched over a small table reading a book.

Glancing about at the sawdust on the floor, the simple wood, and leather furnishings, and the brass-trimmed glass wall sconces, he sighed with mock disappointment. "I had hoped for lazy ceiling fans and palm trees, and a gentleman at a piano playing 'As Time Goes By.' "

In spite of my intention to remain cool, that amused me.

"You have a lovely mouth," he said. "I hope to see that smile of yours more often."

If he wanted to see my smile, he'd have to earn it. We took an empty booth along the back wall and sat opposite each other. I saw his driver come through the door and note where we were sitting. He chose a place for himself on the opposite side of the room at a small wooden table between the bar and the front door, but where he could keep us in sight.

After we ordered coffee, Abacasas asked, "Have you been to the real Casablanca?"

"No."

"You would dislike it. Infested with flies. Not at all romantic."

Whispering the word "romantic," he aimed his intense gaze at me and I felt as though he had pinned me with invisible arrows against the back of the booth. It was exhilarating. And *insane*. I tried to pretend I wasn't altogether discombobulated by this mystery man.

"If I wanted to go to a romantic city, what would you suggest?" I asked.

"Venice. But you must not be alone in Venice."

I glimpsed a momentary expression of pain in his eyes. I wanted to reach out and touch his hand, to ask him what had caused the look of hurt, but instead I clasped my hands together. I reminded myself that the only reason I was here with him was to learn what I could, for Cybelle's sake.

I tried to sound casual as I asked, "Do you have a favorite city?"

"Different ones, for different reasons. Madrid for the Prado, and its magnificent black Goyas."

I felt myself smile, and he cocked his head in silent inquiry. "Those particular Goyas fascinate me, too," I said. "Go on, please."

"Vienna is a favorite, for the music, and for the pastry. Gstaad for the skiing, London for the theater, and for the British Museum. Athens, all of Greece, in fact. It is the closest I've ever come to having a homeland." A warm light shimmered in his eyes. "Have you been to Greece?"

"No, but it's a place I've wanted to visit."

For a moment he looked almost boyish. "You must see the country with a Greek," he said. "Or with a demi-Greek, like me."

He had given me an opening to pry for information. "Were you born in Greece?"

"My father was Greek. My mother was Norwegian and French."

That was interesting, but it didn't answer my question. Before I could ask it again, he turned the tables.

"And what is your lineage?" he asked.

My lineage. I wasn't about to tell him that I didn't know what I was, or where I came from—that I only know where I was *found*.

"Mine isn't as exotic as yours." I tried to make my manner offhand. "Americans are little bits of many things."

He leaned closer, studying my face. "Light hair, blue eyes, fair skin . . . You could be Scandinavian, or Slavic, or German," he said. "Your name, Morgan, means 'morning' in German. Were you named after your father?"

"No, after an actress my mother saw on television." That was a lie. The truth was I had picked the name myself when I was six years old, out of a little book called *What to*

Name the Baby. I chose it because it sounded strong. Even as a child I understood that I needed to be strong.

Steering the conversation away from the uncomfortable subject of myself, I asked, "Are you in a business, or do you just make investments, as you did in Global?"

"I have many interests in many enterprises," he said.

"What attracted you to Global? Growth potential?"

His eyes lost their warmth. He leaned across the table until his face was just inches from mine. There was an edge in his voice as he said, "I took a significant position in Global Entertainment because the company has something that I want."

The sudden coldness in his voice made me draw back from him slightly. "I don't understand."

"Oh, yes—you do. Or rather, you *think* you do. But what you think you know is wrong." His tone was serious, but his voice was gentle again. "I have come to New York to recover something that was stolen from me. If you will help me do that, I can be a powerful friend."

That fired my indignation. "Are you also saying that if I'm *not* helpful you can be a powerful enemy? Your assumption that you can buy my friendship is insulting."

"Forgive me, please. I meant no offense."

"Then tell me what this is about. Just straight, without thinking you have to dangle some reward in front of me. You don't have anything I want."

It was his turn to be amused. "We shall see about that," he said. Once more he became serious. "For now, I will tell you straight, as you put it. It was not an accident of timing that I was at Winston Yarborough's dinner party tonight. Nor was it a coincidence that you were invited. I asked to meet you."

"Why?"

"Yarborough wanted to know that, too. I told him it was because my wife was a fan of the show you write. When he heard the word 'wife' he relaxed and agreed to honor my request." Abacasas chuckled. "I failed to mention that I do not intend to remain married much longer."

"You haven't told me why you wanted to meet me."

"Because you employ a certain actress. You know her as Cybelle Carter. I know her by a different name. We were . . . together . . . briefly a few years ago. She stole something from me and disappeared. I found her, although it took me longer than I thought it would because I made the mistake of underestimating her intelligence. I have had her watched secretly for the past several months, and during that time I made it my quest to learn about the people with whom she works."

"Learn? You mean you had us *investigated?*"

"Certainly, but you have nothing to be concerned about. At least, you need not be concerned about *me,*" I caught his emphasis on the last word.

"What do you mean?"

"The woman you know as Cybelle Carter. Be careful how much trust you invest in her. She is not what she seems to be."

"You said she stole something from you. What was it?"

"Aside from my trust? Several million dollars, which she concealed in the palm of one of her delicate little hands." At my puzzled expression, he added: "Two ancient Greek coins, silver, struck around five hundred B.C. They are so rare that I can name my price for them from any number of great museums or private collectors. She removed them from my safety deposit box just before she disappeared—but then those coins helped me to find her."

"How?"

"She tried to sell them to a dealer in New York, but she didn't know that coins of such rarity and value, unless they are very recent discoveries, are known to dealers and curators all over the world—and they know the provenance of the coins. When the dealer she approached asked to see her proof of ownership, she didn't have it, of course. She snatched back the coins and left, and the dealer reported his experience to the Swiss banker from whom I purchased the coins. The banker got the word to me. Knowing she was now in New York, I hired detectives to find her."

Cybelle Carter and Philippe Abacasas were telling two very different stories. Who should I believe? And what would it cost me if I guessed wrong?

My coffee sat untouched as I leaned back against the cool leather of the booth. "You said you could name your price for the coins. Why hadn't you sold them?"

"Because they have a value to me far beyond the money they would bring."

"I don't understand."

"Perhaps I will explain, one day," he said. "When I know you better."

He aimed those eyes at me again. I felt weak in the knees, even though I was sitting.

He glanced at my unfinished coffee. "Have you had enough?"

"Yes." *For now.*

He signaled for the check. When the waiter brought it, Abacasas handed him a fifty-dollar bill and told him it was "also for whatever the gentleman in the corner had." He added that the waiter was to keep the change.

The chauffeur, seeing we were ready to leave, saluted Abacasas and left Rick's to get the car.

Outside, the late November night was considerably

colder than it had been earlier. I pulled my cape tight around my shoulders. Abacasas, who didn't wear a coat, seemed unaffected by the near-freezing temperature, but he noticed that I was cold.

"Would you like my jacket?" he asked, and started to take it off.

I shook my head emphatically. "No, thank you. I'm fine."

The chauffeur came toward us, a grim expression on his face.

"Sir, there's a problem with the car."

"What is it?"

"The tires have been slashed."

,Chapter 23

I FOLLOWED ABACASAS around the back of the limo to examine the tires. On the driver's side, front and rear, something had sliced into the rubber multiple times, leaving the car to rest on the steel rims of the wheels.

Abacasas turned to the chauffeur. "Handle it."

"Shouldn't we report this to the police?" I asked.

"To what purpose? They'll never find who did it. I doubt that they would try."

I had to admit he was probably right.

"Come," he said, "I'll take you home in a taxi." Without being told, the chauffeur hopped to, hurried into the street and raised his arm to signal.

"That's not necessary," I said, as an empty cab pulled up in front of us. The chauffeur opened the rear door.

Abacasas helped me in, and then climbed in after me.

"One West Seventy-second Street for the lady," he told the driver. "Then take me to the Carlyle."

So he knew my address.

And he had let me know he was staying at the Carlyle.

Abacasas was quiet, seemingly deep in thought, until the cab was halfway through the park. He looked out the window, turned to me and asked, "Do people skate on the lake in Central Park?"

"I don't know."

"Do you skate on ice?"

"Only when it's *thin*," I said.

He got the joke and laughed. An easy, hearty laugh.

"No, I never learned," I added, in answer to his question.

"There is a magnificent freedom of the soul when one skates outdoors in winter, across a frozen pond. Perhaps you will allow me to teach you."

The reckless part of me almost said yes, but the sane part of me got control of my mouth first. "My life is a little complicated right now."

"As is mine," he said. There was a wistful note in his voice.

The cab pulled up in front of the Dakota. I saw Abacasas take a quick, covert glance through the rear window, then get out first. He extended his hand to help me. As I stepped onto the sidewalk, I noticed a dark sedan had pulled up behind the cab. I could see the outline of a broad-shouldered man at the wheel. He was making no move to get out. I gripped Abacasas around the wrist, nodded toward the darkened car and whispered, "I think he's watching us."

"That man is with me," he answered, steering me toward the entrance to the courtyard.

"*With* you? A bodyguard?"

"An unfortunate necessity of the times. Do not concern yourself." We stopped just inside the archway. "Business compels me to leave the country soon, but I would like to see you again."

I glanced back at the bodyguard. "Whatever happens," I said, "we'll always have Rick's."

He recognized my parody of the famous "We'll always have Paris" line from *Casabalanca* and laughed.

I thought again that Philippe Abacasas had a very nice laugh.

A FEW MINUTES later, as I unlocked my front door, I heard the phone ringing. It was Nancy, eager to tell me about her plans to join Arnold on an out-of-town trip. "A couple can't really know if they're compatible until they travel together," she said.

"That's probably a good test," I agreed.

Nancy took a deep, satisfied breath. "Now, what were you doing tonight?"

"I spent the evening with Philippe Abacasas," I said casually. "He wants to teach me how to ice skate."

On the other end of the line, I heard Nancy gasp.

Nineteen minutes later, she rang my doorbell, wearing a coat over silk pajamas and carrying a small bag.

"I'm not going to let you stay here alone tonight," she said.

After she brushed her teeth, Nancy climbed into the never-used side of my king-size bed. She adjusted the pillows against the headboard, leaned back and said, "Now, tell me *everything*."

I did, including the awkward admission that I found myself attracted to this mystery man. "So his name may or may not be Philippe Abacasas, he may or may not want to murder Cybelle, who may or may not have stolen a treasure from him," I concluded. "And Cybelle tells a completely different story."

"Her bit about his bringing a riding crop to bed," Nancy said after a moment. "Did he give off any vibrations of *weird?*"

"Not at all!"

I answered so vehemently Nancy laughed. "So maybe Cybelle is lying." Nancy's fingers traced the English ivy design on my comforter as she thought. When she looked up at me she said, "You could find out."

"Go to bed with him?" I asked flippantly.

"That's *your* idea, not mine," Nancy said. "*I* was going to suggest you spend some time with him, get him to relax, then ask him questions. Of course, your way would be quicker. And might be a whole lot more fun than a Q and A session."

"Forget for a minute how I find out who's telling the truth. I've got other problems."

Nancy guessed what they were. "If you should tell Cybelle that Philippe is here in New York. And if you should tell Matt."

"I'd vote for staying out of this drama entirely, except for the fact that Jeannie Ford was murdered. I can't forget that. I hired her to be Cybelle's double."

Nancy sat up straighter. "But you didn't invite her to stay in Cybelle's apartment, or to rummage around in Cybelle's refrigerator."

I appreciated Nancy's passionate defense. "You sound like my lawyer."

"I am," she said, "plus your closest friend. Now, let's go

over your possible courses of action. One: If you tell Cybelle, what's likely to happen?"

"She could panic and disappear, leaving me without an actress vital to the show. Or, if she tells Johnny Isaac, which I'm sure she would, he might make a preemptive strike and kill Philippe."

"That would be terrible, even if Philippe *is* the monster Cybelle claims he is," Nancy said. "Number two: If you tell Matt, what will he do?"

"He and G. G. would probably hound Philippe, causing him to disappear before we find out who's telling the truth. And that could put us farther away from learning who killed Jeannie."

Nancy nodded sympathetically. "What's behind door number three?"

"I keep Philippe's whereabouts to myself until I have a better idea about whether he's dangerous to Cybelle, or if he's really here to recover his ancient coins and divorce her."

"Good. Your hormones aren't preventing you from thinking this out. But there's one thing about the charismatic Mr. A that bothers me," Nancy said.

"What?"

"He's had Cybelle watched for months. Why hasn't he confronted her yet?"

"I'll ask him," I said. I glanced at the inch-high glowing red numbers on my bedside clock radio: one in the morning. "I agreed to see him this afternoon."

Chapter 24

SATURDAY MORNING NANCY and I were having coffee in the kitchen when the phone rang.

"I've got *fantastic* news!" Tommy Zenos said. He was so excited he'd turned "news" into a three-syllable word.

"What is it?"

"Can't *tell* you—got to show you. Can I come up?"

"Up?" I glanced at Nancy, who was pouring herself another cup of coffee. "Up from where?"

"Downstairs. I'm at your reception desk. Are you dressed?"

"More or less."

"That knock you'll hear on your door in twenty seconds—that'll be me." He was almost singing as he disconnected.

"Tommy's on his way up," I told Nancy. "I should have

called him back when I got home, but after I talked to you, I forgot."

Nancy got up to take a cup and saucer from the cabinet. As she set a place for Tommy at the table, she narrowed her eyes and regarded the china pattern. "You've lived with other people's china and things . . ." she gestured vaguely toward the rest of the apartment ". . . since you bought this place furnished. When are you going to pick out dishes and furniture that reflect your *own* taste?"

"Penny said the same thing to me a few weeks ago," I said.

"I want you to have the fun of finding things that have special meaning to *you*. You've never had a home that was really yours."

That was true. "Tell you what—when it's calmer, I'll give everything that came with this place to charity. I'll pick out my own china and silver and start decorating. You and Penny can help."

Nancy was gracious in victory. "That's terrific," she said. "When?" Before I could respond, she extracted a date book from her handbag on the counter and flipped through the pages. "Let's start right after Christmas."

We were interrupted by the sound of an assault on the front door.

"Pounding on wood with his fist is Tommy's idea of knocking," I said.

I hurried down the hall to let him in. The first thing I noticed was the widest grin I'd ever seen. The second was the manila envelope he was waving above his head.

"What's that?" I asked.

He sniffed the air like a hound dog. "Do I smell coffee?"

"In the kitchen. Nancy's here."

He followed me down the hall, tight on my heels.

"Hi, Nancy," he said. He gave her barely a glance and went directly to the refrigerator. "What have you got to eat?" His happy expression vanished when he opened the door. "Pickle relish and Half and Half?" He looked at me accusingly. "What kind of a way is that to live?"

"I haven't had time to go to the market."

Disappointed, he sat down at the table. Nancy handed him a cup of coffee. "Lots of cream, lots of sugar. Right?"

"Right. Thanks, Nancy."

I sat down across from him. "What's in the envelope?"

"The answer to our prayers."

"Be more specific."

He opened it and removed a dozen eight by ten photographs, which he put face down on the table.

"I loved your February sweeps idea—the big adventure with lots of action on a Mississippi riverboat."

Now I was excited, too. "They approved the budget?"

"Well, not exactly . . ."

Nancy raised an eyebrow. "What does 'not exactly' mean?"

I translated for her. "In TV-speak it means 'no.' "

"Yes, it means no," Tommy said, "but I found another way to make your story happen." He turned over the photos and spread them out across the table. They were color pictures of a handsome old paddleboat, taken from a variety of angles.

"That's beautiful," Nancy said. I agreed.

"Going down the real Mississippi on a working riverboat was a total budget-buster. Sooo . . ." He paused for dramatic effect. "I worked out a deal to shoot the scenes on *this* boat. It was built for filming; all the walls are movable. It's on the back lot of the Olympic Pictures' studio. We're going to Hollywood!"

"When?"

"We can have Olympic's facilities, the riverboat set, and whatever technicians we'll need—*if* we can leave for the coast in two weeks."

"Two *weeks*? I've got the story roughed out, but the scripts aren't written yet."

Panic filled Tommy's eyes, and color literally drained from his face. "But I can't go back to them *now*. They agreed to the budget for this shoot. You can be ready, can't you? Oh, please."

"Yes, I can. It'll just mean some very late nights."

He expelled a huge sigh of relief and color returned to his cheeks.

"I'll need a diagram of the boat, room measurements, and a list of furnishings and props on board," I said. "And whether there's a gangplank onto the deck, and if not, can we get one."

He nodded vigorously. "I'll get the production people at Olympic Pictures to overnight what you need. Anything you want, just ask me."

"Then I guess we're going to Hollywood."

Jubilant, Tommy high-fived me. For good measure he high-fived Nancy, too, before tearing out of the apartment.

Watching me, Nancy had guessed that something was wrong.

"You don't want to go to Los Angeles? You might meet Brad Pitt," she teased. "Or, better yet, Dr. Phil."

"I'm excited about the shoot. But Los Angeles is the home base of Lori Cole."

"Ah, the new vice president. If she makes trouble, take her out to your riverboat and push her overboard. Should you get caught, I know a *wonderful* criminal lawyer."

I laughed, appreciating Nancy's fierce loyalty. Then I remembered something I had meant to ask her.

"Are you using your car tomorrow afternoon?"

"No. You can have it. Arnold went up to Boston to see his daughter, so I'm going to stay in all day and go over contracts."

Nancy reached for her purse on the counter. She fished around inside, found her car keys and handed them to me. "I'll tell the guys at the garage you'll be picking it up."

"Thanks," I said. "I made an appointment at the shooting range in Spring Valley."

"A little Annie Oakley action. Good—keep your skills sharp." She looked at me, a trace of sadness in her eyes. "Did you ever imagine that life in New York City would be more dangerous than it was when you lived in Africa?"

It was a question that didn't require an answer. Instead, I steered the conversation back a few beats.

"Arnold has a *daughter*?"

Nancy nodded. "Didi—she's twelve. Arnold's ex-wife moved to Boston with her four years ago. I think it's terrible what she did, taking the child away. Arnold's a wonderful father. He goes up there every weekend unless he's in the middle of a trial."

"What's she like—the little girl?"

"I haven't met her yet, but I'm looking forward to it."

An ex-wife and a twelve-year-old daughter. Yikes.

I didn't say anything.

Chapter 25

AFTER NANCY LEFT, I spent several hours outlining scripts that would include the riverboat adventure scenes we'd shoot in Los Angeles. While other story lines involving the citizens of our fictional city of Greendale would continue on their separate and previously laid out dramatic tracks, this new February sweeps material had to be inserted into those planned episodes. I would assign writers to turn the breakdowns for the laid out story lines into scripts, but I would have to write the love scenes and the action sequences for the riverboat myself. It would be faster than to explain my vision to someone else.

I'd made a good start when I realized that it was nearly three o'clock. Time to get ready to meet Philippe Abacasas.

I wanted to look good, but I didn't want to look as though I was trying to. Mascara, lipstick, and a few swipes of the hairbrush. Black jeans, tan sweater and a dark brown sleeveless faux mink vest that covered me from shoulders to derriere. I chose a pair of gloves, but then put them back in the drawer. If my hands got too cold, I'd shove them into the deep, lined pockets of the vest. I slipped a small comb and an emergency twenty-dollar bill into a pocket, grabbed my keys and was ready to go.

Abacasas had said he would be waiting for me just inside the West Seventy-second Street entrance to the park. As I darted across Central Park West, I saw him there. Today he was wearing dark brown slacks, a brown jacket, and another turtleneck sweater. This one was a soft butter-yellow cashmere. No coat, even though it was almost December and the temperature had dropped to forty degrees.

Seeing me, he raised a hand to wave, and I noticed that he wasn't wearing gloves either. I had sworn I would not react to him as I had last night. Absolutely, positively, definitely not. I refused to allow myself to feel irrational attraction. He had surprised me at the Yarboroughs' party, but this time I was ready.

Then he took my right hand in greeting, enclosing it in both of his, and what seemed like a hundred little jolts of electricity shot through my system.

Abacasas held onto my hand as he surveyed my outfit. Frowning at my minkless mink vest, he asked, "Are you warm enough?"

"I'm fine," I said.

I noticed a man by himself, standing a dozen steps away from us. All in gray, including a cap, his clothes were so bland he almost vanished into the background. I had seen elephants do that in the African bush—hide behind a few bare twigs. The unwary could suddenly find themselves only a few feet away from a jumbo who might not be in a live-and-let-live mood.

Mr. All-in-Gray had the wide, thick shoulders and narrow waist of a competitive weight lifter. I couldn't see his hands because they were jammed into his pockets. He seemed fascinated by the stones in the wall that separated the park from the street, but I caught him darting a glance toward us. It made me uneasy.

I inclined my head closer to Abacasas and whispered, "Another bodyguard?"

"An assistant." Taking my arm, he gently steered me toward the interior of the park. "It has been many years since I was here. Will you show me your favorite places?"

"Will you answer my questions?"

"Every one that I can," he said.

"Every one that you can." My tone was mocking. "In America we call that line the advance cop-out."

"That is an Americanism with which I am familiar."

"I'm not surprised," I said wryly.

Our threesome—with the "assistant" keeping about twenty paces behind us—strolled through the strawberry fields to the large circular mosaic set into the ground. In the center of the design was the word "IMAGINE." A fresh white calla lily lay on the gray and white tiles, its tubular blossom almost touching the *N*.

" 'Imagine.' That is a word with consequences," he said in a muted tone.

"It's a memorial to John Lennon. He was murdered outside the Dakota."

"And you were nearly murdered *inside* that building." Seeing my surprise, he added, "I read the New York papers. You were very brave to capture your associate's killer."

"Not brave—desperate." We resumed our stroll.

"I hope you will not continue to take such chances," he said.

I'm taking a pretty big one right now.

Within a few minutes we had reached the Shakespeare Garden, which is planted on the vertical slope of Vista Rock. A rustic wooden fence encircles the garden, while the path coils up the hillside to Vista Rock's peak where Belvedere Castle looked particularly beautiful at the moment, set against the darkening November sky.

Whether it was because this was a cold day with a hint in the air of snow to come, or because there were football games on television, few other people were exploring the garden. We had this little wonderland virtually to ourselves.

I led Abacasas to a viewing deck under the shelter of an ancient mulberry tree. He was studying me. To pretend that he wasn't making me nervous, I pointed to a tree near the bottom of the garden.

"That white mulberry is supposed to be a graft of a tree planted by Shakespeare himself at Stratford-on-Avon," I said.

Abacasas nodded politely, but he didn't seem interested in the history of mulberry trees.

I continued doing my impression of a tour guide. "Only the flowers that are mentioned in Shakespeare's plays are planted here," I said.

Abacasas indicated a particular plant a few feet away. He closed his eyes for a moment, then quoted, "There's rosemary, that is for remembrance. Pray, love, remember . . . '"

"You'd be miscast as Ophelia," I said. Okay, I admit I was showing off, letting him know I recognized the line.

"I dislike Hamlet," he said. "Nasty, petulant boy. Ophelia deserved a better man."

Enough of this Freshman Lit chat. I had questions to ask.

"You have just the slightest trace of an accent," I said casually, "but I haven't been able to figure out what it is."

"So, you have been thinking about me?"

He was flirting! I couldn't let it distract me.

"In daytime dramas," I said, "it's a tradition—and the audience *knows* this—that people with accents are up to no good. The only exception is Australian, and you're not an Australian."

He threw back his head and laughed. The gesture exposed a little bit of his throat, and I saw something that made me catch my breath. On the left side of his neck, the skin was puckered into an ugly scar. It was an old scar, faded to white against the darker skin of his face and hands. Mute testimony that in the past he had suffered a terrible burn.

With a gesture that seemed casual, Abacasas adjusted the neck of his sweater and the scar disappeared.

"You suspect that I am 'up to no good'?" he asked.

"I don't know what you're up to. I want to find out."

With a skeptical expression on his face, he locked his gaze on me. I felt the silent question in those mesmerizing eyes: *Is that the only reason you're here?*

I decided if I wanted honesty, I should offer some of my own.

"That's not the only reason I'm here with you," I said. "You're . . . an interesting person. But a woman who was staying in Cybelle's apartment was murdered. The police, and I, think Cybelle was the real target. She thinks that if you find her, you're going to kill her."

"I located her months ago, and she is still alive."

"But Jeannie Ford is dead. Do you know anything at all about that?"

"No." He paused, his eyes narrowing. "The woman you call Cybelle—have you questioned her brother?"

Cybelle never told me that she had a brother.

Abacasas correctly read the expression on my face as surprise. "You did not know about him."

"No. You keep referring to her as 'the woman I call Cybelle.' What was her name when you met her?"

"Sara Gilley. Her brother's name is Floyd. When I met her in Houston they were sharing a miserable little apartment in a bad area. She was paying their bills because she said the brother had been injured in an accident and could not work. Also, he appeared to be . . . not quite right in the head." His tone became as cold and sharp as the blade of a knife. "I was sympathetic to their plight. I gave them money. When Sara and I went to Europe, I established a bank account for her so she would not need to ask me when she wanted something. She sent him money regularly. I was touched." He laughed, but this time it was a short bark without a trace of humor. "In the English language, I have learned that 'to be touched' means both to be *moved*, and to be a bit insane."

The story sounded convincing, but Cybelle's wildly different story had been convincing, too. "Speaking of real names," I said, "is Philippe Abacasas your real name?"

"One of them. Is Morgan Tyler *your* real name?"

"One of them," I admitted.

"Then we have both told the truth, but still we have our secrets," he said.

I had to agree with that.

"You should continue to create mysteries for your pro-

gram," he said. "Trying to solve them in real life is dangerous."

Before I could respond, Abacasas tilted his head to stare
at Belvedere Castle above us. "I have a castle," he said.

"A castle in Spain?" I kept my tone light. "A castle in
the air?"

"In Belgium. It is an undistinguished castle, although
quite beautiful from certain angles. Small, only fourteen
bathrooms." He was self-mocking and rueful as he said,
"Not one of my wiser decisions."

"Bad plumbing?"

"No heat. But it is refreshingly cool in the summer
months."

I astonished myself by blurting out a question I'd had
no intention of asking. "Why did you marry her—Sara?"

Mentally, I kicked myself for asking something that had
no possible relevance to finding out who killed Jeannie,
and that was also none of my business.

Abacasas was silent for a long moment. "When I met
Sara," he said at last, "I was at a very low point in my life.
Something had happened to me . . . that is to say, I had lost
faith in things in which I had believed. Things I had
thought were important. There was no joy in life for me
then." He paused, shook his head, then went on. "Sara was
a wounded little bird, or at least that is how I perceived her.
I thought I could help her. The fact that she is so pretty was
no small part of my attraction, I admit, but I have known
many pretty women. Sara's greater allure was that she
seemed helpless. Rescuing her became my project. It re-
vived my enthusiasm for life. Then came the day when I
realized that the creature I had sheltered was not a soft little dove, but a raptor."

A faint ringing sound interrupted us. I looked in the direction that Abacasas was staring, and saw the assistant take a cell phone out of his pocket. He hunched over slightly and listened for a moment, then mumbled something, pressed a button and nodded to his boss.

Abacasas expelled a sigh of resignation. "That call means I must leave. There is only time enough to escort you home."

As we made our way back through the Shakespeare Garden, I asked, "When are you going to tell Cybelle— Sara—that you're here?"

"Not today. I must leave the country in less than two hours. When I have retrieved the coins she stole from me, I will divorce her." He looked at me, and I saw concern in his eyes. "Be wary of her, and of that brother. I hope you will not believe what they may tell you about me."

"I make up my own mind about people," I said.

It was dark by the time we reached Central Park West. As we waited for the traffic light on Seventy-second to turn green so we could cross, Abacasas said, "There is a man walking up and down in front of your entrance. Is he perhaps one of your suitors?"

"My suitors?" I followed his gaze and was surprised to see the wiry, wild-haired figure of Link Ramsey pacing back and forth in a more agitated state than I had ever seen him. "Good lord, no," I said. "That's one of the actors on our show."

Link spotted me and waved. He loped toward the corner on the opposite side of Central Park West from where we were standing. I gave a responding wave, then turned back to speak to Abacasas—but Abacasas was gone.

Chapter 26

THERE WASN'T TIME to think about the vanishing act Abacasas had pulled because I saw Link step off the curb against the light—right into the path of a speeding taxi. I screamed a warning and with no more than a second to spare, Link jumped out of the way.

The instant the light turned green, I sprinted across to his side of the street. I was shaking. "For God's sake, Link—didn't your mother teach you not to play in traffic?"

"She taught me to stick on seventeen, and not to draw to an inside straight."

I sucked in air to calm myself. "I think I'd like your mother."

"She'd like you, too," he said, "because you're one tough little cookie."

In the light from the street lamp, I saw that Link's face

was unnaturally pale beneath his dark hair, and that the skin over his prominent Slavic cheekbones was stretched tight with tension. Something was bothering him, so much that it had brought him to my building, and sent him rushing recklessly into the path of a zooming car.

"What's the matter?" I asked.

"Can we go somewhere for coffee? I need to talk to you."

I made a beckoning motion with my hand. "Come upstairs. I've got the best brew in the neighborhood."

WE WERE SETTLED in the club chairs in my den, feet propped up on the big, shared ottoman, steaming mugs in our hands. Link was so tense I could see a tiny muscle throbbing beneath his left eye.

"A pair of cops came sniffing around my place, asking questions," he said.

"What did you tell them?"

"Nothing. I went out of town for Thanksgiving. My landlord clued me in." There was a note of urgency in his voice. "I have to know why they're looking for me."

"Don't worry about it," I said. "It's just routine. They're asking questions of everyone who worked with Jeannie."

"The questions won't be so routine with me. Jeannie and I dated for a few months."

"I didn't know," I said. I touched his hand in sympathy. "If you two were close, her death must have been hard on you."

"Yeah, she was a good kid. But when a woman gets popped, the cops always look to the husband or the boyfriend." He gripped the coffee mug so hard I thought it might shatter. "If I find out who killed her before the cops do I might save the taxpayers the cost of a trial."

A few months earlier I wrote a scene for Link that he liked immensely. He had expressed his gratitude by asking if there was anybody I wanted to have killed. I'd thought he was joking. Now more than ever I wanted to believe that he was joking.

Link's stress level was in the red zone. To relieve it, I decided to tell him a little of what I knew.

"This isn't the usual murder situation," I said. "Jeannie wasn't supposed to be the victim. Cybelle was."

"Jeezus, that's bad news."

"I know," I said. "But Cybelle's being protected."

He shook his head impatiently. "No, I mean that *still* doesn't let me off the hook. Puddin' Pop an' I are the hottest romance in daytime. That puts me involved with *both* girls." He looked at me speculatively. I realized that he was coming to the point of this visit.

"The word around the studio is you're pretty tight with the cops," he said. "With one cop, anyway—a good-looking cat, not the heavy guy they say makes 'Hello' sound like an accusation. Can you keep them off my back? We've all got stuff we wouldn't want dug up. Am I right?"

Link was more right than he knew, but I wasn't going to admit it. Instead, I asked, "Do you have any idea who could have killed Jeannie?"

He shook his head. "Tommy told me the creep she was living with is in the clear."

"Hal Meeks. He was in jail before Jeannie went to Cybelle's until after her body was discovered," I said. "Do you have any idea who might want to kill Cybelle?"

He thought for a moment, then lifted his shoulders in a shrug. "She's a pussycat," he said. "Nice to everybody. Lends money, doesn't do the diva thing. Even the other actresses on the show like her." He chuckled. "You gotta know how rare *that* is."

I did, but didn't comment.

"Have you ever been to Cybelle's apartment?" I asked.

"Sure, half a dozen times, to work on our scenes. But we were never alone. That pit bull agent was always there, watchin' where I put my hands."

"Do you know anything about Cybelle's family?"

"She doesn't have any. Her parents died in some kind of accident when she was a baby." There was a sympathetic expression in his eyes, as though he, too, had suffered painful losses. "She told me she grew up with an elderly aunt who passed away just before she came on the show."

"No brothers or sisters?"

He shook his head again. "She's an only child." He gazed across the street at the lights glimmering like diamonds against the black velvet swatch of Central Park below us. "She told me she uses her sadness about not having any family in scenes where she has to make herself cry," he said.

Another contradiction. The more I learned, the further away I seemed to get from the truth.

My thoughts were interrupted by the phone. I put the coffee mug down on the small table between our chairs and answered on the second ring.

"Where've you been? I've been trying to reach you all afternoon," Matt said. "What happened to your cell phone?"

"I forgot to take it with me."

"Never mind. I've got news about Philippe Abacasas."

I fought to keep my voice steady. "What's happened?"

Link, sensitive to vocal nuances, picked up on my fear and was watching me.

"I reached out to a contact in Customs," Matt said. "Abacasas arrived in New York yesterday afternoon."

"Oh, that," I said. A wave of profound relief swept over me.

"What do you mean—'Oh, that'?"

"I was going to call you," I said quickly. "I met him at the business dinner I went to last night, at the Carlyle. Winston Yarborough's party."

"Last night . . ." His tone hardened. "You were at a *party* with him last night?"

"Not *with* him," I said. "We were both guests. Yarborough introduced him as a major stockholder in Global. It gave me a chance to question him."

"Where in hell do you get off questioning—"

"Don't yell at me."

He ratcheted down to sarcasm. "Funny," he said, "I hadn't heard that the phones went out all over the city. That must have been what happened, because I can't think of any other reason why you wouldn't have told me."

"I didn't call because I didn't know what to say."

"'Abacasas is in New York.' Five words. It's a simple sentence for a writer."

"Don't talk to me in that condescending tone."

Silence. I imagined him counting to ten to get control of his temper.

"Abacasas listed his New York address as the Carlyle," Matt said. "When I couldn't reach you, G. G. and I went over there to talk to him, but he'd checked out. Or do you know that, too?"

"He's gone."

"Gone where?"

"Out of the country. I don't know when, or even if he'll come back."

"Did you tell Cybelle that he was here?" he asked.

"No. Did you?"

"No. I thought Isaac might go off his nut and do something crazy."

"That was my fear, too," I said.

Silence. For the sake of our relationship, whatever it was, I thought I had better offer Matt something. "I asked him if he knew Jeannie Ford, and—"

Matt exploded. "You talked to a suspect about my murder investigation! What the hell were you thinking? You've probably ruined—"

"I didn't ruin anything," I snapped. "You never said he was a suspect! He wasn't even in this *country* when Jeannie was killed!"

"I *earned* my gold shield. I didn't get it by writing a soap opera!"

"Well, *Detective* Phoenix," I said. "*We* don't call it soap opera—it's *daytime drama*!" I slammed my fist against the disconnect button.

Chapter 27

I EMPTIED ROUND after round at the silhouettes hanging at the end of my practice alley. Arms extended in the classic two-handed grip—right hand around the stock, index finger pulling the trigger while my left hand supported the right hand from underneath—I didn't put down my Glock 19 until my shoulders and forearms ached from the strain and my .40 caliber ammunition was exhausted.

When I removed the ear defenders that protected me from noise assault, I was surprised to hear a familiar voice behind me.

"That's some good shooting, gorgeous."

I whirled around to see a tall, athletic figure with curly hair the color of paprika.

"Chet!"

He was removing a pair of ear defenders. He'd been watching me drill cardboard hearts and heads.

He opened his arms and I rushed over to give him a hug.

"Are you that glad to see me," he asked after a moment, "or just out of ammo?"

"Glad," I said.

"Where'd you learn to shoot like that?"

"Africa."

He cocked his head at me. "You hunted with Glocks?"

"We *never* hunted, except for food, and then we used rifles." I wanted to get away from a conversation that might lead to questions about Ian. "What are you doing here?"

He grimaced at the bursts of gunfire in the practice alleys on either side of us. "Let's get out before we damage our eardrums."

I slipped the Glock into its carrying case and we hustled toward the soundproof exit door leading to the reception area.

Targets is set up in an old warehouse. Practice alleys take up the rear three quarters of the building. The soundproofed front section is divided into a trio of offices separated by plasterboard walls that don't go all the way to the ceiling, and a reception counter where appointments are booked and people sign in and out. Chet glanced around the reception area and smiled at the décor— posters depicting Mel Gibson and Danny Glover playing cops in the *Lethal Weapon* movies, Clint Eastwood as *Dirty Harry*, Harrison Ford as a cop in *Witness*, and Al Pacino as a cop in *Sea of Love.* The posters were supplemented by dozens of eight-by-ten glossy photographs of actors—many of them old and badly faded—who played popular cops on television, going all the way back to Jack Webb in *Dragnet*. Next to the publicity stills were framed, poster-sized blowups of newspaper articles and photos showing the triumphs and tragedies of real police officers.

At the reception desk, we turned in our ear defenders and I signed out.

"Can I buy you lunch, or dinner, or breakfast? I'm still on Dutch time, so my stomach doesn't know what it wants."

"About half a mile from here there's a restaurant that looks pretty good," I said.

"Let's go."

Outside, I scanned the parking lot for Chet's Range Rover, but I didn't see it.

"Where's the Jolly Green Giant?"

"In the garage in Greenwich," he said. "I hired a car and driver at Kennedy to bring me up here, but I let him go. Can you give me a lift back to the city after we eat?"

"Of course."

Chet followed me toward Nancy's sky blue Mercedes. I took her keys out of my jacket pocket and unlocked the doors, then went around to the trunk. I removed a metal box and secured the Glock inside, then took a full box of cartridges out of the trunk and locked it.

Chet climbed in the passenger side as I put the box of cartridges into the glove compartment and locked it.

"What are you doing?" he asked.

"I only have a Premise permit for the Glock. When I'm transporting it, the pistol has to be unloaded and in a metal box, and the cartridges have to be in a separate place. In case I'm stopped, I don't want the police to have a reason to yank my license—they're too hard to get nowadays."

"Oh, right, since the License Division scandal." He felt around under the seat until he found the lever that adjusted its position and moved it back to accommodate his long legs. "I was following a team of FBI agents through a swamp in Louisiana when that story hit the headlines."

"It's wonderful to see you," I said, "but why are you back so early? What happened?"

"You sounded strange when we talked. Yesterday, when I couldn't get you at home or on your cell, I called Penny. She told me a girl who worked for you had been murdered. I had to see for myself that you were all right, so I caught the first plane I could get out of Amsterdam. And here I am."

I was stunned. "You haven't even been home yet?"

He shook his head.

"That's *crazy*! I can't believe you did that. But I'm very grateful. I need your expert opinion."

"At your service, ma'am."

It was late in the afternoon, and very cold. I switched on the heater and made a right turn to get back onto the highway. "How did you know I was up here?"

"Nancy told me. She even gave me the make, model, and plate number of the car. She didn't say so, but I could tell she's worried about you." He stretched his legs out and rotated his shoulders, trying to loosen muscles tightened by hours on a plane. "Your determination to solve murder mysteries makes me wonder if you're thinking of changing professions," he said wryly.

"The advantage in creating mysteries for the show is I can control the outcome. Real life is a lot messier."

"And full of unintended consequences." He reached out and touched my hand. "But one of those was that you and I met," he added. I gave his hand a gentle return squeeze, then put both hands back on the steering wheel. Because Chet had flown all the way from the Netherlands, I realized—with a clarity I hadn't had before—that his feelings for me were *serious*. Why couldn't Chet just want to go to bed with me? When he's not angry, that's what Matt wants. At least I think that's what he wants. . . .

The restaurant I'd spotted was just off SR-59, the Korean War Veterans Memorial Highway. The sign said The Cottage Inn. It looked clean and cozy: Cape Cod architecture, faded blue clapboard siding, and pitched roof with a weathervane figure of the fabled Headless Horseman who haunted nearby Sleepy Hollow.

Soft, golden light shone through the small front windows, and plumes of silver smoke rose in lazy curls from the red brick chimney. There were only a few vehicles in the parking lot; at four-thirty in the afternoon it was late for lunch and early for dinner.

A smiling host greeted us at the door, and showed us to one of the red leather booths that flanked the wood-burning fireplace.

After giving us menus, he returned to his post. Almost immediately a cheerful teenage waitress in a starched white pinafore over a pale blue gingham dress came over, carrying a tray with a basket of assorted dinner rolls and two small wooden tubs of whipped butter.

"Would you like something to drink?"

"Just coffee for me," Chet said.

"Me too."

She filled our cups with hot caffeine that smelled freshly brewed.

"Tonight's specials are roast loin of pork with homemade applesauce, sirloin tips with mushrooms on rice, and chicken pot pie made with fresh vegetables," she said.

My salivary glands sprang into action. "Mmmmmmmm."

Chet looked at me, amused. "They're all tempting. How's the chicken pot pie?"

"Fab," the waitress said with enthusiasm. "The crust is made from scratch." She nodded toward the door to the kitchen. "The dough falls apart while he's rolling it out. That's what I'm going to have later."

"Sold," I said, handing her my unopened menu.

"Two chicken pot pies." Chet handed her his menu.

"Good choice." She scribbled on her order pad. "Do you want the soup of the day, or a salad?"

Simultaneously, we said, "Soup."

"Don't you want to know what it is?"

"Surprise us," Chet said.

"You two are easy." She was grinning as she bounced off.

Chet leaned part way across the table. "I liked that sound you made."

"What sound?"

"That 'mmmmmmm.' I'd like to hear you make it again, without three feet of wooden table between us."

"You're just hungry," I said, handing him the basket of rolls.

"Yes," he agreed. "And for food, too."

He selected one of the warm, fragrant dark pumpernickels and began to butter it.

While he ate the roll and sipped his coffee, I told Chet what I knew about Jeannie, her death, about Link's fear of being investigated, and Cybelle confiding in me about having married Philippe Abacasas, and then running away from him, and now fearing he was going to kill her.

"Is your detective friend investigating Abacasas?"

"Matt hasn't been able to learn anything about him yet, but—"

I broke off as the waitress came back, bringing two crocks of onion soup with a thin crust of cheese.

Chet inhaled the soup's aroma. "If a woman wore a perfume that smelled like this, she'd have a block-long line of men following her."

The waitress giggled and hurried away. We tasted the soup, and it was delicious.

Chet picked up the conversation, repeating my last word. "But . . . ?"

"Friday night at Winston Yarborough's dinner party, I met Abacasas."

"In journalism, dropping a bombshell like that into the middle of the story is called *burying your lead*. What's he like?"

"The first thing I noticed was he didn't have devil horns and a tail," I joked.

Chet didn't laugh, so I repeated what Abacasas told me. Then I said, "Everything he said totally conflicts with Cybelle's version."

"What's her story?"

I told Chet exactly what Cybelle had told me, including her claim that Abacasas kept a riding crop under his bed. "You're a psychologist, what do you think?" I asked.

"If you're asking my opinion about the riding crop," he said with a teasing smile, "it depends on what he planned to do with it."

"I don't care about his sex life," I said quickly. Before Chet could see the lie in my eyes or the heat on my cheeks, I asked, "Be serious—do you think Abacasas could be a killer?"

"Any human being with the physical ability is *capable* of killing," he said. "*Why* someone kills is a matter of character."

Chapter 28

OUR DISCUSSION OF murder was interrupted by the arrival of the main course. The waitress put two individual baking dishes in front of us and warned, "Careful, they're hot." The pie's golden top crust had been woven into a lattice design, which allowed steam to escape. "Enjoy," she said, and left us alone again.

One thrust of our forks into the flaky crust told us what a good choice we'd made. We ate in silence for a few moments, appreciating the delicacy of the flavors.

"This is the best pot pie I've ever had," Chet said. "I wonder if Penny can make this."

"Probably. I'm glad you didn't ask if I can."

"Can't you cook at all?"

I shook my head. "The only thing I can do is bake bread. But it has to be on hot stones, buried in the ground.

The bread doesn't rise, but it tastes good, if you're hungry enough."

Chet chuckled. "Lucky for you you're gorgeous."

We were halfway through our meal when he said, "You've listened to Cybelle and to Abacasas. Which one do you believe?"

"That's my problem, doctor," I said wryly. "I don't know."

"Let's go at it another way: What do you want to do?"

"Find the murderer and get on with my life?"

Chet was a skillful psychologist before he packed away his PhD and took up writing books on crime; what he said next surprised me.

"You care the most that Jeannie Ford is dead."

I put down my fork. "What do you mean?"

"I did a nexus search after Penny told me about the murder. One and two paragraph articles, buried in the back of the New York dailies—on Thanksgiving, when not many people read the papers. There've been no follow-up stories, and no mention that it happened in Cybelle's apartment, or that Jeannie Ford worked on your show. Either of those bits make it a hot story." Chet was staring at me intently. "Why do you suppose the murder of an attractive young woman, an aspiring actress, was dropped by the media so quickly and completely?"

I knew the answer to that. "Nathan Hughes, Global's head of publicity. Winston Yarborough didn't want *another* murder associated with the network only a couple of months after the publicity firestorm those first two caused."

"You're right. Hughes and Yarborough hushed up Jeannie Ford's death." Chet reached across the table and took my hand. "There hasn't been any media pressure on the cops to find Jeannie Ford's killer, and it's likely the case will just go cold. Much to your network's relief." Chet squeezed my hand. "You're in an ugly business, honey. Why don't you chuck it? Give Global the old middle-finger goodbye wave. Write true crime books with me."

"Come on, Chet. You don't even know if I'm a good writer."

"I think you probably are."

"Based on what? You've never read anything I've written. No, thank you for the offer, but I already let one man choose a career for me." I realized that sounded harsh, and unfair to the old life I shared with Ian. "Don't misunderstand," I said quickly, "I'm *glad* I did it, but I'll never do it again."

He let go of my hand and leaned back against the booth's comfortable padded leather. The expression on his face was sympathetic, but he watched me keenly. Then he repeated the question he had asked earlier. "So what do you want to do?"

This time I was ready to answer. I sat up straight. "Several things." I ticked the list off on my fingers. "One: find out who killed Jeannie. Somebody's got to be held accountable. Two: find out if Cybelle really was the intended victim. I *think* she was, but I need to know the truth. Three: keep Link Ramsey out of the investigation. I'm sure he had nothing to do with Jeannie's death, and that he's no threat to Cybelle." I paused for a moment to swallow a sip of coffee. I wanted to make sure I didn't betray any emotion when I mentioned the final item on my list. "Number four," I said, "eliminate Philippe Abacasas as a suspect."

"Let's begin with four. Why do you want to eliminate Abacasas?"

That startled me. Why did Chet pounce on *four*? In trying to seem casual about Abacasas, did I actually betray

my curiosity—no, my embarrassing *interest*—in him?
Chet was watching me. Did he think I was taking too long
to answer?

I tried my best to sound relaxed as I said, "If Matt and
G. G. waste time concentrating on him, the real killer
might never be found. That's the same reason I don't want
them going after Link Ramsey. Link's currently the most
important actor on our show. If he's not the killer, and I'm
convinced he isn't, I don't want whatever he's hiding coming out and damaging the show."

Chet studied me quietly. "You're a new kind of hyphen-
ate," he said. "Part compassionate human being and part
loyal corporate soldier."

"What did you do, look me up in your DSM-IV?" I
asked.

He was surprised I'd referred to the manual of psychiatric disorders. "How do you know about the DSM?"

"I have a copy. A lot of writers do, the ones who want to
create characters with as much reality as invented drama
allows. Back to the subject: do you have a suggestion about
what I can do for Jeannie?"

"Yes, but Super Cop's going to hate it, if he finds out."

"Matt's not too thrilled with me at the moment. What's
your idea?"

Chet took a small address book out of his jacket pocket,
thumbed through it until he came to a particular name. He
tore a blank page out of the back and wrote on it.

"This is the name, address, and phone number of a
smart investigator. You can trust him. I met him when I was
working on the Three Rivers murder book," he said, nam-
ing the first of his true crime best sellers. "I've used him
more than once."

He handed the piece of paper to me.

"Robert Novello, Discreet Investigations," I read. I looked up at Chet. "I hadn't thought of hiring a private detective."

"Bobby's handled some sensitive matters for me over the years. We got to be friends, and meet for drinks once in a while," Chet said. "He has a master's degree in criminology, he trained with one of the top P.I. firms in the country, and he's a genius with technology. Bobby's a bit eccentric, but he's a good guy. Tenacious. When he thinks he's got something, he fastens on like a barnacle."

I turned the paper over and wove it through my fingers, as though feeling its texture would tell me what to do.

"You're right about one thing," I said. "If I hire a private detective to investigate Jeannie's death, Matt will react like a hiccupping volcano."

Chet smiled. "I'd like to see that."

"I wouldn't." I folded the piece of paper and slid it back across the table. "It would be an insult to Matt, and a betrayal of his trust. I can't do it."

"Keep Bobby's name and number, just in case."

"No." When he saw I wasn't going to change my mind, Chet picked up the paper and crumpled it. "Just trying to help," he said.

"And I appreciate it." I reached for his hand and touched it with affection. "I'm glad you're back."

"And I wish I could stay," he said. With his free hand he reached into his inside breast pocket and showed me the top of a KLM airline ticket. "Now that I know you're all right, I have to get back to the Netherlands ASAP."

I was astonished. "You mean you came *eight thousand miles just* because you were concerned about me, and after a few hours you're flying another eight thousand miles right back?"

"Yep." There was a teasing tone in his voice. "I want you to think about how you can show your gratitude when I return for good in a couple of weeks."

"By then I'll be in Los Angeles, supervising the filming of our February sweeps scenes!"

I saw disappointment in his eyes.

"We're victims of bad timing," I said. I wanted to tell him that no one had ever flown sixteen thousand miles just to make sure I was alive. I wanted to tell him how very much he meant to me, but I was afraid my saying that would lead to a conversation I wasn't ready to have, to a decision I wasn't ready to make.

BECAUSE WE CAUGHT considerable end-of-the-weekend traffic going back to the city, it took more than an hour to drive the thirty miles from Spring Valley to John F. Kennedy International Airport. We didn't talk much on the trip, but our silence was an easy one. For the first time in the few months I'd known Chet, I felt completely relaxed with him.

When I came to a stop in front of the entrance to KLM Royal Dutch Airlines, I leaned over to kiss him goodbye.

"No." Chet held me at arm's length. "I *want* to kiss you. But if I start, I won't want to stop."

"You don't have to explain."

"Yes, I do. We need some time alone together, away from all the distractions in both of our lives. Morgan, I want you more than I've wanted anybody in years, but I want you in the right way, when your desire for me is as strong as mine is for you."

I was about to make a joke to cover my confused feelings, but then I saw the serious expression in his eyes.

"That was a statement of my intent," he said. "Don't say anything now, just think about it."

Car horns honked, clamoring at me to move. Chet gave me a farewell wink and climbed out onto the sidewalk. He was about to leave, but he turned back to tap on the passenger's window. I rolled it down and he leaned in.

"Don't fall in love with somebody else while I'm gone," he said.

Without waiting for an answer, he turned and hurried into the KLM terminal. I felt terrible as I watched him disappear. Chet thought Matt was his only rival. Until forty-eight hours ago, that was true. In a spasm of guilt and confusion, I leaned forward and hit my head against the steering wheel.

Chapter 29

ACCORDING TO THE dashboard clock it was only a little after eight-thirty when I worked my way out of the concrete
labyrinth that was JFK. It wasn't too late on a Sunday evening to call somebody at home.

At the first opportunity, I turned off the busy thorough-
fare onto a residential street, pulled over to the curb and dialed a number on my cell phone.

After several rings, I heard Betty Kraft's bright
"Hello?"

"Hi, Betty—it's Morgan. Hope I'm not disturbing you."

"No, I was just reading. What's up?"

"I have a favor to ask. May I come over to your place? I
won't stay long."

"Sure," she said. She gave me her address and I told her
I'd be there in about twenty minutes.

* * *

BETTY KRAFT LIVED in a nice ten-story apartment building on East Eighty-sixth Street, in a section of Manhattan called Yorkville. I cruised the street, scanning for a parking space. It was practically a miracle, as anyone crazy enough to drive a car in the city knows, that I found an empty spot only half a block from her entrance.

In the building's small vestibule, I pressed the call button for apartment 2G. Without using the intercom to ask who was there, she buzzed me in through the locked front door.

I ignored the elevator, took the stairs and found Betty waiting for me in her doorway. She had a book in her left hand, using her index finger to mark her place. I noticed it was one from the stack that Bud, Johnny's driver, had delivered.

Betty greeted me cheerfully and stepped back to invite me in.

Her living room was neat, but not obsessively so. White walls, dark rose-colored carpet, large pieces of furniture of mixed periods and styles that somehow looked comfortable together. Floor to ceiling bookshelves covered two walls. Sketches and paintings of felines, domestic and wild, flanked the gas fireplace. Little cat figurines made of materials ranging from crystal to steel were scattered along the mantelpiece, and on most flat surfaces. Stretched lazily along the back of the massive big burgundy velvet couch that dominated the room were two examples of the real thing: a pair of exceptionally large calico cats. So secure were they in their environment that when I came into the room, they looked up at me with only the slightest interest.

"Do you like cats?" she asked.

"Very much." I reached out to stroke the shining fur of the nearest one. "These two are beautiful."

Betty smiled with pleasure as the cat I was petting began to purr.

"The black and gold is mother Jezabel, and the gray and gold is daughter Annabelle. Sit down," she said, gesturing toward the deep cushioned wing chair at one end of the couch. "Can I take your jacket?"

"No thanks, I'm not going to stay long," I said. "I appreciate your letting me come up tonight."

"Happy to see you, but I was surprised by your call."

I took the wing chair and Betty sat down on the corner of the couch nearest me. As soon as she settled onto the cushion, the cats climbed down from the back. One hopped into her lap and the other snuggled against her thigh. I glanced at the titles on her shelves. Her books were all mystery novels, ranging from classics to current.

"That's a great collection," I said.

"Like you, I'm a crime nut." Indicating the book in her lap, she said, "Mysteries are my drug of choice."

The novel she had chosen to borrow was a Robert Crais, featuring private detective Elvis Cole.

"Is it good?"

"One of his best." Her eyes were bright with enthusiasm. "At *last*, Elvis broke up with that pretentious prig from New Orleans he was involved with for several books. She wasn't good enough for him, but Elvis was the only one who didn't know that."

"Some detective." I said it as a joke, but Betty took the comment seriously.

"He's an excellent detective," she said, defending Elvis Cole as though he were a real person, and a friend of hers.

"He just has rotten taste in women." She added, with a self-mocking smile, "But I suppose I'm in no position to criticize. I married three different wrong men. Kept the first one long after his expiration date just because I liked the sex. The other two I married after I was old enough to know better." She regarded me shrewdly. "You didn't come over here on a Sunday night to hear about my bad choices. What can I do for you?"

I liked her directness. "It's something that I want you to keep in confidence. Will you be comfortable not mentioning this conversation to Tommy?"

"I wouldn't do anything to hurt that boy," she said, "but I don't think you would, either. So yes, whatever it is stays between us."

"I need to see Cybelle's personnel file, without anyone else knowing."

The wattage in Betty's eyes shot up from interested to gleeful. "What's she done?"

"Why do you think she's done anything?"

"Oh, come on, Morgan. She's too sweet, too soft, too polite. Always has something nice to say, always complimenting somebody. She's so eternally *agreeable* that I'd like to smack her." She shook her head at the irony of what she was saying. "Never thought I'd criticize an actress for being too agreeable, but I might like her more if just *once* she'd throw a fit like a normal person."

I almost laughed, but caught myself at a quick chuckle. Betty promised to have the personnel file for me in the morning and we said good night.

Out on the street, I pulled my jacket tighter against the cold. Hurrying toward the spot where I'd parked Nancy's car, I realized that because Betty was over fifty and not conventionally attractive, I'd never thought of her as a sexual being. It occurred to me that we hadn't done a love story featuring a woman Betty's age, certainly not within my memory. It was time I created a story about an older woman who was the object of passion. Perhaps a younger man—somebody sexy, with a sense of humor—who could have his choice of younger women, but who fell genuinely in love with . . . Whom? I smiled, remembering Betty's admission that she had married three wrong men. It reminded me of Doctor Johnson's famous line that a person's decision to remarry was "the triumph of hope over experience."

I had made my own biggest decisions on the basis of hope over experience, and when Ian was killed I plunged into the world of daytime drama.

I had gambled my life on hope, and I wouldn't change either of those decisions.

Chapter 30

MONDAY MORNING AFTER the long Thanksgiving holiday weekend, Tommy Zenos was working hard at one of his favorite activities: casting. His side of our partners' desk was covered with pictures and resumes of actors who might be right to play the new character, Ben. When I came into the office he was watching a reel of audition tapes our casting director had put together.

"Any luck?" I asked.

"Not yet." Tommy turned off the TV and began to examine the photos. "Johnny Isaac called. He heard about the new role and asked if we'd audition that driver of his—Bud something."

"Bud Collins. He's too young for the part."

"That's what I told Johnny." Tommy looked up from the photos. "God knows why, but he's taken an interest in this

kid." He thought about it for a moment. "You know . . .
Johnny Isaac's an important agent. If he's sticking his neck
out to push this Bud, maybe we should let him play one of
the three bad guys on the boat. What do you think? They're
Under Fives."

Under Fives are parts with fewer than five lines; a
newcomer could get a little experience without damaging
the show.

I nodded in agreement. "That young, innocent face of
Bud's will make an interesting contrast to the usual toughs
who play bad guys," I said. "Good idea."

As he always did when a sign of approval came his way,
Tommy beamed. "I'll tell Casting to do the paperwork.
How are the scripts coming?"

"It'll be tight, but they'll be ready," I said. "I wrote a
scene between Ben and Dinah that'll be good to use when
we find actors we want to have read with Francie." I took
those new pages out of my briefcase and handed them to
Tommy.

Smiling and nodding as he read, Tommy finished the
scene and looked across the desk at me. "This is good.
Gives us a chance to see Ben being funny, and then being
serious when they're trying to figure out how to get away
from the bad guys."

He reached into his top drawer, pulled out a Mounds bar
and tore at the wrapper. "I didn't have much breakfast," he
said. He demolished the first half of the candy, then, realizing that he was eating in front of me, he asked, "Want one?
I've got plenty."

I shook my head and made a list on my scratch pad of
things I had to do that morning before I could get back to
writing.

Tommy finished the candy bar, licked his fingers and

tossed the wrapper into the wastebasket next to the desk. Indicating the pages I had given him, he said, "I especially like the subtext, that undercurrent of growing attraction between Ben and Dinah. Now we just have to find a guy who can act, memorize lines fast and whose chemistry clicks with Francie's."

"I wish we could order actors from QVC, the way I order clothes," I joked, "in exactly the right size and style. And if we didn't like them, we could send them back within thirty days, no questions asked."

Tommy didn't laugh. "I wish we could order our parents that way." He heaved a deep sigh and went back to business. Selecting a pair of photos from the array, he held them up to face me. "I'm going to have these two come in, to see what they look like in the flesh."

I studied the pictures. "They're possibilities for Ben. It would save us time if actors and their agents would get it into their heads that we want to see what they *really* look like, without all the retouching and artful lighting."

Tommy nodded. "I don't know who said 'pictures don't lie.' It couldn't have been a photographer." He put the two pictures aside and shuffled the others together into a stack to be put back into the files, then stood up and stretched. "I'm going downstairs to talk to the *Trauma Center* guys. Maybe they'll remember somebody they liked but couldn't use."

As he started out, Tommy passed Betty in the doorway. He patted the bulge in his jacket. "If you need me," he said to both of us, "I've got my cell."

When he was gone, Betty handed a brown accordion envelope to me. "Here's that thing we never talked about," she said. "This is a copy. The original is back in the file where it's supposed to be."

"Thanks. Oh—we're going to use Bud as one of the Under Five bad guys on the riverboat."

Betty smiled. "He's going to be thrilled," she said. "I hope he doesn't freeze on camera."

"If he does, I'll cut his lines, or give them to the other two bad guys. But at least we'll have given him a chance."

I spent a few minutes while Tommy was gone going over the papers Cybelle had filled out when we hired her. It listed her New York address, phone number, social security number, the name of the bank and the account number where her salary was to be electronically deposited.

On the line asking who should be notified in case of emergency, Johnny Isaac's name, address, and numbers were listed. As an alternate, in case Johnny could not be located, I saw my own name and information. In answer to the question about next of kin, one word was typed: "None."

Under the heading "Confidential Information, Not For Release" it said that Cybelle Carter's birth name was Sara Gilley. That was the name she gave Abacasas when he met her in Houston.

The last page in the file, behind several eight-by-ten publicity stills Betty had included, was the shortest actor's bio I'd ever read. It said only that Cybelle was born twenty-two years ago in Thomasville, Georgia, and that 'Kira' was her first acting role.

THE NEXT WEEK passed—as the cliché goes—in a flurry of activity. After I told Johnny Isaac that we would let Bud play one of the bad guys in our location shoot, he sent Tommy and me each a bottle of Cristal champagne, with notes thanking us for "giving a newcomer a break."

While Tommy and I were producing daily episodes of *Love of My Life* we also had to deal with off-camera problems as diverse as an epidemic of colds striking the actors in the Jillian-Gareth-Sylvia-Brad story line, and the "plot idea notes" with which daytime VP Lori Cole bombarded us. We brought a doctor to the studio for the cast, but I suspected we might need an exorcist to deal with Lori Cole.

Tommy had seen dozens of actors of the right age to play Ben. They hadn't generated the excitement we needed, but now Tommy was enthusiastic about someone named Rod Amato. He'd discovered Amato just the previous night, in a Diet Dr Pepper commercial on TV. He'd immediately tracked down the actor's agent and told me that Amato would be coming in to read with Francie in twenty minutes.

Tommy was out on the floor, setting up a corner in one of the studios where the Amato audition could be taped. I was alone in our office, studying diagrams of the cabin layout of the riverboat on which we'd be shooting, when Betty opened the door.

"New York's cutest—oops, I mean New York's *finest* is here to see you," she said. "Shall I send him in, or can I keep him?"

My smile was her answer. Betty went back to her desk and Matt was standing in the doorway. I stood up to greet him with a cheerful hello, to let him know that I'd forgotten the argument we'd had the last time we'd talked. The smile on my face died when I saw the morose expression on his.

"What's happened?" I asked.

"We've been pulled off the Jeannie Ford investigation. An eight-year-old boy was found early this morning. Murdered. The whole squad's working it."

The image of a child victim caused a physical pain in my stomach. "That's terrible," I said. "I want you to get the s.o.b. who killed him."

"Thanks."

"When you do, you'll go back to Jeannie's case, won't you?"

"It'll stay open because we never close a murder investigation," he said, "but the truth is we haven't made any headway."

I gestured for him to sit down on one of the Queen Anne chairs. He did, and I perched on the edge of the chair opposite him.

"If not you and G. G., then isn't *somebody* working on her case?"

"With the load our squad's got, unless we suddenly get a new lead, it's cold."

"A cold case . . ."

"It'll be reviewed periodically," he said, trying to reassure me, "but without new information, it has to go on the back burner, with other cases that haven't been cleared."

That was deeply disappointing, and exactly what Chet had predicted, but I knew it wasn't Matt's fault. I didn't want to make it harder for him. "Would you like some coffee?" I asked.

"No, thanks. Look, I'm sorry things have been tense between us."

"My fault," I said.

"Mine, too. Forget it. We've got to work long hours for a while, but maybe you and I can get together for a late supper sometime?"

"I'd like that," I said. "It's hard for either of us to make plans right now, but I don't mind being spontaneous."

"Spontaneous is good." He got up, leaned down and

kissed me lightly on the forehead. I felt the faint scratch of his emerging beard against my skin and realized that it had been hours since he'd shaved. And he didn't look as though he'd had much sleep.

He tugged gently at a lock of my hair. Meaning the kiss, he said, "I can do that, because now you're not part of a case I'm working."

Chapter 31

AFTER MATT LEFT, I went around to my side of the partners' desk, sank into my chair and swiveled back and forth. The mechanism under the seat creaked as I thought about Jeannie Ford, and pictured her face. I remembered the day a few months ago when I hired her. We'd needed a body double for Cybelle, because her leg was in a cast. Jeannie had told me how happy she was to get the job. Now her face haunted me. First Global, and now the police had abandoned her.

Somebody had to get justice for Jeannie Ford.

Turning to one of the shelves behind me, I pulled down the Manhattan Yellow Pages and flipped through it until I found what I was looking for. I dialed the number.

"Robert Novello," said a lilting tenor. "You've reached the man himself."

I told him my name, and that Chet Thompson had recommended him. We made an appointment to meet the next night—Saturday, at eight P.M. I scribbled his name, address, and the time on my desk calendar.

Betty poked her head in just as I hung up the phone.

"Tommy said to tell you the actor's here, and he's setting up for taping in Studio thirty-seven."

"Thanks. Would you tell Francie to meet us there?"

"Already did," Betty said. "She was in her dressing room doing crunches."

"Good for Francie. Oh, Betty, come in for a sec. Close the door."

She did. "Double-Oh-Four reporting for duty."

"Double-Oh-Four?"

"Licensed to *wound*."

"Cute, but I don't need anybody wounded—just more secret photocopying."

"Of what?"

"Any information we have on Jeannie Ford," I said. "Could you put it in my briefcase before I go home tonight? And a good picture of her."

Betty didn't ask questions, just nodded.

"I'm going to meet Tommy over at thirty-seven. If anybody calls, I'll be back in half an hour."

"Okey dokey," she said, flashing me a conspiratorial smile. Her steps were jaunty as she went back to her desk.

A SCENE FROM the day's script was taping in Studio 35. From the bit I saw and heard as I made my way past, it was going well. The actors were remembering the lines and were delivering them with the requisite passion.

I continued on to Studio 37, where Tommy was waiting

for me in the far corner of the set that's used as the living room of one of our core families, the Richardsons.

Standing beside Tommy was a man in his early thirties. Attractive in an intriguing, irregular weave sort of way.

His nose was a little long, his eyes were set a little too far apart, and his ash blond hair fell in a jagged clump over his high forehead. Unambiguously masculine, there was nevertheless an impish quality to him. Physically, his light hair and fair skin would make a nice contrast to Link Ramsey's brooding darkness. He was shorter than Link, and more compact. If they were likened to athletes, Rod Amato was a quarterback, and Link Ramsey a long distance runner. I had a double purpose in mind for the character of Ben. He was going to be Francie's love interest, but he was also going to become the buddy of Link's character, so it was important that the two men be physically different from one another.

Tommy introduced me to the actor.

"Thank you for seeing me," he said. His tone was husky and distinctive.

I was about to reply when I heard a soft voice behind me. "Hello, I'm Francie James."

While Tommy introduced the two actors, and explained to Francie that he wanted her to read with Amato, I gave Francie an appraising glance. It was only a little more than a week since I had outlined her new fitness routine. Her cheekbones were slightly more prominent. Her complexion without makeup was clear and glowing.

I noticed that Amato didn't have any script pages in his hand and volunteered to get a copy of the scene for him.

He shook his head. "Mr. Zenos e-mailed the pages to me this morning. I memorized them."

"That's impressive," Francie said. She turned to me.

"We're doing the scene where we're hiding in the boat's costume room, trying to figure out disguises to wear?"

I nodded.

"Good, I'm ready on that one."

All Amato knew about his character, Ben, was what was contained in the pages he'd received, so I explained that Ben had amnesia and didn't know who he was.

"Someone tried to kill Ben, but bungled the job. He was discovered by Francie's character, lying semiconscious in an alley in the rain."

Amato gave Francie a friendly wink. "Thanks for saving me."

She replied, "My pleasure," and I think she meant it.

Then he told her he admired her work on the show, and she told him she'd enjoyed his performance as Thomas in the off-Broadway revival of *The Lady's Not For Burning*. When they began comparing acting coaches, it was clear that they were getting along. Tommy and I grinned at each other like a pair of successful matchmakers.

When they were ready to run the scene, Tommy had the property master bring a trunk full of costume parts onto the lighted corner of the set. I signaled the video-cam operator that we were ready.

Even though they were working without benefit of either rehearsal or the help of a director, they were terrific in the scene. I expected it from Francie, who'd played Dinah for six years. Rod Amato was a revelation. His line recall was perfect, but he also brought surprising nuances to some of his speeches that gave me ideas about further developing Ben's personality. I love it when that happens.

The scene ended. Tommy and I knew we had found our Ben.

"I'm calling your agent today to make a deal," Tommy

told the actor. "We're going to need you right away, and in a week you'll have to go to Los Angeles for a few days. Is that a problem?"

"No conflicts," Amato said, sounding very happy. "Except for the six-week run of the play, and that soda commercial, I've been out of work for a year."

"We'll get you set up with a shooting schedule, and make appointments for wardrobe, and publicity photos."

"You're going to like it here," Francie said warmly. "Nice people." She looked at me. "I'm finished for the day. If Rod has time, I can show him the layout, and introduce him to whoever's around."

"Great," Amato said.

Tommy turned to me. "I've got an appointment to get my teeth cleaned. Walk me to the elevator."

Tommy was practically skipping as we made our way across the twenty-sixth floor. "Sometimes you just get lucky," he said.

I agreed that this was one of those times.

When I got back to the office, I checked my briefcase and saw that Betty had slipped in a copy of Jeannie Ford's personnel file. I planned to pick up a quart of chicken matzo ball soup from my favorite deli on the way home, and—even though I'd instructed Francie not to read while she ate—I was going to examine the file over soup.

I was putting together a pile of pictures and sketches showing the interiors and exteriors of the riverboat Tommy had located on the Hollywood studio's back lot. I'd need them to write scenes this weekend.

Betty buzzed me. "Mr. Isaac is here."

"Send him in." I should have realized he'd be somewhere on the premises; Cybelle was working. "And Betty—why don't you go home? It's been a long week."

"Thanks, I will. See you Monday."

Johnny Isaac's mood was jaunty as he strutted into my office. "Thanks for giving Bud that bit in your show. He's a good kid."

"I'm glad the opportunity came up."

Johnny closed the door behind him and reached into the breast pocket of his suit jacket. He extracted two folded pages. "Wait'll you see *this!*" he said triumphantly. "I got it." He was keeping his voice low, but his tone was practically a whoop. "The advance copy of Cybelle's 'Junior Divas of Daytime' interview."

Mentally, I smacked myself in the head. A lot had happened since Cybelle asked me to concoct a past for her—something she could tell the press.

"I'm sorry. I forgot all about that," I said.

Johnny, always so protective of Cybelle, was surprisingly magnanimous. "No problem. I know how busy you are."

A sudden realization made me look at Johnny quizzically. "I thought *Time* didn't give out advance copies of their stories."

"They don't. I got my ways and means, so to speak. Want to read it?"

"I certainly do." What in the world, I wondered, had Cybelle told that reporter? Johnny unfolded the pages and handed them to me. I skipped the paragraphs on the other three actresses and went right to the part about Cybelle. I was so astonished at what I read I felt my mouth open.

I snapped it closed.

"That's good, isn't it?" Johnny was standing close to me, reading along, even though I was sure he'd already memorized the piece.

For a moment I was rendered speechless, but I recovered my voice and read aloud. " 'It has caused Cybelle

Carter a great deal of pain, she said, not being able to talk about her background, not being able to give credit to the people who were kind to her when she was growing up . . . because *her only living relative is in the government's Witness Protection Program*'?"

"That was my idea," Johnny said proudly. His chest puffed out and he stretched up enough to seem two inches taller. "The rest of the article is all true—how she used to dream of becoming a veterinarian but she wasn't any good at chemistry, and so now she spends time when she's not here at the studio volunteering at animal shelters. And about how she's organizing a 'Fan Weekend with Soap Stars' to raise money so people can get their pets spayed and neutered and vaccinated for free."

"This is truly amazing," I said. Love-besotted Johnny missed the irony in my tone.

"Oh, yeah. Oh, yeah. She's got a big heart in that beautiful little body." Gently, he removed the pages from my hand and put them back in his pocket. "The magazine'll be out next week. We can't let anybody see this before."

Chapter 32

BY LATE SATURDAY afternoon, I had finished writing the scenes we were going to shoot in Los Angeles. I e-mailed the pages to Tommy, along with a list of the props and furnishings we would need.

There was time to unwind before my meeting with Robert Novello, so I set my portable CD player on the counter in the bathroom, filled the tub with hot water and lilac body wash, and soaked to the strains of the original cast recording of *Brigadoon*. I would have sung along, except I can't carry a tune.

With my hair pinned up and my body covered in lilac-scented foam, I lay in the tub until the lovers Tommy and Fiona were finally reunited.

* * *

ROBERT NOVELLO LIVED and worked on MacDougal Street, which is a little more than four miles south of the Dakota—too far to walk on a cold evening in early December, even for me.

At twenty minutes past seven on Saturday night, foot and vehicle traffic along Central Park West was thick. After a few minutes of shivering on the corner without spotting an empty cab, I warmed myself with a brisk hike west on Seventy-second to Columbus Avenue, where I thought I might have better luck. The theory worked. I hailed a cab, climbed in and gave the driver Novello's Greenwich Village address.

The Village got its name in 1731, when Peter Warren, commander of a fleet of English warships, bought what had been a Dutch West Indies Company tobacco village plantation. He built a mansion overlooking the Hudson River, and named his lush acreage *Greenwich*. If that grand house still existed, it would sit right where Perry and West Fourth Streets meet. Modern Greenwich Village is a horizontal strip informally bordered by Fourteenth Street on the north, and Houston Street on the south. Above Fourteenth is the beginning of midtown Manhattan, and below Houston is the island's trendy SoHo area—SoHo being a name created from "South of Houston."

It was ten minutes to eight when the cab came to a stop on MacDougal. I paid the driver and got out.

The sight of the narrow street filled me with a pleasant sensation of familiarity—Novello's address on MacDougal was only half a block from number 130, where Louisa May Alcott wrote *Little Women*. When I first came to New York City to attend Columbia, I visited that house, and other Village literary landmarks: nearby Grove Street, where the gate at Number Ten gave O. Henry his inspiration for *The Last Leaf*, the club on West Third where Edgar Allen Poe wrote "The Raven," and the house on Bedford Street where Edna St. Vincent Millay had lived.

Little Women, and the novels of Dickens, Trollope, Thackeray, the Bronte sisters, Henry James, Jane Austen, and others with multiple characters and stories that unfolded over decades, were the soap operas of their day. I enjoy thinking about that when critics who never watch daytime drama dismiss our endless-novel form of storytelling without considering the root and enduring strength of its appeal.

Novello's address was a well-maintained, nineteenth-century four-story apartment house with a red brick façade. At the front door I found "Novello" and pressed the button next to 1B.

The intercom crackled and a male voice asked, "Who is it?"

"Morgan Tyler. I'm a few minutes early."

"Early is good."

I heard the sound of the buzzer, and the click of the door unlocking to let me in.

Novello's apartment was at the rear of the building. I knocked, the door opened, and I found myself facing—although we were not exactly face-to-face—a handsome man with large, intelligent brown eyes, a cap of rose gold hair, and a truly great set of rock solid shoulders and upper arms. His face was smooth and unlined, except for the creases around the eyes and mouth: hallmarks of a man who laughed a lot. He might have been in his late thirties, or ten years younger, or even a decade older.

Chet had referred to Novello as "a bit eccentric." What he hadn't mentioned was that his detective friend was a dwarf, or—as I had learned from another I had known—a Little Person.

"Welcome," he said. "I'm Bobby Novello." His pleasant tenor rose to be heard above the chirping of a dozen birds. "Come in. I hope you don't mind informality. My office is also my living room."

He opened the door wider, stepped back, and I saw that I was entering an aviary. It was filled with large antique cages containing a virtual catalogue of colorful "merry minstrels of the morn," as poet James Thomson had described the feathered friends. The cages were exquisite works of craftsmanship, and immaculate.

Birds weren't the only unusual sight in the room. Visible through the cages were bookcases filled with hand-labeled videotapes. Lots of people have large video collections, but Novello's was the only one I had ever seen that was in the smaller, and I had thought long discontinued, Betamax format. Behind Novello's desk were DVD and video tape players, editing machines, two big-screen television sets, and an assortment of electronic gadgets. The only decorative items in the room—aside from the spectacular birds—were two framed posters of paintings by Toulouse-Lautrec.

Novello's furniture was covered with many different types of reference books, and telephone books from what looked like all five boroughs and several surrounding states. The four chairs, two end tables, the couch, and Novello's desk were of traditional size, but supplementing these pieces were several fine antique step stools.

Novello grabbed a stack of maps from the seat of a red leather chair that faced his desk. He gestured for me to sit there, and I did. Next to the chair was a small, narrow table, elbow high. It wasn't large enough to hold my tote bag; I put that on the floor. There was something vaguely familiar about the red leather chair, its placement, and the little table adjoining, but I couldn't place my sense of *déja vù*.

Novello picked up an armful of fabric covers from one of the end tables, climbed onto an antique stool and began shrouding the cages.

"Eight o'clock," he said. "Time for all good birdies to go to sleep."

He repeated the process of climbing and covering until all of the cages were darkened, and the birds had settled down for the night. Except for the faint hum of distant traffic, the room was quiet. On the business side of his desk, Novello stepped up onto another stool and settled himself in the high-backed leather wing chair to face me.

"Before we get to your problem, I'd like to know a little bit about you," he said. "Start with how you met Chet Thompson."

"He was considering writing a book about someone in my business—"

"Your business is crime?" His sly smile told me he was joking.

I answered in kind. "In a way—I work in television."

"That's not against the law, but some of the things they're putting on should be," he said.

"I'm the head writer and co-executive producer of *Love of My Life*. It's a—"

"Hey, I know, I watch your show every day! I got hooked a few years ago, when you had one of us on it."

"Jerry Daniels," I said, mentioning the name of an actor who had played an important role for us until last year. He was the one who told me 'Little Person' is preferable to 'dwarf.'

"Jerry was very popular with the audience, with all of us," I said. "We didn't want to see him leave."

"What happened?"

"His health wasn't good. He decided to retire."

Novello's tone was wry. "Yeah, it's not enough that we're four-foot guys in a six-foot world, we get stuck with extra medical problems, too." He shrugged, throwing off any suggestion of melancholy. "What the hell—we play the cards we're dealt, right?" He winked good-naturedly. "At least God made me good-looking." Without waiting for a response, he said, "Okay, let's get down to business. What do you need me for?"

I took the two personnel folders out of my tote bag, leaned forward and handed one of them to him. He opened it and looked at the photograph clipped to the pages inside.

"That's Jeannie Ford," I said. "She worked for us."

"Pretty girl."

"She was nice, too. A couple of weeks ago she was murdered. Poisoned. Yesterday the homicide detective on the case told me it was 'cold' and that while they wouldn't close the file, they have to concentrate on other cases. I want you to find out everything you can about Jeannie, and, if possible, I want you to find out who killed her, or at least come up with some evidence that will get the police seriously back on the case."

He scanned the information I'd supplied. "There's not a lot here, but it gives me a couple places to start." He closed the file. "Why are you so interested in this murder? Were you related to Jeannie?"

"No, but I feel partly responsible because I hired her. If

I hadn't, she might still be alive. I can't bring her back to life, but I can do my best to see that whoever killed her is punished."

"Okay, I'll buy that. But it's a little unusual to meet somebody who feels guilty about a crime she *didn't* commit." He indicated the folder I was holding. "What's that one?"

I opened Cybelle's file and gave it to him. He recognized her picture immediately.

"Cybelle Carter—she plays Kira. What a hottie." He looked up at me and added, "I like it that she's got a thing going with Cody now. The story's much better than when she was supposed to be with that wimp, Nicky."

Everybody's a critic.

"What do you want me to do about Ms. Carter?" Novello asked.

"Jeannie was Cybelle's stunt double, and she was killed in Cybelle's apartment. She died because someone put strychnine in the chocolate pudding which a lot of people knew was Cybelle's favorite treat. Cybelle isn't under suspicion, but she's told some conflicting stories about where she came from, and what her real name is. I'd like you to find out the truth about her. Everything you can learn. But I don't want her to know that I'm having her investigated."

"Got it," he said. "I guess show business is tough enough without one of your actresses getting mad at you."

Ain't that the truth.

"Cybelle invited Jeannie to stay in her apartment so she could hide out from a violent boyfriend," I said. "He's a jerk named Hal Meeks, but he was jailed on a charge of drunk and disorderly before Jeannie knew she'd be staying at Cybelle's, and he didn't get out on bail until after Jeannie's body was discovered."

"*Maybe* Meeks is out of it," Novello said thoughtfully,

"but I don't want to start an investigation with precon-
ceived notions. Tell me about Cybelle Carter." He added
with a charming smile, "Just the facts, ma'am."

I told him what little I knew about Cybelle. Included in
my recitation was her close relationship with her agent,
Johnny Isaac, and the fact that four years earlier Cybelle
had lived in Houston, Texas, possibly under the name of
Sara Gilley, and worked as a waitress. He made a few
notes.

"She may or may not have a brother named Floyd
Gilley," I said. "She told me she married a wealthy man
named Philippe Abacasas, and later ran away from him.
Abacasas may or may not be *his* real name."

He looked up from his notebook. "Anything else?"

"Since you watch the show you've seen Link Ramsey.
He's the actor who plays Cody."

Novello nodded.

"Link is worried about being investigated. He swears he
had nothing to do with Jeannie's death, and I believe him,
but he's afraid of something being uncovered. I want you
to find out what it is, but very discreetly. I don't want to
know his secret—*unless* it falls into one of four categories:
he murdered someone, he abused or molested children, he
beats up women, he abuses animals. If he's done any of
those things, he's off the show and I'll turn him over to the
police with whatever evidence you uncover. But if it's anything else, don't tell me. Let him keep his secret."

I saw a smile curve Novello's lips. He put down his pen
and studied me.

"Are you available to start working on the case, Mr.
Novello?"

"Call me Bobby. Now here's the deal, Morgan. You people in TV get paid top dollar, so I'm going to charge you

double the fee I'd ask from a regular person. That lets me help out other people who can't afford my services."

"At least you're honest about it," I said.

"I'm always honest, except when I have to lie on behalf of a client. How about we start with you giving me a retainer of ten thousand dollars?"

I didn't blink. "All right." It was more than I had expected, but I had come willing to agree to whatever figure he named. Hiring Bobby Novello was my gift to Jeannie.

Chapter 33

I REACHED DOWN into my tote for my checkbook and the pen I use to write checks. It was my favorite, an old Montblanc Ian's father had given to him when he graduated from college.

I put the pen and the checkbook on the little table beside me—and at that moment I realized what was familiar about Novello's arrangement of furniture. Stroking the arm of the chair, and then the surface of the little table, I laughed.

He grinned. "You figured it out, didn't you?"

"Clever," I said. "The red leather chair, this table that's just exactly the right size for writing checks, the lemon yellow couch . . . You've duplicated Nero Wolfe's office. Except that he didn't have these beautiful birds."

"No, he had a roomful of orchid plants on his roof, but

orchids aren't very good company. I started reading Nero Wolfe when I was a kid," he said.

"Me, too." I wrote a check for ten thousand dollars, tore it out and handed it to him. He waved it in the air to dry the ink.

"When it looked as though I wasn't going to grow up to play for the Knicks," he said, "I had to figure out what I was going to do with my life. If I couldn't be a basketball player, the only other thing I wanted was to be a detective."

"Chet says you're good. I'm counting on that."

He looked at my check. "This investigation—how high are you willing to go?"

"Whatever it takes," I said.

"Music to my ears." He put the check in the top drawer of his desk and locked it. "I'm wrapping up a case now. I can start on yours by Wednesday."

I agreed to that, and gave him a card listing all of my numbers. "You can reach me at one of those any time, Bobby. I don't care how late you call."

As I got up to leave, I added, "Please send your report to my home. The address is on the check. Don't send anything to my office."

"You got it."

"May I ask you a question?"

"I'm unmarried, available and looking," he said with a wink.

"That wasn't my question. I'm curious about why all of your video tapes are on Betamax."

"Superior technology."

"Nobody's used Beta for years."

"*I* do. In fact, we've got a club of Betamax diehards. But, I have to admit, we could all meet in a telephone booth—except there aren't any telephone booths around anymore. One by one the big, bad 'Whoever's-in-charge' is getting rid of all the best stuff."

Indicating his collection with a sweeping gesture, he said, "My tapes are important to me. If somebody breaks in here, they won't steal old Betas. Anything else I can replace."

Bobby escorted me to the door and opened it.

"When I have results, I'll call you to tell you the report's on its way to your house. But I have to warn you, an investigation like this can take a while."

DELICATE FLAKES OF snow were drifting down onto Mac-Dougal Street. As I reached the sidewalk, I tilted my face up toward the sky and closed my eyes, letting the gossamer bits settle onto my eyelashes and my skin. This little flurry was just the first gentle preview of winter weather yet to come.

MacDougal Street seemed a lot darker than when I had arrived barely an hour earlier. Glancing around, I saw that the street lamp nearest Bobby Novello's building was broken, shards of milk white glass littered at its base. I was sure it had been working when I arrived. I glanced in both directions, trying to decide which way to walk. Novello's section of MacDougal was bounded on the north by West Third Street, and on the south by Bleecker Street. Looking to the north I could see a stream of traffic flowing steadily, but the glowing lights from the coffee houses and the small shops on Bleecker were more inviting.

Inhaling a few blocks of fresh, cold air before I caught a cab home appealed to me. I turned and began walking south toward Bleecker. Before I had gone more than a few feet I heard the scrape of footsteps on the sidewalk behind me. The hairs on the back of my neck tingled a warning, but it was too late. A hand grabbed a fistful of my hair and yanked me backward. Simultaneously a gloved hand slapped tight over my mouth. I shot an elbow back and connected with a chest as hard as cement. I heard a grunt of pain. My assailant let go of my hair and pressed the cold steel tip of what felt like a knife against my throat, so painfully deep I knew he had broken the skin. I stopped struggling. He squashed the side of his face against my right cheek and whispered, "Scream and I'll kill you."

I froze. My heart was pounding, but I willed myself not to scream. I was in survival mode, determined to do whatever it took to stay alive.

"This is a warning. Mind your own business. If you don't, you'll die." A hard object crashed against the back of my skull. A thousand shooting stars exploded behind my eyes—and my lights went out.

Chapter 34

I STRUGGLED UPWARD from a deep black void into a lighter darkness. My head throbbed. As my vision cleared, I began to make out objects around me and saw that I was in a stone stairwell a few feet below the level of a street, just outside the closed door of a basement apartment. The front window was dark, so either no one was home, or it was so late that the residents were in bed. I felt my wrist and discovered I was still wearing my watch, but it was too dark to see the time.

My tote bag—upended, its contents scattered—lay crumpled beside me. I saw my discarded wallet, reached for it and discovered the money was gone, but I could feel that my driver's license and credit cards were still inside.

I had a moment of panic as I thought about my keys. My hand groped toward a side pocket of my jeans, and a profound sense of relief flooded over me. *He didn't get my keys.* Gently exploring for damage, I felt a lump on the back of my head. It was sore. My fingers touched the front of my throat and came away just slightly sticky with blood. The sharp tip of whatever he had pressed against my throat had broken the skin, but I wasn't seriously injured.

I determined that none of my extremities were broken. I scooped my things back into my bag, then, fighting waves of dizziness, I managed to get to my feet, and climb the several steps up to the sidewalk. Looking around, I tried to orient myself. When I saw the shards of white glass at the base of a darkened light pole, I realized I was still on Mac-Dougal Street, and only a few yards from Bobby Novello's house. If I didn't move too fast, I could make it to Bobby's without falling down.

I leaned on his bell, and to his "Who is it?" I managed to croak out my name. His buzz unlocked the door immediately.

"Good God." He put an arm around my waist to steady me as he guided me into his apartment. "What happened? Were you mugged?"

"A man grabbed me. He had a knife. He hit me on the head. . . ."

Bobby swept books and magazines off his sofa and propped me onto it in a sitting position. "Don't lie down—you might have a concussion. I'll call a doctor, or an ambulance. Or do you want me to take you to a hospital?"

"No, don't. I think I'm all right. . . ."

"Want me to call the cops?"

"There's nothing they can do now. And I'm not really hurt. It's just my head . . ."

"Don't move, but stay awake." He hurried out of the room, returning shortly with a bowl of ice water, a roll of

LOVE HER TO DEATH 221

paper towels, and a first-aid kit. He dipped several paper towels into the bowl. With delicate fingers he explored the back of my head until he found the lump and applied water-soaked towels to clean it.

"The blow broke the skin, but not badly," he said. "You don't need stitches, but be careful how you brush your hair for a few days."

He put fresh cold towels into my hand and told me to hold them against the lump. While I did as instructed, he opened the first-aid kit to remove a bottle of antiseptic and a gauze pad in sterile wrapping.

"This'll sting a little," he said. It did.

As I turned my face to thank him, he winced. "Your neck is bleeding."

"Isn't it just a knick?"

"Yeah, it's only superficial," he said with relief. A relief I shared. "But we don't want it to get infected."

Bobby ripped open another sterile pad, soaked it in the antiseptic and pressed it against the wound in my neck. That hurt like hell.

"Jeez, you were lucky. What happened? Tell me everything, exactly."

It didn't take long. When I finished, I asked, "Do you think he was some mental case who goes around grabbing people and telling them to mind their own business? Or was he giving a message to *me*, in particular?"

He didn't answer directly. "The streets are full of nut jobs who should be locked up. Describe him."

"About five feet ten. Wiry build, no fat. Strong. Something that felt like a ski mask covered his face. Wool gloves. I think he was disguising his voice."

Bobby chewed his lower lip thoughtfully. "It's a coin toss. Could be just a mugger. Or maybe he was following you."

"If I'm in danger, then you might be, too, because I came here—"

"This isn't an office building. All that's on the bell is my last name. Even if he knew what apartment you went to, he wouldn't know I'm a P.I." He wiggled his eyebrows and teased, "But he might think you've got a thing for little guys." His expression turned serious again. "How about letting me take you to a hospital?"

"No, I'm okay, really. But he took my cash. Can you lend me cab fare?"

"I'll do better than that. I'll take you home myself." Bobby went to a closet by the front door, removed a heavy leather jacket with a lot of zippers and put it on.

"You look pretty dashing," I said.

"Think so? Wait'll you see the rest." He pulled a black helmet painted to resemble a skull out of the closet, plopped it on his head and bent over. When he straightened up, he was brandishing a duplicate. "You can wear my guest helmet."

The image in my aching head was bizarre. "You're going to take me home on a motorcycle?"

"Not just any old motorcycle—an American Iron Horse, the Stalker model. It's been modified for me with hand controls. Tell the truth, Morgan Tyler, have you ever ridden through the streets of Manhattan on a snowy night, hanging onto the back of a handsome dwarf?"

"Little Person." I had to admit that this would be a first.

THE SIGHT OF two people in skull helmets zooming up to the entrance of the Dakota on an American Iron Horse motorcycle was such a surprise to security man Frank he squeezed his hero sandwich hard enough for a meatball to pop out and roll across the sidewalk. I stepped over it as I climbed off the back of Bobby's Stalker.

My cycle pilot used a special hand lever—one of his machine's modifications—to lower the prop for when it was standing still. I waved a cheerful hello to Frank. His shock-meter shot into the red zone when I removed the guest helmet and he recognized me.

Surveying the Dakota's grand gothic—some called it *Grand Guignol*—façade, Bobby said, "Who was the architect? Dracula?"

I laughed and handed him the helmet. "Thanks for the ride."

He indicated the building with a nod of his helmet. "Impressive digs. I should have charged you a bigger retainer."

"You'll probably make it up in the *per diem*."

He chuckled. "I bet you think you're joking." Turning the Stalker around, he said, "I'm worried about that blow on the head. If you won't see a doctor, will you call somebody to come over and stay with you tonight?"

"As soon as I get upstairs. I promise."

That satisfied him. "Watch your back," he said. "I'll be in touch."

BEFORE MY WILD ride with Bobby was over, I had decided I wouldn't tell Matt I'd been struck on the head by a masked man who warned me to mind my own business. He'd insist on knowing why I was on MacDougal Street, and I had no intention of telling him I'd hired Bobby Novello.

Unless, or until, Bobby discovered significant information about Jeannie's murder, our arrangement had to be my secret. Matt was going to be furious regardless, but the storm would be a lot less severe if I could give him something to help arrest the killer.

There was another consideration that meant I had to keep the attack to myself. It was essential that the riverboat adventure scenes be filmed for the February sweeps, and we could only get the location, sets, and technicians we needed in Los Angeles, and only during their four-day window of availability. If I told Matt what had happened, he might get it into his head to try to prevent me—and Cybelle—from leaving New York.

Upstairs, I kept my promise to Bobby and dialed the number I knew best.

Nancy was home, and awake. As soon as I told her someone had whacked me on the head, she said, "You can't be alone tonight. I'll be right over."

Twenty minutes later, Nancy had gently felt the bump on my head, looked into my eyes, checked my pulse and finally admitted that I *probably* didn't need to go to a hospital. The intensity in her eyes signaled that she was going to be watching me.

"Tell me everything."

I did, then I said, "I've been thinking about the early part of the evening, tracking myself from the time I came out of the building and started looking for a cab. I've been visualizing the street, trying to discover if I have even the tiniest fragment of a memory, any glimpse of a person following me. There wasn't anybody."

"How can you be so sure? You weren't expecting to be followed, so you weren't checking the area out."

"Because I walk all over the city. I've developed a kind of interior radar. Nobody followed me from the apartment. And there weren't any other vehicles behind when I got out on MacDougal."

"Are you sure no one knew you were going to see him tonight?"

"Only my P.I. and me."

"So it was just some roving nutcase? That's better than if the attack was really meant for you."

I was about to agree, when I remembered something disturbing.

Nancy saw the changed expression on my face. "What?"

"I wrote Bobby Novello's name, address, and the time of our appointment on my desk calendar. Betty's not always at her desk to keep people out of my office . . . Anyone who was on the twenty-sixth floor could have come in, seen the notation and known where I'd be."

"So somebody you know—work with—could have been responsible. Oh, God . . ."

"I hate that thought, too."

"What are we going to do?" Nancy asked. I loved her for that "we."

"Call Bobby."

It was after one, but he hadn't gone to bed yet. When I finished telling him what I suspected, he said, "Sounds like you work in a nest of vipers."

"Vipers—that reminds me. I forgot to tell you that a few weeks ago somebody sent me a live rattlesnake." Briefly, I related *that* story.

"I am *definitely* not charging you enough," Bobby said.

I hung up the phone, said goodnight to Nancy and turned off the lights.

Even though we both needed the sleep, Nancy woke me up every hour, checking to see if I was still all right.

Chapter 35

MONDAY MORNING, WHEN I realized that I was dawdling over coffee, and had just read the entire police blotter column in the *New York Post* for the second time, I had to admit to myself that I was stalling. For the first time since I joined the *Love of My Life* family five years ago, I wasn't eager to get to work.

I was afraid that when I stepped off the elevator, I would assess every expression on every face, search every pair of eyes, looking for a telltale flicker of guilt, because I believed that a person who worked there had seen my calendar and seized the opportunity to threaten me. I chided myself for being idiotic. The idea that I could discover who was behind the attack by scanning faces was absurd. Recognizing that yanked me out of my paralyzing funk.

* * *

TOMMY ZENOS LOOKED up from his side of our partners' desk and greeted me with a scowl.

"I just got off the phone with Lori Cole," he said.

I glanced at my watch. "It's three hours earlier in California. She called you before five-thirty in the morning, her time? What's the problem?"

Tommy picked up the large box of donuts next to his elbow and passed it to me. Half of the donuts were gone, but my favorite, a warm chocolate cruller, remained. When I bit into it, the dough was so light it practically dissolved on my tongue. "Okay, I'm sitting down and I've had some tranquilizing carbohydrates, tell me."

"She wants us to put two new characters into the story—a vampire and an angel."

"What!" I shot up to a standing position.

Tommy quickly offered me another donut, but I waved the box away.

"That's a terrible idea." I sat down again. "Vampires and angels are absolutely wrong for *Love of My Life*. Our appeal is in the flawed humanity and the vulnerability of our characters. It's the complication-filled love stories and the mystery stories that keep people tuning in—"

"You're preaching to the choir," Tommy said. "When you get to Los Angeles you'll have to talk her out of it."

"What do you meant—when *I* get to L.A.? Aren't you coming, too?"

He shook his head. "Wish I could, but I realized that with episodes taping here every day, we can't both be out of town. And if there's any emergency rewriting to be done, you're the one to do it. We're the perfect team: you steer the boat while I keep it afloat."

I had to agree that he was right. "But I'll miss your company," I said.

"Thanks, I'll miss you, too." His voice took on that familiar sing-song quality. "I've got a little surprise." He removed a photograph from the top drawer of his desk and handed it to me. "What do you think of this?"

It was a four-by-five-inch color picture of a house that was similar in style to Spanish, but more open and with larger windows. Two stories, cream stucco exterior, a pale terra cotta tile roof "It's pretty. But why am I looking at it?"

"It's Rocky Castaneda's Mediterranean villa," he said, mentioning the name of a boyhood friend of his who had become an international movie star in action pictures. "I borrowed it for you, for the five days you'll be in L.A."

"Borrowed it?"

"Rocky's in Spain, shooting some big Bible epic with a French director and an Italian crew. He was renting his house to an actor who was out there making an HBO series, but they've finished up, so the house is empty. Rocky'll be back in a couple of weeks. There isn't time to rent it to somebody else."

I studied the picture, then did a quick tally in my head. "It's a beautiful house, but it looks too small to accommodate all of us."

"Forget *all of us*," Tommy said. "It's just for you. I've made arrangements for the actors, the director, and the others to stay at the Crown Colony Hotel. It's a few blocks from the studio, and it's fabulous. Two super size pools, six tennis courts, a huge gym, a spa with masseuses, or masseurs, or whatever. Anyway, it's got the works. They'll love it. Johnny Isaac wanted to take a suite for himself and Cybelle at the Bel Air Hotel, but I vetoed that." Tommy's face took on his naughty-little-boy expression. "I told him that if they stayed at the Bel Air, it would make the others jealous and they might take their resentment out on Cybelle." Tommy grinned. "I can get Johnny to agree to practically anything if he thinks it's good for Cybelle."

"Tommy, I really appreciate your thoughtfulness, but shouldn't I be at the hotel too?"

"Absolutely not. Somebody would be bothering you every fifteen minutes. Joel Davies will be there. As unit production manager, he can keep everybody in line. He'll be the only one who'll know how to reach you when you're not on the set, in case of an emergency."

"It seems as though you've thought of everything."

"Organization, making deals, hiring the right people—those are *my* talents," he said proudly. Then his tone became somber. "But I'm not much good at handling difficult people, like Lori Cole."

And your tyrant father.

"Oh—I almost forgot to tell you the juicy news."

"I hope it's not about me," I said wryly.

"You? Oh, no. You're dull. This is about Lori Cole."

"What's she doing?"

"It's more like *who* she's doing, although I guess, in this case, the *who* and the *what* go hand in hand. Or blank in blank," he said. "I don't want to be vulgar, so you fill in the blanks with the relevant body parts."

"Tommy, you're making me crazy. Details, please."

He was positively chortling. "She's fallen for an *actor*."

"Anyone we know?"

"Nobody we ever heard of. She *discovered* him—wink, wink, nudge, nudge—in an Equity waiver production. She's got the hots for him, so she's thinking up new characters, like this vampire-angel thing, to make him a TV star, on our backs." Tommy reached into his desk and took out a candy bar. "I know you'll find a way to save the show."

Chapter 36

BEFORE I LEFT for the airport on Saturday, I called Bobby Novello. "I'm going to be in Los Angeles until Friday," I said, "but you can reach me on my cell phone any time."

"I'll be out of town for a few days myself, on your case."

"Sounds encouraging. What have you found out?"

His tone was cautious. "I'm following an interesting trail, but I don't want to talk about it until I have something concrete for you."

AFTER GETTING THROUGH the long process of security checks at JFK, the trip to Los Angeles was uneventful. That's exactly how I want a flight to be. I like my excitement on the ground.

Tommy told me he'd have a car meet me at LAX. As promised, a barrel-chested man in a white shirt, dark tie, dark jacket and slacks, and a chauffeur's cap waited at Baggage Claim, holding a white sign that said "Tyler."

I waved to him and introduced myself. He told me his name was Hugh and took my tote and my carry-on duffle bag.

"This is all my luggage."

"Smart," he said, nodding toward the growing crowd around the baggage carousels.

On the sidewalk outside the terminal, it was a warm, sunny afternoon. I inhaled my first breath of California air, and guessed that the temperature on this tenth day of December was in the high seventies. I took off my suede blazer, glad I'd worn a silk shirt underneath instead of a sweater.

Shortly after we left New York, I'd set my watch back three hours. I was already on West Coast time when I glanced at my wrist and saw that it was three in the afternoon. Back in New York it was six in the evening, dark and cold. People with fireplaces would be lighting fires in them.

"If you'll wait here, ma'am, I'll bring the car around."

"I'll walk with you," I said. "I need to stretch my legs."

The car was a black limo, so clean it seemed to dare any speck of dust to land on its pristine surface.

Hugh stowed my two small bags in the trunk and opened the rear door for me.

"Do you have the address where we're going?"

"Yes, ma'am. Eleven four oh three Mulholland Drive."

"This is my first time in California. I'm curious about Beverly Hills. I'd like to see it, in case I ever need to write about it. Would it be out of the way to drive through?"

"You're the boss, ma'am. If that's the way you want to go, that's how we'll go."

Saturday afternoon traffic moved swiftly along the freeway. While there was no attractive scenery to view through the car window, at least it didn't take very long to get from the airport to the point when Hugh announced, "This is the beginning of Beverly Hills. It's only five square miles, so I'll go up and down some streets to give you a look."

My first impression of residential Beverly Hills was that most of the houses were enormous, and had been designed by architects who not only wore blinders, but who never spoke to each other. Sprawling Spanish haciendas were jammed to their property lines against enormous pseudo-Tudors, which reached to the borders of bloated French Chateaux. Next to these were replicas of Margaret Mitchell's Tara and Middle Eastern palaces. As we cruised through wide, immaculate, palm tree-lined streets, it appeared that each property owner had constructed according to his personal desires, without consideration given to the neighborhood's visual harmony.

Hugh gestured toward a line of incompatible mansions and dryly repeated an old joke, "Goes to show what God could do if he had money."

We reached the business district of Beverly Hills, a several-block grid that ran north-south and east-west. Christmas lights and decorations were everywhere. Rodeo Drive, the premier street of expensive stores, swarmed with shoppers wearing casual slacks and shorts, tee shirts and sunglasses. They carried packages wrapped in Christmas paper, or bulging shopping bags decorated with reindeer, elves, and smiling faces of Santa Claus.

Christmas would be here in only fifteen days and I

hadn't thought about the holiday yet. I promised myself I'd
start making lists of things to do and gifts to buy.

There were several new people in my life to shop for, in
particular Penny Cavanaugh, Matt Phoenix, and Chet
Thompson. I looked forward to finding presents for Nancy
and Penny; that would be easy. But what should I do about
Matt and Chet? It was a delicate matter, choosing presents
for a man with whom there was the possibility of romance.
The first gift shouldn't be too personal, but it shouldn't be
too *impersonal*, either. Part of the difficulty was that I
wasn't sure what messages I wanted my presents to con-
vey. After five years of having no romance in my life, now
there was the possibility of *two*. I refused to think that
there might be *three*. Admittedly, I was attracted to the
mystery man, but I put those feelings into the category of
fantasy. When I committed myself to a real romance, I
wanted more than just the initial excitement. I couldn't picture myself going to the movies with Abacasas, or shopping for lamps—normal things. He was surrounded by a
wall of secrets. I leaned forward and said, "I've seen
enough."

"Yes, ma'am."

He turned left at the next street and headed north on
Beverly Drive. In a few minutes, we passed the palatial
Beverly Hills Hotel on Sunset Boulevard. Further up Beverly Drive the street curved, narrowed, and flowed into
Coldwater Canyon. The houses along Coldwater were
mostly large, too, but unlike those I'd seen between Sunset
and Santa Monica Boulevards, these were older, set further
back from the street, and had much more space between
them. They looked like *homes* instead of monuments.

Deeper into the canyon, the houses were smaller. Some
were balanced precariously on stilts overhanging the road,

which was now twisting into serpentine curves. This stretch of Coldwater had narrowed to one scant lane in each direction. Because the series of blind curves prevented drivers from seeing what was coming, there was no way that one car could safely pass another.

At the top of the canyon, Hugh turned right onto Mulholland Drive. Mulholland was as narrow as upper Coldwater, virtually a country road. On one side were banks of rock and ground cover, alternating with steep paved driveways leading to elegant houses.

On the other side was a sheer drop, so sharp and perilous that it made my insides clench the first time I looked down. Hugh was a skillful driver, and was piloting a heavy vehicle that hugged the road. Soon I was confident enough to enjoy the spectacular view into the San Fernando Valley below. Way below.

Number 11403 Mulholland was set high, and far enough back on the property that I saw only a corner of the house from the road below. Mercifully, the driveway had been graded into a gentle slope, instead of being virtually perpendicular as were many we'd passed.

That was comforting, because a Global loaner car waited for me at the house, and I would have to drive myself to and from the film studio along an unfamiliar route.

According to the plans we'd made in New York, Jim Hudson, Olympic Pictures' production facilities man, would meet me at the studio's main gate at eleven o'clock on Sunday morning. We would go over the sets and the locations and make whatever changes might be necessary before filming on Monday.

Our group would arrive in Los Angeles early Sunday afternoon, and I'd meet them at the Crown Colony Hotel after my trip to the studio, to help Joel Davies get everyone settled, and to distribute Monday's schedule. They already had script pages for the scenes we'd be shooting.

Link, Cybelle, Francie, Rod, and the three actors playing the Bad Guys would be made up, their hair done and their costumes donned in a suite Tommy had reserved at the hotel for that purpose. Our own makeup, hair, and costume team was necessary so that the California shots would match what would be taped in New York. Once the actors got inside Olympic's studio gates, camera ready, any necessary touching up of hair and makeup, and any changes of costume would be handled by studio people. Our hair, makeup, and costume team could amuse themselves during the day at the lavish hotel facilities, or by using the bundle of tickets Tommy had provided to the Universal Tour, and for a VIP excursion to Disneyland. Thanks to Tommy, everybody was happy.

Hugh glided the limo up the driveway and came to a stop at the entrance to Rocky Castaneda's Mediterranean villa. The basic lines of the house were simple, but graceful. The cream stucco façade was framed by great bursts of trellised scarlet bougainvillea. Their spectacular blooms climbed up and spilled over onto the roof of terra cotta tiles. Extending from both sides of the house and going to the back was a six-foot high fence made of heavy boards, which made it impossible to see anything behind the house.

Hugh removed my bags from the trunk and carried them to the massive oak front door. Before I could ring the bell, the door opened and a short, dark-skinned woman greeted me cheerfully. She was somewhere in middle age, attractive and dignified. Her dark hair, streaked with gray, was swept up to the top of her head and secured by a silver comb. She introduced herself as the housekeeper, Lupe Gonzales.

Hugh put my tote and duffle down just inside the door.

"Do you have anything for me to sign?" I asked him.

"No, ma'am. All taken care of."

I handed Hugh a twenty dollar bill. He thanked me, pocketed it and took a folded sheet of paper from inside his jacket. "This is a page from the Thomas Guide," he said. He indicated a particular spot. "The circle—this is where we are right now." He used his finger to trace an already highlighted route. "And this is how you get to the studio from here. It's a short ride, ten minutes."

"Seems simple. Thanks again."

"Part of my instructions." He handed me his card. "I'm supposed to pick you up at six o'clock Friday morning to go to the airport. If there's any change in plans, call me at this number." He gave me a sprightly salute and left.

Lupe reached for my bags, but I stopped her. "Don't bother, I'll take them."

She insisted that it was her job, so we compromised; each of us took one light bag. She led me through the cool interior of the house to the master bedroom and opened one panel in a wall of mirrors, exposing an empty closet. More room than I needed for the few things I'd brought with me.

Lupe conducted a tour of the house, showing me which switches controlled which lights, instructing me on how to use the Jacuzzi, and explaining the intricacies of other amenities that I wouldn't have time to enjoy.

When we got to the security system, she pointed out a special feature in the master bedroom. "With the gate and the house secured, there is a bypass switch here." She pointed to a small rectangle set into the wall, next to the bathroom door. "That switch allows you to open the bedroom doors to the patio while every other part of the protection system remains in place. Mr. Castaneda is very proud of this," she said in an admiring tone. "He helped to develop the bypass."

"I'm impressed," I said.

"Shall I come in tomorrow, Miss?"

"Sunday? No, Lupe. Please, stay home. I'll be fine."

She smiled, seeming relieved. "Are you going out tonight, Miss?"

I told her no, that I'd be staying in.

"Then I'll turn the security system on when I leave," she said.

Chapter 37

AFTER I'D UNPACKED and gotten myself settled, I called Tommy to tell him what a great house he'd borrowed.

"Oh, expect a call from an Yvette something-or-other. I couldn't understand her last name. She's a reporter for *Paris Match*. We're doing so well in France she wants to interview you. I gave her the phone number at the house."

"Okay. Do you want me to let her watch any filming?"

Tommy thought for a moment. "Use your judgment. If she's a fan, that might be good. But stay with her if she talks to Link or Cybelle. Or Francie. Try to get her excited about Rod. We could use some advance buzz on him."

"Got it."

We talked for nearly an hour, going over upcoming shows and story lines.

When we finished, I poured myself a glass of fresh orange juice from a pitcher Lupe had left, went back to the master bedroom and flopped onto the king size bed. It was eight o'clock. Eleven in New York; Nancy would still be up. I dialed her number.

In answer to her hello, I said, "I'm in a movie star's bed."

"Knowing you, either the movie star is a dog or a cat, or if it's a man, he's someplace else."

"He's in Spain, earning a few million dollars. You must think what Tommy does—that I'm dull."

"He doesn't know you as well as I do." I heard the smile in her voice. "Good flight? Nice house?"

"Any flight that lands in one piece is good. The house is beautiful. Not too big, not gaudy." I reached for a colorful folder on the nightstand. "The actor who owns the place rents it out regularly. I'll read you highlights from the brochure his realtor made." I sat up and leaned closer to the bedside lamp. " 'Three bedrooms, three and a half baths, eight-foot doors, eighteenth-century tiles, three limestone fireplaces. Four thousand square feet of magnificent appointments, on nearly an acre of parklike grounds. Idyllic landscape features a lagoon-style pool with cascading waterfall, and a garden filled with prize-winning roses. The breathtaking great room brings the outdoors in by floor-to-ceiling glass doors.' "

"What's a 'great room'?"

"It looked like a living room to me," I said, "but what do I know? This is my first time in a movie star's villa. Oh, there's an upstairs, too, but it's sealed off. The housekeeper says he uses it for storage."

"Sounds suspicious," Nancy said teasingly. "Maybe he keeps his mad wife locked up there. Or the mummified body of someone from his past, someone whose footsteps you'll hear shuffling piteously above your head just before dawn."

"Thanks a lot. Remind me never to talk to you before I go to sleep in a strange place. And for your information, footsteps can't be 'piteous.'"

Nancy told me about Arnold's latest legal triumph, and about a new case of her own. "My client had an oral agreement to buy a major sports team, but the other man's claiming there was no agreement. A 'he said / he said' with no witnesses. It's going to be tough to win this one, but I believe my client."

"Do you believe him *because* he's your client?"

"No, I really do believe his version of the story. He's used our firm for years, and he's always been honorable. The team owner's background is littered with people he's cheated, so for me this case is a mission."

"I almost feel sorry for the other side," I said, "Hurricane Nancy's heading for their shore."

After I told her that I'd call Monday evening to let her know how the shooting went, she joked, "Sleep well, sweetie. If you can . . ." I laughed and we said good night.

While it was only nine o'clock in California, my internal timekeeper insisted it was midnight. I didn't want to eat the shrimp salad Lupe had left for me in the refrigerator, even though it looked delicious. I didn't want to watch television, or read the new Carolyn Hart novel in my bag.

My clothes were rumpled, and my skin felt sticky with grit from the plane ride. I stripped off shirt and slacks and underwear, and put on the navy blue silk robe Tommy had given me just before I left for California.

"You're going to Hollywood," he'd said as I unwrapped the package from Dior. "In case there's an earthquake and you have to be evacuated in the middle of the night, I want you to look smart."

All I had planned to do was take a shower and fall into bed, but before she left, Lupe had opened the drapes across the French doors. Outside, beyond the tree-shaded patio, I saw moonlight shimmering on the dark surface of the pool. Faint little wisps of rising steam told me that the water was heated. An irresistible invitation. I flipped the security system's bypass switch and went outside.

Rocky Castaneda's rental brochure hadn't exaggerated. His pool did look like a lagoon: free form, and encircled by large, smooth stones. The waterfall at the far end wasn't cascading tonight. There must be a switch somewhere that activated it, but I didn't care enough to look. On one side of the pool was a life-size statue of a striding black jaguar, and on the other was an arbor. Inside the arbor, I made out the shape of a double chaise. Such a beautiful night. Maybe, after my swim, I'd pull the chaise out beside the pool and spend the night here. It had been years since I'd slept outdoors.

I dropped my robe onto the decking and stepped into the water, standing still for a moment to enjoy the sensation of the cool night air on my body and the warm water on my legs. A moment later, I plunged in, letting the liquid envelop me. With leisurely strokes, I swam the length of the pool and back again. As I moved through the water, the tensions of the past few weeks began to wash away. So peaceful, so nice to be all alone . . .

Suddenly, I wasn't alone anymore.

At the deep end of the pool, I looked up to see a man's shoes and pants.

Chapter 38

I GASPED, ACCIDENTALLY gulped a mouthful of water, and started coughing.

"I am so sorry!" It was too dark to see his face but I recognized the voice: melodic, with an accent difficult to identify. "I didn't mean to frighten you," Philippe Abacasas said.

I sputtered with anger. "How the hell did you *think* I'd react?"

He knelt at the edge of the pool. Moonlight sculpted his features, emphasizing his high cheekbones, his full lips, and the expression of concern on his face. "This was a foolish impulse. I apologize." He sounded sincere. "Tell me to leave and I will, immediately."

I had a better idea. Extending my right hand to him, I said, "Help me up, please?"

Philippe reached out—and took the bait. The moment I had a grip on his wrist, I *yanked*. Off balance, he tumbled forward into the pool and hit the water with a mighty splash. Fully dressed.

He emerged from beneath the water, laughing. That surprised me as much as his suddenly materializing out of the darkness.

"I deserved this . . . dunking," he said.

"You certainly did. What are you *doing* here?"

"I came to talk to you, where no one would see us together."

"That's a pretty lame excuse, if you're telling the truth."

In the moonlight, I saw him smile ruefully. "Sometimes the truth is not as believable as a well-crafted lie."

We swam side-by-side to the shallow end of the pool.

Philippe took off his wet jacket and tossed it onto the decking. His nearness was making me nervous. The water and the night covered my nakedness, but the fact remained that I was naked. I should have thought of that before I pulled him in with me.

"You are so beautiful . . ." He moved toward me, extending his hands, palms up. There was no menace in his gesture.

Drawn by the irresistible force of desire, I moved closer to him, and suddenly we were in each other's arms.

His first kiss was gentle, but I kissed him back with a passion that had been dormant five long years. I slipped my hands beneath his lightweight turtleneck shirt to help him out of it, and he threw it onto the deck. We were in each other's arms again, our naked torsos pressed against each other, kissing hungrily.

Philippe stepped out of the pool, slipped off the rest of his clothing and helped me out. Guiding me into the arbor and onto the chaise, he kissed my eyelids, my lips, and the hollow of my throat. Lying down beside me, he kissed and caressed my breasts as I moaned with pleasure. He was careful, moving slowly until my body welcomed him. I felt myself soaring, and exploding, and soaring again, lost in the magic of yearning and release. All of my senses had come back to life when, with a cry, he exploded, too.

We collapsed in each other's arms.

LATER, WHEN WE had rested, I asked how he knew where to find me.

"My secretary telephoned your office, posing as a writer from *Paris Match*. She asked to interview you this week, and was told you were going to be in Los Angeles, but your Mr. Zenos was eager to have international publicity. He told her where you would be staying."

"You have a devious secretary," I said. "What's her name, Miss Moneypenny?"

For a moment he didn't get my joke, then he remembered. "Ah, yes, Miss Moneypenny—from James Bond."

He got to his feet, held out his hand and helped me up from the chaise. He whispered, "That concludes the foreplay."

"If I had the strength, I'd laugh."

Together, we picked up his soaking clothes and spread them out on the chaise to dry, then, holding my hand, Philippe led me toward the open French doors into the bedroom. He stepped aside to let me enter, but he didn't follow me inside; instead, he stood, a dark silhouette, in the doorway. Gesturing toward the small bedside lamp, he said, "Turn that off, please. We will have enough light from the moon."

As I reached down to snap the switch, he came into the room, and I had a glimpse of his body. The burn scar that I'd noticed on his neck was matched by several other burn marks on his chest. Before I could ask a question, Philippe drew me into his arms and kissed me. I forgot everything except the thrill of his mouth on mine and of his hands caressing me.

We made love until the last of our energy was spent. I luxuriated in the glow of absolute contentment as we burrowed against each other. Even after hours in each other's arms, it seemed as though we still could not get close enough.

I thought Philippe was on the verge of sleep when he surprised me by asking, "The film star who owns this house—have you met him?"

"No. He's in Spain, making one of those sex and swords epics with thousands of people in sandals."

Philippe laughed quietly. "Your business—your *show* business—has done much good for the world."

"Is that a joke?"

"Not at all, my darling, it's a rather amusing fact. Filmmakers have kept Spain and its neighbors at peace since the end of World War Two by renting the Spanish Army to play in their big productions. In the cafes of Madrid and Seville, one can see Spanish soldiers reading your *Variety,* where once they studied books on war."

I snuggled closer to him. "That's an interesting theory. Do you have any others?"

"Many . . ."

I remembered something. "How in the world did you get into this house?"

With a smile in his voice, he said, "One of my skills."

I had experienced some of his other skills, and none of them involved a riding crop.

"Seriously, how did you? The alarm system is supposed to be state-of-the-art."

"It is little more than a toy." He gave a grunt of contempt. "I escaped from a place infinitely more secure than this."

I felt a stab of dread as I asked, "Were you in prison?"

"A sort of prison," he said carefully. "But not because I committed a crime." His voice was steady. "Do you believe me?"

"Yes." I did, but I could not give a rational explanation as to why.

"We should rest," he whispered, and cradled me in his arms. In a few moments his breathing became deep and regular. He was asleep.

I wanted to sleep, but then I remembered the puzzling scars on his chest. Old scars. Small, oval-shaped burn marks, spaced several inches apart . . .

With a sudden jolt, I realized the significance of what I had seen. There was nothing natural, nothing *accidental* about those scars. Philippe had been tortured. I held him tighter, and squeezed my eyes shut, forcing myself to push away hideous images. It took an enormous act of will but, finally, I was able to fall asleep.

MORNING LIGHT AWAKENED me. I stretched long and languidly, like a cat. A very happy cat. I awoke facing Rocky Castaneda's rose garden. The blooms looked even more spectacular than they had yesterday.

I turned carefully, so as not to awaken Philippe. I

wanted to watch him while he slept. I fantasized that he would sense my eyes on him, awaken, and that he would reach for me. . . .

Philippe was gone.

I looked out to the decking around the pool. His wet clothes were gone. I called his name, but there was no answer. I didn't really expect there to be; instinct told me that there would be none. The house felt empty.

On the pillow next to mine, which still bore the impression of Philippe's head, lay a small, slender leatherbound book: Shakespeare's *Sonnets*.

A large, fragrant, pale lavender Sterling rose—like those that grew in abundance along the edge of the patio off the bedroom—had been inserted about a third of the way into the book. It marked Sonnet 29. He'd put little black ink brackets around the first line, a middle line and the final two. I read:

{ When, in disgrace with fortune and men's eyes }
{ Haply, I think on thee }
{ For thy sweet love rememb'red such wealth brings
{ That then I scorn to change my state with kings. }

That's easy for you to say, I thought.

"Bastard!" I said aloud.

Philippe Abacasas had disappeared again.

I removed the rose and snapped the book closed. The urge to hit something was powerful, but nothing in the house except my clothes and my laptop belonged to me. I went into the bathroom to fill a glass with water for the rose, and glanced in the mirror. The woman who stared back at me had bed-tangled hair and lips slightly swollen from hours of kissing. Okay, let's keep this in perspective,

I said to myself. I'd spent a night engaged in the most magnificent lovemaking. That was a *good* thing . . . right? I shook my head violently to dislodge the memory of being in his arms. What a corny farewell stunt—leaving a rose inside a copy of the *Sonnets*. Yuck! And it was so *practiced*. He actually brought a copy with him! He could be driving around with a trunk full of *Sonnets*! He'd probably done this dozens of times before.

Maybe hundreds.

I wondered: did he always mark that same sonnet? Or did he choose a different sonnet for each woman? I had to make myself stop thinking about it. About Abacasas.

Unless . . . unless I thought of him as *medicine*. As the cure for having denied my sexuality for five years. That's what I would do.

I put the flower in the trash.

Chapter 39

AFTER TAKING A bath, washing my hair, dressing in khaki slacks, a cotton shirt, and Nikes, I made a pot of strong coffee and scrambled a couple of eggs. The phone rang.

"Welcome to the coast," said Lori Cole.

Still in a foul mood, I was tempted to tell her that the United States has *two* coasts—more, if you count all the places where water laps up against the Hawaiian Islands and Alaska.

But all I said was, "Thank you, Lori."

"I have the most wonderful treat for you," she said.

"That's what the Greeks told the King of Troy when they gave him that big wooden horse."

Her laugh was tentative. "Good one," she said without conviction. "Anyway, since you don't have plans for to-night, I'm taking you to the theater."

"How do you know I don't have plans?"

"I called Tommy."

Thanks, Tommy. "What play are we going to see?" I asked.

"*Uncle Vanya.*"

I wanted to scream. I hate that play!

"I'll meet you outside the Crown Colony at six-thirty. We'll take your car. I don't like to drive at night."

DURING BREAKFAST I'D memorized the route from the house to Olympic Pictures. With all of the twists along Mulholland, I didn't want to risk my life by checking Hugh's map while I was driving.

I took my blazer and shoulder bag from the closet. Because I doubted that I would have time to come back to the house and change for my evening with Lori, I grabbed a silk shirt, a pair of black twill stacks, and high-heeled ankle boots for a change of clothes.

Turning onto Mulholland from Rocky Castaneda's driveway was easier than I had thought it would be because there was no traffic. It was late Sunday morning and I had Mulholland all to myself.

The new white Saturn the network had left for me was an easy car to handle, but I was negotiating an unfamiliar, narrow, winding road, so I didn't allow myself the pleasure of looking at the view below. When I reached the turnoff from Mulholland and started down a broad avenue leading into the heart of the San Fernando Valley, I caught my first glimpse of the Olympic Pictures lot. An impressive sight.

The famous aerial photograph of the studio's hangarlike sound stages is the image of Hollywood to many moviegoers around the world. Even more so than Paramount's majestic DeMille Gate with its ornamental wrought iron curlicues. Hollywood legend has it that Olympic's founder, Rudolph Metz, insisted that a shot of the Olympic lot be in every picture the studio released, appropriate or not. In one movie filmed entirely on a desert island, the photo appeared on the front page of a newspaper that washed up onto the beach.

I saw a man standing just outside the studio's security gate, chatting with the guard on duty. In his late forties, medium height, lean build, with light brown hair cut military style, he wore faded jeans and a lightweight navy blue sweatshirt that bore the title of one of the studio's recent movies. He gave me a cheerful wave as I drove up, loped over to the Saturn's passenger side, opened the door and leaned in.

"Morgan Tyler?"

"Yes."

"Hi, I'm Jim Hudson." We exchanged friendly greetings as he climbed into the passenger seat. "I got you a drive-on pass," he said, slapping a yellow rectangle of paper onto the inside of the windshield. Glue on one end made it adhere to the glass. When Hudson signaled the guard, the gate swung open and I drove through.

"Speed limit is fifteen on the lot," he said.

I kept the car to fifteen.

"We'll have the place pretty much to ourselves this morning, except for routine maintenance. No shooting on Sundays, unless there's some catastrophic emergency." He rapped his knuckles on the plastic dashboard "Knock wood, we've been on a long lucky streak, catastrophe-wise."

"That's good," I said. Glancing around curiously, I asked, "How big is the lot?"

"Three hundred acres, and we use every inch of it.

We've got the biggest standing sets in the world, plus there's a five-acre jungle in the back which looks just like anything you'd find in the Philippines, and we've got a lake that's ten feet deep in the middle."

He pointed to the corner just beyond a motel-like structure with a weathered sign that said Sound Mixing. "Turn left there."

Following his instructions, I found myself cruising along a pretty little town square. Fanning out in two directions from the center statue of Benjamin Franklin and the fountain and the band shell, were tree-lined streets on which stood upper middle class houses, many bracketed by white picket fences. Red geraniums grew along paths to front doors, or sprouted from terra cotta pots and window boxes.

Romanticized, idealized Small Town, U.S.A. It was a mythical kingdom, where boys and girls pedaled their bikes safely down the streets, grandparents drank iced tea on porches, happy in retirement, mothers were nurturing, and fathers wise and kind. Children grew up to work hard, vote in every election, and never beat their own kids. Unfortunately, nothing was real. The buildings were false fronts, supported from behind by a skeletal frame of two by fours and steel braces.

When we reached the dock and I saw the riverboat, it was even better than the photographs. "It's really beautiful," I said.

Jim grinned with pride. "That's our *Mississippi Princess,* even though she'll never see the Mississippi."

The *Mississippi Princess* rose up from its waterline like royalty preening before her subjects. We spent three hours going over every inch of her, and another hour inspecting additional sets and props on Stage 14, one of the sound stages between Small Town, U.S.A. and the studio's permanent standing New York Street set.

Back at the lake where we'd left my car, I gave *Mississippi Princess* one last admiring look. "Our February sweeps scenes will be terrific," I said.

"Yeah . . . unless we get another big earthquake—or the boat sinks."

That got my attention. "Are either of those things likely?"

"Well, I wouldn't say *likely* . . ." He shrugged. "I was on a shoot down in Brazil—we'd built a whole village in a place where they hadn't had a flood in three hundred years. Suddenly there was this wall of water comin' at us. Swept everything away, and injured a bunch of extras and some of the crew."

"That's terrible!"

"One thing I learned during twenty years in the movie business: expect the unexpected."

Chapter 40

THE *LOVE OF My Life* group had arrived in Los Angeles and was settled comfortably into the Crown Colony by the time I reached the hotel to check on them. Unit Production Manager Joel Davies had preregistered everyone from New York, so all that was necessary when the hired cars pulled up to the entrance was for Joel to collect the keys at the desk and direct our team and the hotel porters to the assigned rooms.

Before I went into the building to look for Joel, I took a walk around the grounds. Tommy had not exaggerated the merits of the Crown Colony. With its tennis courts, spas, large, well-equipped gym, three restaurants, and two huge pools, the place was as comfortable as a fine resort.

I spotted Joel and Johnny Isaac sitting at a table beside one of the pools. The two men were a study in contrasts.

Joel, out of shape and seemingly indifferent about it, was lounging in rumpled swim trunks, enjoying a cold beer. Johnny was dressed in perfectly pressed slacks and a designer polo shirt, twirling the stem of a glass of white wine. This was the first time I'd seen Johnny in anything other than a suit or a sports jacket. His chest was hard and his arms tightly muscled; obviously, he'd not let himself deteriorate in the twenty years since he'd boxed professionally.

Johnny stood up politely when he saw me. Joel said, "Hi," but stayed slumped, his pale legs stretched out and crossed at the ankles.

"Hello, guys." I gestured for Johnny to sit back down as I slipped into a chair between them. "Everything okay?"

"Things are going so well it's making me nervous," Joel said. He leaned over to extract a page from a folder of papers on the table and handed it to me. "Here's a list of where everybody is." He rolled his eyes and said in amazement, "We've been here two hours and nobody's complained about their rooms. Never happened to me before."

"You did a good job arranging," Johnny told Joel.

"The sets and props are ready," I said. Scanning the list of room numbers, I saw that Johnny's room was next to Cybelle's—no surprise. Bud Collins had the room on the other side of Cybelle; I guessed that Johnny had managed that lineup with Joel, to keep Bud on bodyguard duty. Link Ramsey's room, I noted, was on a separate floor, between Francie James and Rod Amato.

"Any changes in tomorrow's schedule?" Joel asked.

"No, I can say with a sigh of relief. Hair and makeup should start here at seven A.M. Cybelle, Link, Francie, Rod, and the three baddies should be camera-ready for arrival at the studio by nine. Jim Hudson will be at the gate to meet you. I'll be on the set with his production people."

Joel nodded, finished his beer and burped discreetly. "We're screening an unreleased movie here tonight," he said. "Olympic sent a print over, with a projectionist. That should keep everybody entertained until I herd 'em off to beddy-bye."

I MADE THE rounds, finding everyone in our group and asking if they had everything they needed. Thanks to Joel, they did. When I got to Bud, he told me how much he appreciated my giving him a part.

"I've been working with an acting coach all week, so I can make something out of my lines," he said.

My heart sank. Bud's lines were: "Hey, look out!" and "I wouldn't do that if I was you," and "I bet you think that's funny." The *last* thing the producer or director of a daytime drama wants to hear is that an Under Five is going to "make something" out of his lines. We just want the actor to *say* them, not try for an Emmy with a part that's little more than visual.

I decided to let the director deal with Bud's line readings, if they were over the top. I had a night to forget behind me, and an evening of Lori Cole and *Uncle Vanya* ahead of me, and that was going to be tough enough.

LORI COLE WAS waiting for me at the hotel's entrance at six-thirty. In spite of the abundant California sunshine, she was as pale as she had been when I met her in New York a few weeks earlier.

"I can hardly wait for you to see this fabulous actor I've discovered," she said.

I gave her a tight-lipped grin.

The valet attendant brought the Saturn, and I tipped him while Lori climbed into the passenger seat. She started talking as soon as she'd strapped herself in.

"Do you know how many big stars came out of daytime TV? Meg Ryan, Julianne Moore, Kathleen Turner, Warren Beatty, Christopher Reeve, Brad Pitt, Marisa Tomei, Tom Selleck, Morgan Freeman—"

"Just tell me about the actor we're going to see tonight."

"He's playing Astrov," she said. "That's the idealistic doctor who comes to visit, between treating poor people and trying to save the forest. Sofya's secretly in love with him, but she's plain so he falls for Yelena, who's the beautiful young second wife of Sofya's boring father—"

"Careful, you'll spoil it for me," I said dryly. "Where's the theater?"

"Go up to Ventura, turn right and go south across Laurel Canyon. When we get to Hollywood Boulevard I'll direct you the rest of the way." She took a deep breath and plunged on. "Now, the actor you're going to see is Paul Magrew—awful name, but we can change it."

By the time I parked the car down the street from the theater entrance, I knew everything about Paul Magrew except how many of his teeth were capped.

Clearly, Lori Cole was obsessed with him, and I was about to step into an emotional minefield.

Uncle Vanya was being performed at a small, Equity-waiver theater called the Kings Road Playhouse, named after the street where it was located. The sign outside described the play as "a Russian drama of desperation." Inside that night, Vanya, Sofya, Astrov, and Yelena weren't the only ones who were desperate.

The production was as turgid as I had feared, but the one good thing about it was Lori's actor, Paul Magrew. He was attractive and charismatic, with a mesmerizing stage presence. According to his brief bio in the photocopied and stapled program, he was dedicating his performance "to God, to my mother, and to my special lady, Miss L." From the way Lori's eyes were shining as she watched him, it didn't take a master detective to figure out who "Miss L" might be.

HALF AN HOUR after the merciful end of *Uncle Vanya,* Lori, Paul, and I were having coffee at a crowded little café next door to the theater. I had just told Paul, sincerely, that I was impressed with his performance in what I euphemistically described as "a difficult role" when I heard the short beep from my cell phone that signaled someone had called me.

"Excuse me," I said, and turned the phone back on. I'd turned it off before the play began.

The message was from Bobby Novello.

"Hello, pretty lady," he'd said on my voice mail. "This is your own personal, private detective, calling to tell you that I'm back *and* I've got something really hot for you."

Glancing at my watch, I saw that it was nearly three A.M. in New York. *Damn.* I'd have to wait a few more hours before I could call him. I erased the message and slipped the phone back into my bag.

Lori was looking at me with impatience. "You were telling Paul how marvelous he was," she said.

Paul lowered his eyes and joked, "Aw, shucks, ma'am. You don't have to say that."

"Oh, she *meant* it," Lori said. "Morgan's notorious for speaking her mind, whether people want to hear what she has to say or not."

I ignored her and addressed Paul, "You are a very talented actor." I added with a smile, "When you were on stage I didn't want to run for the exit."

Paul leaned toward me across the table. Lowering his voice conspiratorially, he said, "Honestly? If I wasn't in it, it would take an electric cattle prod make me see *Uncle Vanya*."

"Kindred souls," I laughed and took a sip of espresso. I was enjoying this part of the evening until I heard Paul Magrew say:

"I'm really excited to be joining *Love of My Life*."

I nearly choked in mid-swallow.

Lori jumped in. "Morgan's just started creating the part, and that'll take a few weeks," she said. Under the table, I felt her press her knee against mine, signaling me to play along with her.

I jerked my knee away.

Paul frowned and his dark eyes narrowed. "Did I say the wrong thing?"

Not wanting to embarrass him, I said, "No, Paul. It's just that the introduction of new characters is a complicated business. Stories are planned months in advance."

"Months?" He looked stricken. I guessed that as a virtually unknown actor in Hollywood he might have been counting heavily on the income from landing a role in a series. My *Sensibility* overwhelmed my *Sense* and I heard myself saying, "Have your agent call me and we'll discuss timing. Perhaps he can squeeze another job in for you before we're ready to talk specifics." I said that because agents often find it easier to get work for an actor when they can say their client is about to get another job.

Paul's handsome features relaxed. Enthusiastically, he

signaled the waitress and asked her to bring me a fresh cup of espresso.

"No, thanks," I said. "I've got to go. Long day tomorrow." I glanced from Lori to Paul. "So, Lori, is Paul taking you home?"

"Uh . . ." He looked uncomfortable. "I've got to go see my mom," he said.

"I live in Encino," Lori told me. "That's not far from where you're staying, Morgan."

AT A LITTLE past midnight, Laurel Canyon was virtually deserted. Because I was furious at Lori, I was driving faster than the posted speed limit. Then I realized that fog was closing in. Laurel was narrow and winding—not a place to be reckless when my visibility was poor. I slowed down.

"Lori, how could you have unilaterally promised him a role on *Love?*"

There was not even a hint of contrition in her voice as she said, "Because, unlike *Love,* the soap we shoot out here isn't network-owned, so I didn't have any leverage, and because I couldn't talk that prick Alexander Zenos into putting Paul on any of *his* shows, and because our *Trauma Center's* ratings are heading south faster than college kids on spring break."

Her arrogance made me steam, but I wasn't too angry to realize that the situation had to be handled delicately.

While I was controlling my temper, Lori said, "Forget who found him. Paul will be great on the show. He could be a breakout star."

Thinking calmly now, I realized I could use what she wanted to solve a *worse* problem.

"I agree with you about Paul," I said, making my voice as warm and sweet as marshmallows in a cup of hot cocoa. "He's a real find. I'm upset because I hate to see us throw him away."

"What do you mean?"

"If we have Paul play a vampire or an angel he won't be able to stay on the show." I shook my head sadly. "Those parts are short-term stunts, and the actors who do them are pretty quickly forgotten. Paul's so talented, I would much rather have created a part that showcased him as a romantic hero, with long-run potential . . ." I sighed and let my voice trail off in an imitation of regret.

Lori leaped at the bait, as I leaned forward to peer through the thickening fog.

"Forget vampires and angels," she said. "My secretary, Lawrence, came up with that idea. He wants to be a writer, but I'll have to put a leash on him." Dismissing Lawrence's ambition as easily as she would have swatted a fly, Lori returned to her favorite subject. "What kind of character will you create for Paul?"

I was spared from having to make something up on the spot because a sudden, extreme brightness in the rearview mirror caused me to squint. Lori squirmed in her seat and shaded her eyes from the glare.

"What's that thing behind us trying to *do*?"

That "thing" was a wide-bodied black vehicle that looked to me like a Humvee. It had *six* headlights across the front, and all of them were on bright. I pressed down on the accelerator, but the Humvee roared up dangerously close behind us.

Lori grabbed the dashboard, her arms straight out, bracing herself. "Let him pass!"

Hoping he *would* pass us, I was already squeezing over

as far to the right as I could—brush that sprouted from the
rocky wall of the canyon scraped the passenger side of the
car. Luckily for Lori, her window was up.

BAM!

Instead of passing, the Humvee rammed my Saturn
from behind!

Lori screamed. I was jolted so hard the chest strap bit
into my skin. Jamming my foot on the accelerator, I sent
the Saturn shooting forward, putting a few precious yards
between us, but my burst of speed bought us only seconds.

BAM!

He rammed us again, harder this time. I tried to get a
look at the driver through the rearview mirror, but in the
foggy darkness it was impossible. The traffic light marking
the turnoff from Laurel onto Mulholland Drive was coming up. I stomped down on the accelerator and blew
through the red light. As I skidded onto Mulholland, I
prayed: *Please, please, let there be a cop here to catch me
running the red light!*

But no police siren came screaming out of the fog to
save us.

The wide-bodied monster ran the light too and he stayed
on our tail.

As I negotiated the tight, perilous curves of Mulholland,
I urged more speed from the Saturn. It was taking every
ounce of upper body strength I possessed to keep from losing control; I knew any miscalculation would send us flying over the edge into the valley below.

BAM! Another jolt from behind—this one even harder.
Lori screamed again, and covered her face with her hands.
I honked the horn furiously, desperate to attract attention
from anyone who might be awake in the houses along Mulholland. But they were set up high and back; there was lit-

tle likelihood I would be heard. I flipped on the hazard lights. Maybe someone would see them blinking and realize we needed help.

"Lori—cell phone, in my bag—call 911!"

She didn't respond, seeming too paralyzed with fear to move. There was no way I could use the phone; I needed both hands on the wheel just to keep us on the twisting road that felt so slippery beneath my tires.

Coldwater Canyon! If I can get to the Coldwater turnoff and turn left, then we've got a chance to get to the populated safety of Beverly Hills. . . .

I gripped the wheel hard. The Saturn was weaving and swaying as I forced it around Mulholland's dizzying curves. I had to put as much distance as possible between the Saturn and the Humvee.

Suddenly the six-eyed Colossus was gone—there were no lights behind us. A wild, irrational feeling of hope soared in my chest. *He's given up—we've escaped!*

Then the big black monster—headlights off—roared up behind us with the fury of a tornado. It smashed into us and the Saturn was air-born. Frantically—uselessly—I pumped the brakes as we sailed through the night, hurtling down, down, down into the canyon below.

Chapter 41

THE IMPACT OF the Saturn hitting the earth was so powerful the airbags exploded. I felt as though I'd been slammed in the chest with a two by four. It knocked the breath out of me and rocketed the back of my skull into the padded headrest. Painful as the blow was, the airbag kept me from going through the windshield, and the headrest probably saved me from a broken neck.

Even though we'd hit the ground, the car was still plummeting downhill, over bumps that thrust the top of our heads up dangerously close to the roof of the car. In those infinite seconds when I believed I might die, the only thought in my head was *It's too soon*.

A terrible jolt rattled my teeth as the earth disappeared beneath the left front wheel, sending the Saturn into a frightening tilt. I thought we were going to turn over, but, miraculously, we remained right side up. The car continued to bounce downhill until, at last, it smashed into a tree that brought us to stop.

Oh, God, thank you . . .

"Lori." My voice was little more than a whisper.

No answer.

Lori had strapped herself in with the seat beat. I knew she must still be in the passenger seat, but I couldn't see her because of the air bags, and the darkness. I was shaken, disoriented from the crash. My head throbbed and my ears were ringing. I couldn't see anything through the window except vague shapes that looked like bushes and boulders. I knew I had to get us out of the car.

Clearing my throat, I raised my voice. "Lori!"

Silence. And then something worse . . .

The smell of gasoline!

The gas tank must have ruptured. Any tiny spark could turn the car into an inferno, and there'd be no escape.

Determining that I could move my hands and legs, I fumbled for the catch that released the seat belt. With the fingers of my left hand, I found the unlock button and grabbed the door handle. I groaned with frustration when the door wouldn't open. Fighting the airbag pressing against my chest, I twisted in my seat enough so that I could use my left shoulder and both hands to push at the door. It gave a few inches. Grunting and shoving with all of my strength, I managed to force the door open far enough that I could squeeze out onto the hard ground.

Stones and brambles tore at my hands and clothes, but I ignored the pain and stumbled around the front of the car to the passenger side.

Through the window I saw that Lori was motionless, her eyes closed. Because the passenger side had landed at a higher angle, when I yanked at the door it opened. Leaning across Lori's body, pushing at the air bag with my right shoulder and elbow, I released the seat belt with my left hand.

The gasoline smell was stronger now.

I put my arms around Lori from behind, beneath her armpits, and locked the fingers of both my hands together over her chest. Backing up, I inched her forward, struggling to pull her from beneath the airbag. I was weak, and fighting waves of dizziness, but somehow I managed to drag her all the way out of the car. Just as I thought I didn't have the strength to get us even one more foot further away from danger, I saw the beam of a flashlight above us. The scraping of leather against rock and a shower of tiny stones signaled that someone was scrambling down the hill toward us.

"Hey! Hey!" A man shouted. "Hang on—I'm coming!"

"Over here," I yelled, even though I had no idea where "here" was. The sound of his voice gave me a fresh burst of strength, enough to drag Lori a few more feet away from the car.

The man's flashlight's beam hit my face.

"Morgan? Lori . . . Oh, my God."

It was Paul Magrew, disheveled from slipping and sliding down the ravine.

"Help me with her," I said. "I'm afraid the car's going to explode."

Paul thrust the flashlight into my hands and took Lori's body from me. He pressed two fingers under her jaw, just below her right ear, searching for a pulse.

"Is she alive?"

"Just barely," he said.

I swept the beam around until I found a reasonably flat

path that led off to the right. "This way," I called, lighting the ground for us.

Scrambling as fast as we could over the rough terrain, we managed to cover about twenty yards when I heard a tremendous explosion behind us and felt a searing flash of heat against my back as a huge fireball shot up into the night sky.

Paul got to his feet first. Carrying Lori, he yelled, "Run!"

We ran, hot bits of metal car falling around us.

I heard the sirens before I saw the whirling red lights of the police cars and paramedic vans that screeched to a stop on Mulholland, high above the burning Saturn.

I was almost giddy with relief. "Somebody must have heard the crash and called it in," I said.

"Me. I was behind the Hummer when it started ramming your car. I couldn't stop him with my little heap, so I called 911—and I got the license plate."

"Good work," I said.

I'm willing to bet that it was stolen.

While I flashed the light to signal the rescue team, Paul spoke urgently to Lori, promising her she would be all right, pleading with her to say something.

"She squeezed my hand!" he cried.

Silently, I gave thanks that Lori was alive.

THE NEAREST HOSPITAL turned out to be one of the best in Southern California: Providence St. Joseph's, in Burbank. Next door to NBC, it was known informally as Bob Hope's hospital because of the late comedy icon's generosity.

Paramedics rushed Lori's gurney through the doors to the Emergency entrance, with Paul and me close behind.

Immediately inside those double doors was an entry foyer, with the Admissions desk off to the left. Directly opposite the Admissions counter, framed by a waist high partition, was a small waiting room with chairs placed along the sides, facing a big screen television set.

A team of doctors—alerted by the medics about the patient they were bringing in—took over and whisked Lori's gurney through the closed door to the treatment rooms.

Paul tried to follow but a large uniformed security guard with kind eyes and a paternal manner gently urged him to wait.

I took Paul's arm, guided him to the chairs, and said, "We were lucky you came along."

Paul looked at the floor, then raised his eyes to meet mine.

"It wasn't *luck*—and I'm a stupid jerk," he said angrily. "If I'd had the guts to insist on taking Lori home, instead of pretending that we're not . . . you know—*together* . . . well, she might not be in there now. If we'd left a couple minutes sooner, or later, that Hummer might have picked on somebody else!"

I had the terrible feeling that the chase and our near-death smash up wasn't a random act of violence. And as irritating as Lori was, I doubted anyone was trying to murder her. That left one other likely target—me.

Paul interrupted my thoughts. "Are you okay?" he asked. "Shouldn't a doctor look at you?"

"I'm bruised and scratched in a thousand places," I said, "but I think my injuries are just superficial. Right now I've got calls to make."

Without thinking, I reached down for my handbag—and realized it wasn't there. My bag, with credit cards, ID, money, and my cell burned up with the car. Indicating the pay phones on the wall at the far side of the waiting area, I asked, "Do you have some change I can use?"

Paul emptied his pockets and gave me all of his coins.

My first call was to Joel Davies. I told him briefly what had happened, and asked him to come to the hospital to handle the paperwork for Lori's treatment. I also asked him to bring me some cash, and arrange for another rental car. He said he'd take care of everything.

In spite of the hour, my next call had to be to Tommy Zenos in New York. He sounded as though he'd been deep in sleep, but he snapped awake when he heard my voice.

"Morgan! What's wrong?"

I told him, and in the next second he was ready to spring into action. One of Tommy's best qualities is his ability to function in a crisis, as long as the crisis didn't involve his father, or the anger of someone who outranks him.

"The good news," I told him, "is that everything's set for shooting tomorrow."

"Will you be able to go to the studio?"

"I'm pretty roughed up, but fully functional. Unlike Lori."

"How bad off is she?"

"We haven't got the official word yet," I said, "but I heard the paramedics say that both her legs and her right arm are broken, and she may have internal injuries."

Tommy was silent for a long moment. I thought we'd been disconnected, but then I heard him sigh. "You know, the word might start to get around that you're a jinx."

"What?"

"Think about it, Morgan. This is the *second* VP of Daytime in a row who's been put out of commission when you've been involved."

"That's a stretch about as high as the Empire State Building."

I heard a chuckle on Tommy's end. "Instead of doing an executive search for the next Daytime head, maybe Yarborough should ask for volunteers."

"Tommy, will you tell him what's happened, and find out if Lori has any relatives we should notify? Oh, and in the morning have Betty report the destruction of my credit cards and arrange for new ones? There's a list of cards and card numbers taped underneath the top drawer of my desk. And ask her to let the DMV know I need a replacement driver's license."

My final call was to access the voice mail messages from my destroyed cell phone. There was only one, from Bobby Novello, telling me he was following a new lead and would be out of town for a few days.

I WENT BACK to Paul. At nearly two A.M. there were only three people awaiting medical attention: a mother and baby, and a man with a crude, blood-soaked bandage wrapped around his left hand. Paul was sitting on the chair closest to the reception desk. As soon as he saw me he stood up. I gestured him back down, and perched on the arm of the sofa next to his chair.

"I saw you go to the desk. Any news?" I asked.

"The lady told me an orthopedic surgeon took Lori to an operating room. They didn't even wait to do the paper work."

"A hospital with a heart," I said, impressed.

At that moment, Joel Davies, followed closely by Johnny Isaac, hurried in. They spoke at the same time.

"God, you look awful!" said Joel.

"What do you need?" said Johnny.

"I'm all right." Turning their attention away from me, I said, "This is Paul Magrew. He's a friend of Lori's who happened to come along just after the crash. Thanks to Paul, we got away from the car before it exploded."

Joel and Johnny shook hands with Paul. Joel squinted at him. "You look familiar."

"Paul's an actor. He's going to play a new role on our show," I said. "Joel, Lori's in surgery. Will you handle the admission forms and insurance information and all that?"

"Roger," he said. Before heading for the Admissions desk, he drew me aside, took a wad of cash out of his pocket and handed it to me. "Here's a thousand," he whispered. "Will that be enough until we get back to New York?"

"More than," I said. Production managers on location routinely have eight or ten thousand dollars with them—money to be used for bribes and payoffs, if an actor or a director gets into trouble. Cash slipped into the right hands can keep a film or TV show from being derailed by an artist's after-hours bad behavior. What isn't used goes back into an office safe when the company returns to home base, where it remains until the next crisis.

I glanced back at Paul and Johnny, who were talking to each other and not paying attention to us. "I suppose this incident will get into the papers?" I asked Joel.

"Two good-looking young women executives from Global Broadcasting run off the road and almost killed? The press will be all over it."

"Then put the focus on Paul Magrew's rescue of us. He's going to be on *Love*. Sell it as 'Actor's Real Life Heroics.'"

Joel nodded. "I like it." He reached into a jacket pocket and pulled out a cell phone. "Here's my spare," he said. "The number's taped to the back. Tomorrow I'll replace the one that got burned up in the car. You want the same number you had?"

"Yes, thanks."

He leaned closer to me. "Just tell old Yarborough how helpful I was, okay?" Giving me a quick wink, he hurried toward the Admissions desk.

I shook my head. How in the world was I going to put that sleeping-with-the chairman rumor to rest?

I returned to Johnny and Paul, and saw Johnny studying me critically. "Have you seen a doctor yet?" he asked.

Paul answered. "No, she hasn't."

"I'll fix that," Johnny said, and marched out of the waiting room, bypassing Admissions and pushing through a double door marked "Authorized Personnel Only."

"Where's he going?" Paul asked.

"To find a doctor and make him an offer he can't refuse," I joked.

In four minutes Johnny returned with a scowling man wearing a white lab coat. The photo badge clipped to his breast pocket identified him as Dr. Eugene Peskow. Johnny introduced him to me. Dr. Pescow's response was only a brief nod, but he ushered me into an examination room.

The hijacked doctor quickly determined what I tried to tell him—that there was nothing wrong with me that couldn't be fixed with a tetanus shot and about a gallon of stinging antiseptic.

"Your escape from serious injury is incredible," he said.

"I don't understand it."

"Some things just can't be explained," he said. "Why

does a tornado destroy a house, but leave the one next door standing? Be thankful you were the house next door."

LORI COLE WAS in the operating room until five A.M. When Dr. William Gaines, a handsome black man who introduced himself as Lori's orthopedic surgeon, finally came out to report to us, his prognosis was guarded.

"Ms. Cole suffered multiple fractures in her right arm. There's just a simple break in her left leg, but the bones in the right leg were shattered. We managed to save the leg, but she'll require more surgery later. Perhaps several more operations."

"What do you predict for her?" I asked.

"It'll take months of painful healing and a rigorous schedule of rehab therapy," he said, "but I *hope* that eventually she'll be able to walk again. Potentially more serious was the fact that we had to remove one of her kidneys."

"A person can live a healthy life with one kidney, can't they?" Paul asked. He seemed eager for any bit of good news.

"Many people do, if they're careful . . . In any event, Ms. Cole is in for a long and difficult recovery."

When we were alone again, Paul said, "Morgan, I guess I'm blowing my big chance, but I can't take that new part you're going to write."

"What?"

"One of my day jobs is working at a rehab center, assisting physical therapists. I don't want to go to New York if something I know how to do can help Lori."

This struggling actor was willing to give up a career-launching role . . . He was a better man than I'd given him credit for.

I gave Paul's hand a quick pat and said, "I'll delay creating that part until you can work in New York. Just give
me at least six weeks' notice so I can weave your character
into the story lines. In the meantime, I'll see what guest
spots the casting people can find for you on our shows that
film out here."

Before he could thank me for something that was much
less than what *he* was going to do, I said goodnight and
hurried outside to the car and driver that Joel had assigned
to take me home.

According to the dashboard clock, it was a little after
six o'clock Monday morning. We'd begin shooting at
Olympic Pictures in three hours.

Chapter 42

MY LACK OF serious injury was followed by another miracle: shooting the difficult riverboat scenes went *smoothly*. The footage I viewed every day was better than I'd dared to hope.

In fact, it was fabulous.

Rod Amato was a terrific match for Link Ramsey. Their scenes crackled with tension, but with a hint of camaraderie developing beneath the surface. Cybelle, whose beauty made the cinematographers look good, was appealing in her terror. She gave the best *gasp* of anyone in daytime drama. Francie James—definitely several pounds lighter—carried off her scenes with charm and wit. Her exchanges with Rod showcased their chemistry, and their ability to play comedic moments in the middle of drama.

Bud Collins proved to be not very promising. Fortunately, his part was so small his lack of talent didn't damage the scenes he was in.

As soon as I could leave the studio each evening, I visited Lori at the hospital. Whatever time I arrived, Paul was there.

Lori's room was filled with vases and baskets of flowers. The largest basket was four feet high and three feet wide. The personal note, pinned to the pink ribbons that encircled the arrangement, read, "Best Wishes for a speedy recovery. Winston Yarborough."

"From the size of this, you'd think you'd won the Kentucky Derby," I joked.

"These legs won't be running for a long time," Lori said weakly. A spasm of pain hit her hard. Paul winced with her, and squeezed her hand. "Do you want something for the pain?" he asked.

"It's too soon since the last one." She squinted at her bedside clock. "Sixty-seven more minutes until I can have the next dose. But who's counting?" She was barely able to manage a chuckle, but made a gallant try. I admired her for it. For the first time since we'd met, I liked her.

"Did they catch the bastard who almost killed us?" she asked.

I shook my head. "The police said the Hummer was stolen in North Hollywood, then abandoned in Burbank. No fingerprints."

THE FILMING OF our February sweeps scenes continued to go so well that we wrapped late Wednesday night instead of our scheduled Thursday afternoon.

Joel changed our airline reservations from Friday to Thursday, and all but three members of our group took the

noon plane back to New York. Johnny, Cybelle, and Bud
weren't traveling with us. Johnny had arranged for them to
fly back on the Olympic Pictures private jet, which left Los
Angeles early Thursday morning.

Joel had booked seats for the two of us in the first row,
where there was more room to stretch out his legs. He'd
put Rod and Link in seats next to emergency doors, "Because they're in the best shape to help out in case we
crash," he'd said.

Cheerful thought.

I'd never flown with Joel before; I hoped he wasn't a
talker, but I needn't have worried. As soon as he strapped
himself in, he took a pillow from the overhead compartment, propped it, and his head, against the window, told the
flight attendant that he didn't want anything to eat or drink,
and fell asleep.

I was too tired to sleep.

I replayed in my mind the scene on Mulholland Drive
with the two police officers who investigated the chase and
crack-up. They were convinced what happened to us was a
kid's prank that went too far. As "proof," they cited the
facts that the Hummer had been stolen in the area, and later
abandoned near where it had been taken.

"You didn't find any fingerprints in it. None at all," I
said. "Thoroughly wiping down a car doesn't sound to me
like the act of a kid."

There was some grumbling and shuffling of feet, but
they admitted that such caution wasn't typical of a joy-
riding or juiced-up teen.

"Then it was probably gang members," the older officer said.

"Is Mulholland Drive gang territory?" I asked skeptically.
They admitted gangs didn't usually run wild "in the

high rent district," as they referred to the area. In an attempt to comfort me, or maybe to shut me up, the younger officer said, "Well, Ms. Tyler, the attack couldn't have been *personal*. You haven't been in town long enough for somebody to want to kill you."

The flight attendant interrupted my musing to ask what I would like to drink. I chose coffee. I looked at my watch. Four more hours before we landed. I was impatient to find out what Bobby Novello had uncovered. I wanted to discuss it with Nancy, and if Bobby had turned up important evidence, with Matt Phoenix. *That* was not a conversation I was looking forward to.

I let my thoughts drift. Our scenes on the studio back lot had gone remarkably well. In spite of Bud Collins's inability to hit his mark until the third try, we finished early and under budget. Bud Collins . . . why was such an inexperienced actor represented by a top agent? It didn't make any sense. I closed my eyes and began to think of what motivation I would come up with if I wanted to explain why a character like Johnny Isaac would represent an inexperienced and untalented actor. Why would he accept him as a client? Did the Bud-character have rich parents who bribed the agent? No, this agent character already had plenty of money. Okay—then what does Johnny want that Bud might have? Nothing I could imagine.

Wait a minute, forget Bud.

What does Johnny Isaac want more than anything else in the known world?

The answer was so simple I could smack myself for not having seen it before: *Cybelle Carter*. Johnny would do anything for Cybelle. Suppose it was *Cybelle* who asked Johnny to represent Bud. Okay—but why would she do that? Maybe because he's an old school friend? Doubtful.

Because he once loaned her money? No, she would just have paid him back as soon as she was working. Then I remembered that Johnny, Cybelle, *and Bud* had celebrated Thanksgiving together. That's a family holiday, not a dinner to which a wildly-in-love man like Johnny would casually invite his good-looking young gofer-chauffeur-client, even if he was a temporary 'bodyguard.' Johnny wouldn't have included him without Cybelle's agreement, or her *request*. There's something special about Bud Collins, something special about him to Cybelle. . . .

What was Bud to Cybelle? Her *brother?* Bingo!

Now that I thought about it, and if I pictured Cybelle with her natural blonde hair, there was a family resemblance between her and Bud. Slight, but recognizable if one looked for it. All at once Philippe's voice was in my head, warning me to be careful of Cybelle's brother—Floyd Gilley—the young man he'd thought "was not quite right in the head."

IT WAS A little after nine P.M. EST when, as planned, Nancy met me outside the American Airlines baggage claim area at JFK International. I'd expected her to cluck-cluck over the bruise on my cheek and the scratches on my hands. Instead, she took one look at me in the bright airport lights and said, "You've had sex!"

My face flushed, and I almost dropped my luggage. Nancy grabbed my free hand and pulled me along, walking us briskly toward the parking garage.

"Don't try to deny it. I can tell," she said. "I'm thrilled, and I insist on *details*." She spotted her blue Mercedes and took the car key out of her bag. Bending over the lock, she asked, "So which one of your hunky guys went to Los Angeles? Matt or Chet?"

"None of the above."

Nancy froze, the car door half open. The smile vanished from her face. "You *wouldn't* have picked somebody up."

"Let's talk in the car."

I tossed my duffle over the back seat, climbed in next to Nancy, and put the tote that was doubling as my handbag on the floor next to my feet.

Nancy locked the doors and inserted the key into the ignition, but she didn't turn it. Instead, we sat, safe in her little steel cocoon.

"Tell me," she said.

And I did. Everything: Philippe Abacasas surprising me by suddenly appearing at the end of the pool, my pulling him into the water with all of his clothes on, how wonderful it felt to be in his arms, making love . . . and how furious I was when he vanished before I woke up.

"Boy, you do go to extremes," Nancy said. "I've been urging you to start dating—but with Abacasas you just skipped right over the dating part." She took a deep breath, frowned, and sat for a moment, thinking. "Okay, you got back on the horse, so to speak," she said. "But I watched you and Ian fall in love at warp speed. You were *lucky* that turned out so well; the odds were against it. What I'm saying is—don't think about marrying this mystery man just because you went to bed with him."

"This is the new me," I joked. "I take my pleasure, then toss 'em aside."

Nancy wasn't buying it. "Enjoy the experience for what it was: harmless fun. He's all fantasy, no future. But Matt and Chet are *real life*. I think that's why the idea of getting

serious with either one of them scares you. It scared you
into the arms of Abacasas. Your night with him was just the
bridge you had to cross to get back to reality."

I smiled. "It *was* a very well built bridge."

Nancy leaned back against the headrest. "I crossed a
few of those before I met Arnold," she said. "I can testify
that all those *structures* are pretty much the same. I don't
want to belabor this bridge analogy any more, except to
say that what counts is where it's going to take you." Suddenly she had a new thought. "I hope you used protection."

"No."

"Dumb! You could be pregnant."

"No, I can't be."

I heard frustration in her voice. "Sweetie, when Part A
is inserted into Slot B—"

"What I mean is—I can't have children."

For once in her life, my never-at-a-loss-for-words best
friend didn't know what to say. I saw the look of concern in
her eyes, and answered the question she didn't ask.

"There was an injury . . . when I was a child . . . I told
Ian before we were married, because I thought he wouldn't
want to marry me, but he said it didn't matter, that we'd be
traveling for years. One day, if we ever decided to settle
down, we could adopt."

Nancy leaned over and gave me a loving hug. "I'm so
sorry."

"It's okay," I said. I forced a smile to let her know that
I'd dealt with it. "Let's go."

Nancy nodded and started the car. As we exited the
garage, my cell phone rang. It was Bobby Novello, and he
sounded excited.

"How soon can you get here?" he wanted to know.

Chapter 43

NANCY AND I reached MacDougal Street thirty minutes later. She found a parking space a few doors down from Bobby's apartment building, locked the car and we hurried up the stairs to the entrance. I reached toward the bell, then saw to my surprise the security door was propped open with a telephone book. I looked at Nancy and she shrugged.

"He's in One B," I said, leading the way down the hall at a trot.

Bobby Novello's door stood open. The first thing I saw was that all of the bird cages were open—and empty. Nancy gasped and pointed to the floor between the desk and the couch. Bobby Novello was lying face down, the hair on the back of his head matted with blood.

"Oh, lord . . ." Nancy whispered.

Horrified, I fell to my knees next to Bobby.

I touched him gently on the side of his throat, under his chin. "He's still alive," I said, "but his pulse is very faint."

Nancy pulled out her cell phone and dialed 911.

At that moment I became aware of something on the floor that was digging into my left knee. I adjusted my position to see what I was kneeling on—and my breath caught in my throat. It was a very old silver coin, about the circumference of a half dollar, but twice as thick and not as perfectly round. The design on the side facing up was of an owl. I was willing to bet that this was one of the two ancient coins Philippe said had been stolen from him. My hand closed over it.

I shoved it into the pocket of my jacket just as I heard a man's heavy footsteps in the hallway. Chet's tall figure filled the doorway, an expression of shock on his face. "Good God! What happened?"

"We found him like this," I said. "The door was open, and the birds were gone."

Chet moved swiftly to stand beside me. "Is he breathing?"

"Just barely."

"I called for an ambulance," Nancy said. "And the police."

An envelope lying near Bobby's right hand caught my eye. It had my name on it, and had been torn open.

I leaned over to pick it up, but Nancy saw me, grabbed my arm and commanded, "Don't touch anything."

"You're right," I said, sitting back on my heels. "I wasn't thinking."

Chet bent down to get a closer look at the envelope. "I'm guessing Bobby's report to you was in it," he said.

The taste of bile rose in my throat. "Then it's *my* fault he's been hurt."

"This is the fault of whoever attacked him," Nancy said.

Chet agreed. "Bobby went into a dangerous business. He knew the risks."

"Don't talk about him in the past tense!" I said sharply.

We heard the scream of a siren racing in our direction. "I'll go guide them in," Nancy said.

Chet moved around to the far side of Bobby's desk. He gestured toward the empty cages and said, "I'll call the SPCA in the morning, and leave Bobby's name and my number in case they find any exotic birds."

I nodded in silent agreement as, directed by Nancy, paramedics came pounding into the room.

TWENTY MINUTES LATER, in the Emergency Room of St. Vincent's Hospital Manhattan, I signed a form guaranteeing to pay Bobby Novello's medical bills, in case he didn't have insurance. While Nancy sat with Chet in the waiting room, I made the phone call I most dreaded.

Matt picked up on the second ring. "Hello?"

"Hi, it's Morgan. I'm sorry to call so late."

"Eleven o'clock isn't late." He sounded happy to hear from me, but I knew that wouldn't last. "Did you just get back in town?"

"A couple of hours ago. I would have called earlier, but . . ."

"What's the matter? Are you okay?"

"Matt, a friend of mine—somebody I hired—has been injured. Attacked in his apartment on MacDougal Street."

"That's the Ninth Precinct. Do you want me to call—"

"We've already notified them. But you need to know

about this because the person who was hurt is a private detective I hired, after you told me Jeannie's murder was a cold case. I think he was attacked because of something he found out."

Silence on the other end of the line. An icy silence.

"Matt?"

All the warmth was gone from his voice. "Where are you?"

"At St. Vincent's Hospital Manhattan. One Seventy West Twelfth. We're in the Emergency Room waiting area."

He hung up without saying goodbye.

PLAINCLOTHES DETECTIVES WALLER (red-haired and thin, sallow complexion, and a smoker's cough) and Jones (blond buzz cut, ruddy skin, and a muscle-heavy torso) barely had time to learn our names when Matt and G. G. arrived.

In a stark reversal of their usual on-duty faces, G. G.'s expression was pleasant and Matt was the one who looked like he was suffering from an abscessed tooth. What might have been an awkward situation—detectives from the Twentieth Precinct showing up on a case in the Ninth Precinct's jurisdiction—was defused by G. G. Flynn, who turned out to be old friends with Detective Waller. From fragments of conversation I heard, it seemed they'd worked together a decade earlier. When G. G. promised to give Waller and Jones "the collar" if G. G. and Matt caught the person who attacked "the vic," the law enforcement quartet became buddies.

Then the "four horsemen" of my personal Apocalypse advanced on me.

"Let's hear your story," Matt said. He sounded as though he was talking to a stranger. My response was just as impersonal.

Because Matt and G.G. already knew the details of Jeannie's death, I confined my "story" to what I knew about Bobby Novello's investigation. It wasn't much. "On the telephone, he sounded as though he'd learned something important," I said, "but I don't know what it was."

"There's an envelope with Morgan's name on it, on the floor," Nancy said. "Torn open. We didn't touch it, but it looks as though there's nothing in it."

"We'll go over Novello's place, see if he has a copy in his files," Waller said.

"Bobby didn't make copies, or keep files," Chet told them.

Matt turned his glare on Chet. "How do you know that?"

"He's done some work for me in the past."

"So you're the one who told Morgan to hire Novello," Matt said accusingly.

"I didn't *tell* her to do anything."

"*No one* tells me what to do," I snapped. "You should know that."

"I did *recommend* him to Morgan," Chet said, "but she turned down my suggestion—out of loyalty to you, as a matter of fact."

Matt switched his glare to me. "I didn't know loyalty had an expiration date."

"Don't you talk to her like that," Nancy said angrily.

"It's all right. Matt has a right to be upset." Keeping my voice calm, I said to Matt, "I changed my mind about hiring the detective when you told me the case was on the back burner, unless you got new information."

Before he could respond, a man in green scrubs
emerged from the double doors leading to the treatment
area and came over to us. "I'm Doctor Kleiner," he said.
"Are you the people with Mr. Novello?"

"Yes," I said. "How is he?"

"I'll ask the questions," Detective Waller said. He
flashed his shield at the doctor. "How is he?"

"Mr. Novello's suffered a severe blow to the head.
We'll have a better idea of his condition when he regains
consciousness."

"When can we talk to him?" Matt asked.

"Perhaps in a few hours, but that's optimistic. It could
be considerably longer."

Detective Waller handed him his card. "Let us know as
soon as he's awake, okay?"

"May I see him?" I asked the doctor. "Just for a
minute?"

He looked sympathetic, but his voice was firm. "I'm
sorry, but I can't allow visitors right now. Check with me in
the morning, after eight."

IT WAS CLOSE to one in the morning when I climbed into
the passenger seat of Chet's Range Rover. He and Nancy
had parked their cars on Eleventh Street, just off Seventh
Avenue, less than a block from the hospital. After seeing
Nancy to her Mercedes, grabbing my luggage, and helping
me into the passenger seat, Chet climbed into the driver's
seat. He expelled a deep sigh and then said, "Hello, you."

"Hello," I said, leaning back against the headrest. Matt
was furious that I agreed to let Chet drive me home. Rather
than remember his awful glare, I asked, "What were you
and Waller and Jones talking about just before we left?"

"I asked them to go through Bobby's wallet and if he had a medical insurance card, to give it to the Admissions clerk."

"Oh, thanks."

"*Then* I asked them when their crime scene unit was going to Bobby's apartment. They said since this wasn't a homicide the techs would get to it sometime tomorrow. Waller told me they'd had the uniform cops seal the place and had the super lock the door." Chet leaned forward, put the key in the ignition and fired the motor. "So we're going back to Bobby's right now, while there's nobody to stop us."

"What? Why? Didn't you just say the place was locked?"

"Reach into my right hand jacket pocket and take out what you find."

I reached in. My fingers closed around keys. "These are Bobby's?"

"His spare set. He keeps them on a hook on the side of his desk," Chet said. "I grabbed them when I heard the paramedics coming."

"But what's the point? If he didn't make copies of his reports—"

"I told them Bobby doesn't keep files or dupes of client reports. And that's the truth. But Bobby *does* keep a copy of every report he makes to a client—on Beta videotapes."

"Are you kidding?"

"No. The labels are in code, so somebody looking at the tape titles won't know what they really are. He told me one night when we were drinking too much."

"This is great!"

"Well—maybe. He didn't tell me what the code was."

So that was our mission: code breaking. "I like puzzles," I said.

"So do I, or why would I want to spend time with *you*?"

The short drive back to MacDougal Street took less than five minutes. Chet parked around the corner, explaining, "In case anyone on the street or looking out a window might remember seeing this Range Rover that didn't belong in the neighborhood earlier and think its return was suspicious."

"Good idea."

"Do you have gloves?"

"Yes." I pulled them out of my jacket pocket.

"Put them on," he said. He took a pair of his own out of the Rover's side pocket and drew them over his hands.

Chet and I walked close together, with his arm around me, like a couple returning home from a night out.

In a matter of seconds, we'd unlocked the front security door and reached Apartment 1B. Chet bent down, inserted the key, pushed the door open and held the crime scene tape up far enough so that I could stoop under it. He followed me in and bolted the door. Before we turned on a light, I closed the drapes over the windows.

I looked at the large wall devoted entirely to Beta videotapes, all labeled with the titles of movies. Some included names of the film's stars or directors.

"You study the labels on that half," I said, gesturing to the right, "and I'll do this side." Chet nodded and started with the bottom row.

"Wait a minute," I said. "Bobby's short. Don't you think he might put something he wanted to hide—hide in plain sight—way up high? When people scan titles on shelves they usually do their looking at eye level. Traditional eye level," I said, indicating the middle shelves.

I pulled one of Bobby's step stools over to the shelves,

mounted it and started at the top of my section. Chet did the same.

So as not to miss a clue, I pulled each movie out of its case to examine it closely.

We'd been at it for twenty minutes when I saw something that looked a little bit off. "Chet, did you ever see an old movie called *The Guns of Navarone*?"

"It's one of my favorites," he said. "Why?"

"Starring Gregory Peck, David Niven, and Anthony Quinn?"

"Yeah."

"Directed by C. Lee Thompson?"

"No, that's wrong—it was *J*. Lee Thompson."

"That's it!" I said, climbing down with the tape in my hand. "*C* Thompson. Maybe that's his code for Chet Thompson. You said he did some work for you."

Chet slipped the tape into the machine and pushed "Play." Instead of the opening scene of *The Guns of Navarone* we saw Bobby Novello, sitting at his desk and looking into the camera. Before he'd said more than identifying the tape as a report to Chet Thompson, I said, "That's enough." I pushed "Stop" and then "Eject." "We broke the code!"

I handed the tape to Chet and climbed back onto the stool. "Let's see if he used some form of my name, or the name of the show."

A few minutes later Chet, with a video in his hand, asked, "Did you ever see *Bonnie and Clyde*?"

"Sure."

"Did you see the version starring Warren Beatty, Faye Dunaway, and *Morgan Freeman*?"

"Give me that!"

We descended simultaneously and Chet inserted the tape and pushed "Play."

Bobby's face came on the screen. "Miss Morgan," he said, "I've got good news, and I've got bad news . . ."

Chapter 44

"FIRST, THE GOOD news," said Bobby's electronic image. "You can keep Link Ramsey on your show. I understand why he was nervous, because he *does* have a secret, but it's not one of the ones you told me would make you fire him, so, as you instructed, I'm not going to tell you what he's hiding."

Out of the corner of my eye, I saw Chet smiling.

"Next, about Jeannie Ford," Bobby said. "As far as her murder is concerned, the boyfriend's alibi is solid, so he's out of it. I was able to track down her mother and got a lot of background on Jeannie. It's not particularly interesting—except for these bits: you think that Jeannie Ford and Cybelle Carter met when you hired Jeannie. Not true. They knew each other at least casually for a couple of years before you hired her to double Cybelle. They met in the act-

ing class Cybelle took a few months before she was hired
to play Kira.

"Also, you think the plan for Jeannie to sleep at Cybelle's apartment was made the day they were together on
the location shoot in Astoria. Not so. According to Jeannie's mother, they'd planned several days earlier for Jeannie to be at Cybelle's that night. I don't know how relevant
these bits are, but you were lied to.

"Now, for the juicy stuff, but this is the bad news. Bad for
your show. If you're in my office when you're reading my
report, I'll make sure you're sitting down before you read
this next part. While you get to keep Link Ramsey, you're
probably going to lose Cybelle Carter, unless she hires herself a good criminal lawyer. I spent a couple of weeks in
Georgia, South Carolina, Tennessee, and Texas—for which
I'm charging you double per diem because the food was so
bad." He flashed a devilish little smile as he said that. "But I
learned a lot. Sara and Floyd Gilley were born in Lofton,
Tennessee, not in Thomasville, Georgia as Cybelle claims.
The brother's two-years older. Lofton's a little town. Barely
even a town, in the poorest section of the state. Sara and
Floyd's mother died of pneumonia when the kids were pre-
teen. It wasn't a secret that their father was a violently abusive alcoholic, but nobody did anything to get the kids away.

"One night when Sara was fourteen and Floyd was sixteen, the father was found crushed to death under an old
car he was repairing. From marks on the ground, the sheriff suspected somebody had pulled away the jack that was
holding up the car, but there was no way to prove it, and the
kids vanished before the body was discovered. In addition
to the marks on the ground, another thing the sheriff found
curious was the fact that, there wasn't even a dime on the
dresser in their shack, in spite of the fact that Gilley

bragged about having a hidden nest egg. Since nobody seemed sorry that Gilley was dead, the event was labeled 'accidental death.' Case closed. I talked to the sheriff. He's retired now, but he remembered the event clearly. He told me he figured the kids had taken old Gilley's money, and they were entitled, considering the hell everybody knew that drunken s.o.b. put them through."

Bobby paused to take a sip of orange juice. "I traced the kids from Tennessee to Georgia to South Carolina. Now Sara was sixteen but passing for eighteen, blonde, and gorgeous. Calling herself Sharon Marie Bowie. Brother Floyd was going by Jim Bowie—like the guy who invented the Bowie knife and died at the Alamo. Anyway, they did odd jobs to survive, until Sara met a rich man in his late seventies, Clayton Anders. In a few weeks, she was Mrs. Anders. They hadn't been married even two months when Anders died. Boating accident, the young widow said. She and her brother and Anders had been sailing on a lake in Anders's boat when he 'fell overboard and drowned,' according to Sara. When the body was recovered, the coroner found it had a bash on its skull. Sara claimed his head must have hit the bottom of the boat. There was no way to prove it happened differently—and Sara was a very appealing figure in her grief. She might have become a rich widow, except that Clayton Anders had pulled a fast one. He turned out to be a dirty old man who lied to Sara about being long divorced. The truth was he was still married, just separated for a decade. The *real* widow made a stink to the authorities, claiming her husband had been murdered. She shut up when Sara and Floyd disappeared and the legal Mrs. Anders collected old Clayton's money."

"Whew!" Chet said. "That's enough material for your show for the next couple of years."

Bobby took another sip of juice and went on. "I traced the kids—I'd come to think of them as Bonnie and Clyde junior—to Texas. Four years ago they lighted in Houston, where Sara, who was now eighteen, got a job as a waitress and met another rich man. That Philippe Abacasas you asked me to check out. I'll get to him in a minute. First I want to tell you that I found a drinking pal of Floyd's who claimed Floyd told him that he and his sister were about to get rich because she was going to marry a really old millionaire who was dying. Floyd told him that when they had money no one could ever hurt them again. 'People with money are safe,' is what Floyd said.

"Floyd lied to his pal. Abacasas wasn't even forty when he met Sara and Floyd, and he was *healthy*. My guess is that brother and sister were planning to change that. The kids had been lucky in that they hadn't had to pay for anything they'd done—presuming that they did kill dear old dad and rich husband number one—but they aren't rocket scientists. When Sara married Abacasas, she and Floyd didn't know anything about him except that he was rich. But it seems he's one dangerous dude who has guards near him all the time.

"This next part is just my guess, but I think Sara discovered Abacasas wasn't going to be easy to kill, so she ran away from him, taking the presents of jewelry and money he'd given her. To bring the story up to date: brother and sister showed up in New York about two and a half years ago. Now Sara was a brunette calling herself Cybelle Carter who said she was an actress. At an audition, she met an important agent, Johnny Isaac. The word is he fell for her and took her under his wing, so to speak. He even hired her brother, who was now going by the name of Bud Collins, to work in his office and to drive for him.

"I ran a Dun and Bradstreet on Isaac. His net worth is

between ten and fifteen million. Professionally, even his competitors regard him as the smartest man in whatever room he's in. If his libido causes his I.Q. to short circuit and he marries her, your actress might finally end up a rich widow before she's twenty-five. Last week, Isaac started trying to arrange a quick Dominican Republic divorce from Abacasas for her.

"As for you, Morgan, my most agreeable client, you'd be smart to regard Cybelle Carter as a time bomb."

Thinking the report was over, I reached for the "Stop" button, but Bobby had more to say.

"Here's another interesting bit: those jobs the kids had when they were chasing around the south? For a few months, they worked at a zoo in Georgia. Floyd's job was in the reptile house. The sheriff back in Lofton, Tennessee, told me that Floyd's hobby when he was growing up was collecting snakes. The sheriff said the snakes had been, turned loose when he got out to their place to investigate the old man's death."

Bobby's right eyebrow went up, he cocked his head and in a wry tone he added: "Maybe somebody sending you a rattlesnake was just a coincidence, but Floyd-Bud was working as a driver for Isaac that night. Drivers have time to run errands while the boss is having a leisurely dinner. Well, I haven't brought you back a killer, but I uncovered some suspicious lies. Let me know if you want me to keep investigating."

The tape went black. Neither Chet nor I said a word while he rewound it. When it was back at the beginning, Chet pushed the "Eject" button. He slipped it into its case, gave it to me and asked, "Somebody sent you a rattlesnake?"

I shrugged. "It was weeks ago, and obviously I wasn't hurt. I don't want to talk about it."

"What are you going to do?" he asked.

"Think, long and hard," I said. "Will you take me home?"

"Would you like some company while you think?"

"Not tonight, Chet," I said softly.

THE FIRST THING I did when I got back inside my apartment was to call St. Vincent's Manhattan Hospital to ask about Bobby's condition.

"There's been no change," the floor nurse told me.

My next action was to make a strong pot of coffee. While it was brewing, I shed the clothes and the high heeled ankle boots I'd been wearing since I left Los Angeles yesterday morning and took a long shower. Afterwards, I slipped into a pair of satin pajama bottoms and an old, oversized red sweatshirt and sat down at the kitchen table with a super-size mug of coffee, a pen, and one of the white legal pads I use to work out story points for the show. But the points I were about to list had nothing to do with *Love*.

In the shower I'd mentally reviewed Bobby's taped report. Now I was going to list the things I hoped would give me what Matt and G. G. called "a theory of the case."

1. Cybelle lied about the fact that she and Jeannie knew each other before I hired Jeannie to be her double.
2. Cybelle lied about when she invited Jeannie to stay at her apartment.
3. Cybelle and Bud *may* have killed their abusive father.
4. At sixteen, Cybelle married a rich old man and she and Bud *may* have murdered him for his money, but they didn't get it.

5. At eighteen, Cybelle married Philippe. She and Bud *may* have planned to kill him, but discovered it was too diffi-cult because of the protection around him.

6. After running away from Philippe she changed her looks and met Johnny Isaac. Was she planning to marry him? If she did, would Johnny meet a sudden death? Or was he too smart?

7. How much does Johnny know about Cybelle and Bud?

8. Why did someone leave an ancient Greek coin—most likely one of those belonging to Philippe—beside Bobby's body? To frame Philippe?

9. Assume that it was Bud who sent me the rattlesnake. Why? A warning? An attempt on my life?

10. Assume Bud or Cybelle sent me the DVD of *Vertigo*. Was it part of a scheme to make it look as though Philippe Abacasas was going to kill her? To deflect suspicion from them?

11. Did Bud threaten me outside Bobby's house because he found out Bobby was a P.I. and guessed that I'd hired him to investigate Jeannie's murder?

12. Cybelle and/or Bud could have killed Jeannie. With Jean-nie's stay planned a week in advance, they had plenty of time to put poison into the chocolate pudding. And who else, other than the two of them, had free access to Cy-belle's apartment? But *why* would they kill Jeannie? Did she know something about them?

13. The attack on Mulholland Drive: Bud could have been driving that Humvee. It was stolen near the Crown Colony Hotel and abandoned not far away. Because of shooting the next morning, everybody was supposed to be in bed when the Humvee came after me. Bud could have sneaked in and out of the hotel without being seen.

His room was at the end of the corridor, next to the fire stairs.

14. Why did Johnny, Cybelle, and Bud take a private jet back to New York, instead of traveling three hours later with the rest of us? Cybelle could have persuaded Johnny to get them back to New York ahead of the rest of us, giving Bud—or even herself—time to go to Bobby's, hit him and steal the report. Knowing how important it was to me to find Jeannie's killer, it would be logical that I'd go right to Bobby's when I landed. But would Johnny have let Cybelle go anywhere alone? Not likely. He would have let her go somewhere with Bud, or would have given Bud time off. BUT: The problem here is that Bobby would have been suspicious if Cybelle or Bud or both came to his place. He would have been on guard if either of them . . .

I stared at the page I'd filled with my scribbles, rereading the list. I knew I was missing something.

But *what*?

Then I remembered one more thing that Bobby said on the tape: about how smart Johnny was. Suddenly I had at least a *theory* of the case, but the thought made my stomach lurch.

The information Bobby uncovered wasn't substantial enough to turn over to Matt. It was full of *maybes*, with no hard evidence. I would have to learn the truth on my own. Completely on my own. I couldn't even tell Nancy because, as an attorney, she was an officer of the court, and what I planned to do was against the law.

Retrieving my laptop from the bedroom, I set it up on the kitchen table, and began to create a new scene for the show. I wasn't writing with my usual care and attention to detail; I wasn't polishing dialogue to the best of my ability. This scene didn't have to be great. All it had to be was *long* enough.

By five o'clock I'd finished this crucial scene, which I was going to insist be taped this afternoon . . . but which I never intended to insert into the show.

Chapter 45

WHEN I REACHED the office a few minutes before eight, Betty was already at her desk. I told her we were doing an extra scene this afternoon, handed her the pages and asked her to make copies—one for each of three actors in the scene, and others for the director and the necessary tech people.

"It uses the Hilltop Restaurant set on thirty-seven," I said. "That stage should be free by four, so I want this new material to begin taping at five. The other actors in the scene are Kitty Leigh and Sean O'Neil. They're already working today; we'll just keep them longer. They can run lines with Cybelle from four-thirty to five. I'll call Cybelle and get her here. Fax her the pages. She's at Johnny Isaac's house."

As I spoke, Betty was scanning the pages. She looked up at me, puzzled.

"This isn't . . . well . . ."

I could see from her expression she didn't like the dialogue. "It doesn't read like a great scene," I said quickly, "but when it's shot, I think it'll play well."

She didn't say anything, just watched me.

"Who's directing today?" I asked.

"Holly Willis. She's in the control room."

"I'll let her know about this extra scene. Thanks for the help, Betty."

"You got it," she said.

Something in her voice told me she didn't buy my story. I hurried into my office and dialed Tommy's number. He was just about to leave his apartment. I told him I wanted to tape an extra scene and he agreed. He only asked a couple of basic questions having to do with production needs. It was awful, lying to people I valued. I picked up the phone and made the other necessary calls, then phoned St. Vincent's Manhattan Hospital to ask about Bobby. When the doctor came on the line, he said, "I've just finished examining Mr. Novello. I'm sorry, but he's still unconscious."

"Please tell me—he's going to live, isn't he?"

He paused for a moment. "We're doing absolutely everything we can."

The doctor's guarded words hardened my resolve.

CYBELLE—EAGER TO please as always—arrived at three o'clock for wardrobe and makeup. I'd told her the new scene was laying the foundation for a subplot that would expand her story line beyond her romantic adventures with

Link. Judging by the smile on Johnny's face, he was happy to hear that.

"Johnny, if you like, you and Bud can wait in my office during rehearsal," I said. "Use my phone if you need to make calls. Betty will let you know when they're ready to tape. I've got to go talk to the director, then I'll be up in the control booth."

"Thanks," he said. "How about having dinner with us later?"

I smiled at him warmly, but shook my head. "I'm going home to crash tonight. Rain check?"

"Any time."

Betty was at her desk. "I'll be all over the floor for the next couple of hours," I said. "Whoever calls, just take messages, okay? And let Mr. Isaac know when they're ready to tape the new scene so he can watch it."

She nodded and gave me a perfunctory smile.

IT WAS A quarter to five when I got out of a cab in front of Johnny Isaac's townhouse on East Seventy-fourth Street, between Park and Lexington. I'd been there once before, when he gave a party for the cast and crew of *Love* to celebrate our rise in the ratings.

Next to the front stoop was a sign identifying the alarm company that protected the house. The front window screens were alarm-wired. Johnny's home was his fortress. As I pressed the bell, I hoped that Mrs. Jeffries, Johnny's housekeeper, would remember me.

She opened the door and smiled pleasantly. I extended my hand.

"Hello, Mrs. Jeffries. I'm Morgan Tyler from *Love of My Life*."

"Oh, yes. Good afternoon." She took my offered hand.

"I'm so sorry to pop in on you," I said in a rush, "but we have a problem at the studio. Miss Carter's shooting a new scene today, and she forgot her lucky charm. Mr. Isaac sent me to get it for her."

She looked puzzled. "I don't know anything about a lucky charm. What is it?"

"An old coin. Cybelle usually has it with her, but she hadn't expected to work today." I smiled ruefully, lifted my shoulders and gestured palms up: *mea culpa*. Then I made a point of shivering, and Mrs. Jeffries stepped back to let me in.

"Thank you," I said, "It's *cold* out there. I'm afraid this is all my fault. I threw new work at Cybelle the moment we came back from California, but that's life in TV!" I took a breath. "Anyway, Cybelle told me she left it in the bedroom when she was rushing around getting ready to go to the studio." I looked at the staircase behind Mrs. Jeffries. "Could I take a quick peek upstairs? I've got to get back as soon as possible so we don't run into double overtime."

"Well . . ." She was frowning, unsure, but she wasn't saying no.

I pressed on. "I'm *so sorry* to intrude on you late on a Friday afternoon. You're probably getting ready to leave?"

"Not quite—I have some more household bills to go over. . . ."

I gave an exaggerated sigh of relief. "Oh, I'm so glad I'm not making this *worse* for you!" My eyes went to the staircase again. "I remember where the bedrooms are. If it's okay with you, I'll just run up and find her lucky charm, then get right out of your hair. Will you be in the kitchen?"

"Yes . . . but I could come up and help you look."

I took advantage of the reluctance in her voice. "That's so nice of you, but it'll be easy to spot. And I don't want to delay you getting home. I'll poke my head in the kitchen to say goodbye as soon as I find it."

With that I hurried toward the stairs and started up. I held my breath, gambling that she wouldn't follow me. She didn't.

I started with the guest room. Pale blue paint formed a lovely background for the gleaming brass queen-size bed and its soft, puffy blue silk spread. Next to it, serving as a night table, was a graceful little walnut chest. Two crystal and brass wall sconces flanked a comfortable, deep-cushioned sofa with rounded arms. Completing the furnishings were a small rosewood writing desk with a lyre-back gilt chair. A wall of mirrored doors concealed closets where Cybelle's clothing hung; one was open and I recognized some of the outfits. Her makeup and grooming products filled the bathroom.

Working fast, I went through Cybelle's jewelry box, the drawers that held her sweaters and lingerie, the pockets of her coats and jackets, and the inside of her shoes, boots, and handbags. Nothing. I had no better luck searching the drawers in the bedside chest and the writing desk. A total strike out.

I'd been upstairs eight minutes. Not very long, but I knew I had to hurry before Mrs. Jeffries became suspicious.

In contrast to the lightness of the guest room, Johnny's master suite was dark and dramatic. For a moment I felt like Jane Eyre entering the bedroom of Mr. Rochester, the brooding master of Thornfield. I recognized the medieval looking furniture—straight lines, sturdy construction, ornate carvings, all with a dark finish—as seventeenth-century English, Jacobean. They weren't my taste, but the pieces looked to be of fine quality. Hanging tapestries covered the walls with designs depicting medieval travelers on a journey. Burgundy velvet drapes framed the tall casement windows, and beneath the windows stood a library table covered with scripts. Next to the table was a chair with a square back, and arms that sloped down to meet the posts from the square seat. Dominating the room was a king-size bed with a massive, carved headboard and an emerald velvet spread.

As quickly as my fingers would move, I went through Johnny's clothes, concentrating on pockets and linings. Nothing. Nor was there anything concealed in his shoes, or the drawers that held his shirts, socks, underwear, and his extensive collection of cuff links and watches. I closed the drawers and closet doors and stepped back into the middle of the room, surveying it as Johnny might have if he'd been trying to decide on a hiding place for something small.

Then I saw it—an object so commonplace I nearly missed its significance. On Johnny's dresser, slightly behind an antique silver-framed picture of his favorite client, was a large cut glass jar of pennies.

I felt my pulse quicken as I picked up the jar. It was heavy, full almost to the top. I carried it to the bed and dumped the contents out onto the green velvet spread. And there it was: an imperfect circle of silver gleaming softly amid a sea of copper pennies.

There was no doubt in my mind anymore: Philippe had been telling the truth.

I grabbed the coin and quickly slipped it into my bra.

"What the hell do you think you're doing?"

I whirled to face Johnny Isaac. The first thing I saw was the burning fury in his eyes. The second was the pistol he was pointing directly at my thudding heart.

Chapter 46

"PUT THAT DOWN, Johnny. I came here to help you." The calmness in my voice amazed me; I was feeling anything *but* calm.

"You're not trying to help me." Johnny closed the bedroom door, and my palms turned clammy with fear.

"Where's Cybelle?" I asked.

"At the studio." He gestured with the pistol, indicating he wanted me to sit down on the side of the bed, next to the lake of pennies. I sat. He loomed over me.

"Pretty damn smart," he said, "getting us out of the house to shoot a fake scene."

"It's not a fake—"

"Don't insult my intelligence," he snapped. "I thought it was a piece of crap when I read it, but with all the close-ups for Cybelle, I figured you were going to do something

clever in the editing room. I didn't catch on to the trick until it was time to tape. You weren't there, and nobody knew
where you'd gone."

"Johnny, listen to me—"

"Shut up! You can talk when I say it's your turn."

Keeping the pistol pointed at me, Johnny went to the far
side of the bed and leaned over to rake his other hand
through the pennies. "Where is it?"

"A silver coin? That's what I was looking for, but I
couldn't find it."

Johnny's free hand lashed out. He slapped my right
cheek so hard my ears rang. "I don't have it," I said softly.
I leaned away from him—enough to lessen another blow if
it came. Tilting as I was toward the night table, I glimpsed
something on it that gave me a flash of hope. "Johnny," I
said, "I'm willing to forget you hit me if you'll let me
leave now."

"Don't bullshit a bull-shitter, baby. You broke into my
house. In a few minutes, I'm going to accidentally shoot
you."

"What about Mrs. Jeffries? She must have told you I'm
up here."

"I had Bud call her from the car and tell her to go home.
I waited out of sight until she left. So I *don't* know you're
in my house." Johnny screwed up his face and said, "Jeez,
officer," in an agonized tone. "I heard footsteps and yelled
'Who's there?' Nobody answered. I thought I saw a gun, so
I fired in self-defense! Oh, God!"

"That's quite a performance."

"Cut the crap," he said. "How did you figure it out?
There's nothing you can prove—I got the evidence away
from your midget P.I."

My fists clenched with anger. "He's not a midget—he's

a dwarf, and they're called *Little People*!" I scooted a few inches further back on the bed—and nearer to the night table.

He waved the pistol at me menacingly. He was close enough that I could see it was a snub nose Beretta. I turned my guess into a bluff. "I *know* you killed Jeannie," I said. "I just can't figure out *why*."

"Before she met me, when she was alone and frightened, Cybelle let something slip to Jeannie Ford. The bitch started blackmailing her. I wasn't going to let that go on."

Playing to Johnny's ego I said, "But if I was blackmailing somebody who had *you* as her protector, I'd stay where I'd feel safe. Why would Jeannie go to Cybelle's?"

Johnny smiled. "I promised a million dollars in cash, one big payoff so she'd go away and leave my girl alone. Then I suggested she stay out of sight at Cybelle's while I got it together. Of course, I knew one day she'd come back for another bite."

"How did you know she'd eat the pudding?"

"I took everything else out of the refrigerator." He frowned at me. "You should have stayed out of this. Jeannie Ford was an unknown, worthless chick. No loss."

"She was a human being."

"Forget her. Give me the coin."

I held up my open hands. "I don't have it."

"Empty your pockets."

I turned the pockets of my jacket inside out. "Maybe Cybelle or Bud took it."

Johnny wasn't buying that. "Take off your boots and give them to me, one at a time."

I tried a joke. "If you've got a deck of cards we could play strip poker."

"Shut up and give me the boots."

I unzipped the right one first, pulled it off and handed it to him. While he turned it upside down and examined the heel, I grabbed a small rectangle of plastic from the night table—his burglar alarm's Panic Button. I pushed it, and kept pushing it as I lurched to my feet.

Still holding the pistol, Johnny lunged at me and tried to grab the Panic Button.

The phone rang.

Gambling it was the alarm company, I threw the Panic Button to the floor and snatched the cordless phone out of its recharge cradle. "Police!" I screamed. "Call the police!"

Johnny slammed me to the floor, knocking the phone out of my hand. I scrambled to my feet. Johnny's finger was on the trigger as we wrestled for the pistol. He was stronger, but survival instinct had kicked in, sending a rush of adrenaline through my system. As Johnny tried to force the point of the barrel toward me, I resisted with every ounce of strength I had. I managed to shove the Beretta's snub nose away just as the bedroom door burst open and a woman screamed.

Then the pistol went off.

Chapter 47

FOR AN INSTANT it seemed time had stopped. As though we were actors in a frozen tableau, Johnny, Cybelle, and I stared at Bud Collins, who was lying on the floor. From the bullet hole in the middle his forehead, I had no doubt he was dead. Cybelle broke the momentary spell by flinging herself down beside her brother. "I hate you!" she shrieked at Johnny. "You shot my brother! I hate you!"

"No, baby, no—it was an accident!"

Johnny stared at Cybelle, tears of agony in his eyes, the Beretta dangling from his fingers. Realizing that I was forgotten, I jerked the pistol out of his hand. He didn't seem to notice. He was focused on Cybelle, who was screaming, "I hate you! I hate you! I hate you!"

Gripping the Beretta in both hands, I pointed it at

Johnny and backed away—just as two uniformed police officers, weapons drawn, came pounding into the room.

I put the Beretta down carefully, and raised my hands.

PLAINCLOTHES DETECTIVES AND the Crime Scene team
went to work at the townhouse. Johnny, Cybelle, and I were
brought to the Nineteenth Precinct, on East Sixty-seventh
Street, in three separate police cars. We were stashed in
separate rooms, each with a "minder."

Mine introduced himself as Detective Mercer. He was
over fifty, with fists the size of water buckets and kind gray
eyes. He let me telephone Matt. It was a short call. Matt
listened to my story—the *Reader's Digest* version, which
involved only what happened in Johnny's bedroom—
grunted once and then asked to speak to Detective Mercer.

They talked for about a minute. I couldn't hear what
Matt was saying, but Detective Mercer mumbled a few
words, while looking at me with just the hint of a smile at
the corner of his mouth.

He put down the phone and asked, "You want some
coffee?"

"No thank you. I'd just like to tell you what happened.
I'll talk into a tape recorder if you want me to, and I don't
need a lawyer."

"You're certainly easy to get along with," he said wryly.

"That depends on who you ask."

DETECTIVE MERCER TOLD me that because their separate
investigations were linked, Matt and G. G. would be allowed to participate with the detectives from the Nine-

teenth Precinct in the interrogations of Johnny Isaac and
Cybelle Carter.

I'd been sitting alone for two hours in the small, charm-
less chamber Detective Mercer referred to as "Interview
room three" when, at last, the door opened. It was Matt. A
great wave of relief swept over me at the sight of him.
"Come on," he said. "I'm taking you home."

On the ride to the Dakota, Matt filled me in.

"Isaac confessed to murdering Jeannie Ford."

That surprised me. "Johnny's a fighter. I would have
thought he'd insist he's innocent and hire the best lawyer
money can buy."

"It started that way—then we let him watch through the
glass as Cybelle was being questioned. She blamed everything on Johnny, said he forced her to invite Jeannie Ford
to her apartment but didn't know why, that when she found
out he'd murdered Jeannie she was terrified of him, too
frightened to go to the police. She said she hated him because he forced her brother to threaten you outside Novello's, that Johnny was the one who saw Novello's name on
the appointment pad in your office. He knew he was a detective and guessed you were hiring him to investigate the
murder. Cybelle said that when you wouldn't be scared off
by threats, he persuaded Bud to kill you on the L.A. trip.

"I watched Johnny watching her. It was like he was becoming a little old man right in front of me. Suddenly, he
didn't seem to care about living anymore. He told us everything, including the fact that he was the one who attacked
Novello, stole the report and let the birds loose to confuse
things. And he said that Cybelle was in on everything,
from the beginning. She should be up for murder along
with him, but because she'd be harder to convict, they'll
probably charge her as an accessory."

We were nearly home when I realized there were some missing pieces. "What about the rattlesnake, and the DVD of *Vertigo*?"

"Johnny said he had Bud deliver the DVD to your home, figuring you'd recognize it as similar to the story Cybelle told you about Abacasas transforming her. He knew about Bud's interest in snakes. When he discovered that Abacasas had located Cybelle and was having her watched, he had Bud send you the rattler, hoping you'd connect it to Abacasas. Isaac thought it would look like Abacasas intended to kill Cybelle, but killed Jeannie by mistake. He was sure the plan would have worked, except that you became obsessed with solving Jeannie Ford's murder. He hadn't figured on that complication."

We'd arrived at the entrance to the Dakota. Matt leaned forward, reached across me—careful not to let his arm brush against my breasts—and unlocked the passenger door.

"Good night," he said.

"Are you angry at me for interfering?"

He stared straight ahead through the windshield. "Yeah. And for almost getting yourself killed. Again." He sighed. "I'll probably get over it."

There was nothing I could say, so I got out of the car. Before I reached the entrance, I heard Matt drive away.

I was about to enter the courtyard when Frank lumbered out of the office and called my name.

He jerked his thumb in the direction he'd come. "There's somebody waiting for you," Frank said.

"Who is it?"

He shrugged his big shoulders. "Never saw him before."

A man stepped out of the office and came toward me. He was a little shorter than medium height, slender, and

wearing an expensive-looking black overcoat. The brim of
a charcoal gray fedora threw half of his face into shadows.

"Mrs. Tyler?"

"Yes?"

"My name is Frederick Lytton. I'm an attorney. May we
speak in private?"

"No," I said. "I'm tired, I'm hungry and I've never
heard of you."

He lowered his voice. "You've heard of my client.
Philippe Abacasas."

I nodded toward the fountain in the center of the courtyard. "We can talk over there."

Obediently, he followed me. I stopped at the point
where we couldn't be overheard, but which allowed me to
keep Frank in sight. My visitor took an envelope from an
inside pocket.

"Please read this."

I opened it, extracted the contents and tilted the top
page so that the corner courtyard light illuminated it. "My
darling, I do not know when, or if, I will be able to see your
beautiful face again." I gripped the page tightly to keep my
hands from shaking. "Whatever happens to me, I want you
to have the document enclosed." It was signed with the single initial, "P." When I unfolded the paper beneath the letter, I stared at it in shock. I took a breath to steady my
voice. "What is this?" I asked.

"Exactly what it appears to be," he said. "The deed to a
house on Mulholland Drive, in Los Angeles. In your
name."

"This is a joke."

"I can assure you that the deed is real. You are now the
owner of that house. Additionally, Mr. Abacasas has en-

trusted me with a sum of money which will pay the property taxes for the next ten years."

"That's very generous," I said. Neatly, I refolded the letter and the deed, replaced them in the envelope—and thrust it back into Lytton's hand. "I don't want it," I said.

I called to Frank, who was standing just outside the archway. "Mr. Lytton is leaving. Now," I said firmly.

As soon as I got upstairs I called St. Vincent's Manhattan. I gave the floor nurse my name and asked about Bobby's condition.

"Good news, Mrs. Tyler—he's been awake for several hours. The doctor left word that you can visit Mr. Novello tomorrow."

CHET AND I went to the hospital together. The moment I saw Bobby's small body in that big hospital bed, I wanted to cry. Instead, I said, "Is there anything I can do for you?"

"Ask me that again when I'm out of here," he said with a Groucho leer. "And when you're not with *him*," he added.

We told Bobby that—thanks in large part to his work— the Jeannie Ford murder case was solved and the killer, who'd also attacked him, was in custody.

"Bobby, I'm so sorry about your birds," I said.

He reached for my hand and stroked it briefly. "Wasn't your fault."

"I know you can't replace creatures you love the way you can replace *things*, but I'd like to get some other birds for you," I said. "Or pay for the ones that you choose."

"*We'll* pay for them," Chet said. He looked at me and asked, "Agreed?"

Before I could reply, Bobby gave me a devilish smile.

"Tell him yes. The birds I like are expensive—and I'm already soaking you with a bill that's going to look like the national debt of Finland."

As Chet was driving me back to the Dakota, he reached over, took my hand and said, "We've only had one real date. That was almost three months ago, and it ended with our being shot at. I'd like to risk a second date."

"Brave man."

"You think you're kidding. Since I met you I increased my health coverage," he said. "Let's have a real New York City night. An early dinner and a Broadway show?"

"How about a *leisurely* dinner, and a walk to look at the Christmas decorations?"

"When?"

"Tomorrow. That'll give you time to get fitted for a Kevlar vest."

Chapter 48

A FEW HOURS after Chet dropped me off, Nancy and I were sitting in my den, feet up on the shared ottoman, eating Japanese take-out. I had just finished telling her about Johnny, Cybelle, Bud, and Jeannie Ford's murder, when the phone rang.

It was Tommy, and he sounded almost hysterical. I listened, then said soothingly, "Don't worry, Tommy. I'll figure out a way to fix it. I promise. Now get a good night's sleep." I hung up. "The thrills just keep coming," I told Nancy. "Cybelle has disappeared—vanished with her jewelry, whatever cash she had, and her passport."

"I thought she was under arrest as an accessory."

"There was a bail hearing this morning," I said.

"Who'd be dumb enough to put up bail for her?"

I grimaced. "Tommy—but he's not dumb, just soft-hearted."

Nancy put down her chopsticks and frowned with concern. "What are you going to do with your story?"

"I'll have to write her out. Maybe I'll have the Los Angeles footage re-edited so that she dies falling off the riverboat. That will give Link some juicy grief scenes to play. And we can do a memorial episode, with lots of her film clips. Then I'll have to create a new love interest for Link."

As Nancy was sipping her sake, I told her about the visit from Philippe's lawyer.

Nancy almost choked on the last of her sake. "Abacasas gave you *a house?*"

"Tried. I gave it back." I aimed my chopsticks at a slice of sweet potato tempura, gripped it and dipped it into the tangy sauce.

Nancy studied me with narrowed eyes. "What do you *do* to men? I'm going to have your lipstick analyzed for drugs."

I poured some more sake into her glass.

"What are you going to do with the two coins Cybelle stole?" she asked.

"Send them back to Abacasas, care of his banker in Zurich."

The ringing doorbell startled us.

"Who could *that* be? And why didn't the desk phone me first?"

Nancy got up. "I'm going to answer it with you."

I squinted through the peephole. "It's Matt," I whispered. "I haven't heard from him since he sprung me from the Nineteenth Precinct."

I opened the door and saw that Matt wasn't alone.

Penny stood beside him. She was grinning and clutching a bulging shopping bag.

"Is this a bad time?" she asked.

"Not at all. Nancy and I are having Japanese. There's enough for four." I stepped back and gestured for them to come in.

As Matt followed Penny into the foyer, I saw something *move* inside his partially zipped up leather jacket—then the small, furry head of an ebony black kitten emerged. I found myself staring into a pair of big green eyes.

"Oh, Morgan—isn't he *adorable?*" Penny sighed. "Matt found him this afternoon, abandoned at a crime scene!"

"He was on the street, *outside* the crime scene," Matt corrected. "He came up and rubbed against my ankle. An elderly woman on the stoop said she puts out food for him when she remembers, but that he doesn't belong to anybody."

"The poor little thing's homeless," Penny said.

Nancy chuckled. "Not anymore I'm guessing."

"You don't have to keep him," Matt said, unzipping his jacket and handing me an incredibly soft bundle of black fur. "I can take him to an animal shelter."

Simultaneously, Nancy, Penny, and I cried, "No!"

The moment the kitten was in my arms he rubbed his little head against my chin, closed his eyes and started to purr.

Penny indicated the bag she was carrying. "Kitten food, dishes, and litter."

Matt aimed a wry smile at me as I gently stroked the little cat's head. "Maybe having a pet will keep you busy," he said.

Nancy arched her eyebrows. "Busy enough so she'll stay out of your investigations?"

Over the kitten's head, I smiled at Matt. "Dream on, Detective," I said sweetly.

Chapter 49

AS SOON AS Tommy told her I had a cat, Betty Kraft rushed into my office with advice.

"You have to understand," Betty said, "that to a cat, *everything* is a cat toy."

"So I discovered when I tried to read my paper this morning."

"How old is he?"

"About four months."

"Too young for catnip. Read every toy label to make sure there's no catnip in it."

"I will."

"He should be fed twice a day."

"I'm doing that. Plus he has a dish of dry kitten food for any time he wants it."

Betty nodded her approval of my cat-care program. "What's the little fella's name?" she asked.

"Magic. He's my little black Magic."

TWO WEEKS LATER, in the early hours of the morning of the last day of the year, I was sound asleep, with Magic's soft body curled around the top of my head. A sharp, jarring sound roused me. Swimming up to consciousness, I realized the phone was ringing. Careful not to disturb the purring kitten, I reached for the receiver and muttered, "Hello?"

Silence.

"Hello?"

Silence.

"Damn all cranks," I said, and hung up.

I had just gotten comfortable when the phone rang again. Realizing it might be an overseas call—Chet had returned to The Hague the day before to interview another war criminal—I resisted the urge to answer sharply and instead said a pleasant, "Hello?"

Silence again. I waited, but no one came on the line.

The red numerals on my bedside clock read 4:25 A.M. Completely awake now, I replaced the receiver, gently moved Magic to the other pillow and sat up.

"How would you like to have an early breakfast?" I asked my furry roommate.

Magic opened his green eyes to half-mast, yawned, folded his little front paws into his chest and went back to sleep.

"Okay, but I made the offer," I told him. Maybe this morning I could actually read the *Times*.

After switching on Mr. Coffee, I went to the front door to see if the paper was there. It was.

Back in the kitchen, I opened the newspaper and saw that something had been slipped inside—a page of notepaper, expensive, faintly textured, pale gray. Attached to it by a pearl-tipped hatpin, was a sprig of what looked like pine needles. The note read:

Rosemary, that's for remembrance: pray you, love, remember . . .

And meet me now.

The handwriting was Philippe's.

I recognized the quotation; it was something Ophelia said to Hamlet. In literary code, Philippe was letting me know where he was.

The telephone calls weren't cranks, but were intended to wake me, so I would get up. And what do most people do when they get up? They bring in the morning paper. . . . My heart pounded with excitement, or apprehension—I wasn't sure which. I studied the spiky sprig in my hand.

So Philippe had returned.

Nancy said he'd served his purpose in my life, but curiosity made this an invitation I couldn't resist.

I flipped Mr. Coffee's off switch, refilled one of Magic's dishes with cool water, and put down another dish with half a fresh can of Natural Balance cat food. His breakfast was ready for him, whenever he decided to get up.

I dressed hurriedly, in black wool slacks tucked into calf-high boots, and the indigo cashmere sweater that was a Christmas present from Penny. On my way out of the apartment, I threw on a faux fur cape.

It was a few minutes after five as I hurried east, toward the corner of Seventy-second and Central Park West. The first pale sliver of morning edged the bottom of the predawn sky. Central Park was dressed in shades of gray, with just enough light for me to find my way to the Shakespeare Garden without stumbling.

I sensed his presence an instant before he emerged from the shadows of Shakespeare's mulberry tree. As usual, in spite of the late December cold, he wasn't wearing a coat, only a dark suit and a smoky gray turtleneck sweater.

Before I could speak, his arms were around me. His lips pressed down on mine. We kissed for what seemed like an instant, but when we drew slightly apart, and I opened my eyes, I saw that the sky had lightened to silver.

Philippe took my hand, drew me toward the Ramble and said, "Come."

In a few minutes we'd reached Bow Bridge, the nineteenth-century cast iron structure with beautiful circular grillwork that connected the Ramble to Cherry Hill, just west of Bethesda Terrace in the middle of Central Park.

He led me to the crest of the "bow," about halfway into its sixty-foot span and stopped. Gently, he turned me so that I was facing west.

"From here I can see where you live," he said, indicating the top three floors of the Dakota, visible in the distance beyond the trees.

"Why did you disappear that morning?" I asked.

"There are things I cannot tell you right now."

I shook my head. My tone had an edge as I said, "That's not good enough. A few months ago, before we met, I created a character something like you—a mystery man named Gareth who keeps disappearing without explanation. He asks Jillian, the woman he loves, to trust him."

"And *does* she trust him?"

"Yes, it's a love story. A fantasy."

Philippe took me in his arms and pulled me close. "How does their story end?"

"I haven't decided yet," I said. "It depends on what kind of man he turns out to be." I raised my face to look at him and said, "Cybelle—Sara—vanished again."

He nodded. "I know. In time my people will find her."

"And then what?"

"I will make it worth her while to give me a divorce."

As much as I wanted to, I refused to ask, "And *then* what?"

"I must go now," Philippe said.

"What a surprise!"

"Don't be angry, please. When it is possible, I will be back."

"The coins Cybelle stole—I sent them to you, care of your bank in Zurich."

"You could have kept them."

"I don't want—"

He kissed me, fiercely. Then he was gone.

Two squirrels, chasing each other past my feet, disappeared into one of the cast iron circles near the far end of the bridge. In nearby trees, birds were waking up and starting their chatter.

I turned and began to walk back through the park, back toward real life—and my New Year's Eve date with Matt Phoenix.

LINDA PALMER was a wildlife photographer in Africa before she tunred to writing. She teaches screenwriting classes at UCLA Extension, and lives with several pets in Studio City, California.

Visit her website at www.lindapalmermysteries.com.